The summer fete was
proceeding smoothly . . .

. . . But the shout they now all heard came from nowhere near the yellow Prize Every Time stall; nor did it sound like the normal joyous shouts of a summer day, a happy gathering . . .

"Help! Someone, quick—help!"

Cherry clutched her husband's arm. "David—listen—"

"Help, for God's sake! Somebody come quick—please!"

"The rose garden," said Margaret Brown, pulling herself together in the startled silence.

"More likely the maze." Caleb frowned. "Though mebbe it's no more than some youngsters fooling . . ."

"Get us out, please! There's a dead body here!"

"It doesn't sound as if they're fooling," said David.

MORE MYSTERIES FROM THE
BERKLEY PUBLISHING GROUP . . .

MURDER IN THE MAZE

SARAH J. MASON

BERKLEY BOOKS, NEW YORK

MURDER IN THE MAZE

A Berkley Book / published by arrangement with
the author

PRINTING HISTORY
Berkley edition / April 1993

ISBN: 0-425-13795-3

A BERKLEY BOOK ® TM 757,375
Berkley Books are published by The Berkley Publishing Group,
200 Madison Avenue, New York, New York 10016.
The name "BERKLEY" and the "B" logo
are trademarks belonging to Berkley Publishing Corporation.

PRINTED IN THE UNITED STATES OF AMERICA

10 9 8 7 6 5 4 3 2 1

One
G. Volk

It was the morning of the summer fete, and everyone in Redingote village had spent the preceding week praying for rain. They told one another this was sure to result in fine weather, since Old Parson, incumbent of the parish for more than fifty years, had recently been translated to a higher congregation, and would doubtless wish to do his best for the flock he had left behind. His muddleheaded ways, however, had long been a byword in that distant corner of Allshire, and it was thought better not to express directly what was required. The poor old gentleman could be relied upon to get it wrong.

Now that the great day had come, the sun was shining, the sky was cloudless, and every twig was alive with a riot of racketing bird life. Old Parson had done Redingote proud—a splendid effort, backed up, no doubt, by patron saints Swythun (Redingote's idiosyncratic spelling of the forty-days-of-weather man) and Jude, he of the Lost Cause. Not that Redingote saw its collective self as in any way lost: it was the rest of Allshire, the village maintained, which had rashly and needlessly abandoned the old ways. The rest of Allshire in its turn maintained that isolated Redingote was the sort of place where scold-ducking, witchcraft, bestiality, incest, and lively pastimes not unconnected with fertility rites were but a few of the vices still indulged in . . . although only the most pessimistic citizens of the county could suppose the village capable of murder, despite the perennial provocation undoubtedly afforded by the Redingote parish fete.

Murder now was far from the thoughts of Cedric Ezard as he went about his business in a mellow mood. Hereditary head gardener at The Stooks, he stumped from tree to tree in the small yet fertile orchard, selecting the finest fruits and placing them carefully in a laden trug. Cedric's very surname gave support to his proud belief that he was related (albeit by some ancestral orgifying on the wrong side of the blanket) to the manorial family of the Izods; he regarded the manor house and grounds as his personal responsibility. But upon the recent decease of Francis, last of the Izods, his relict had removed to the congenial air of Budleigh Salterton; and a soi-disant solicitor had offered cash down for a quick purchase of the property. Cedric had stayed on to tend his inheritance, despite disgust and suspicion of the town-bred newcomer; and now he was rifling the orchards and hothouses of the mysterious Montague Rowles without the knowledge, or permission, of that reclusive would-be squire.

"And," gloated Cedric with grim satisfaction, "if such matters as Christian charity don't meet with his approval, the jumped-up beggar, then so much the worse for him! He'll find it no easier to fit in with our ways here if he's inclined to be surly-minded. . . ."

Mr. Rowles had not realised that the fete would be held in the grounds of his new home. It was not given as a condition of purchase: had it been, the sale would never have gone through. Nobody had troubled to mention this annual invasion to the new owner of the manor because it had been, time out of mind, good enough for the Izods: it must surely then be good enough for one who was, after all, only aping his betters by the assumption of a position to which it was becoming all too clear he had not been born . . . and Redingote rejoiced at the rout of its new squire by churchwarden Caleb Duckels.

"We don't disturb things no more than needful, and we put all to rights by tidying, once it's over," Caleb had advised Mr. Rowles during his brief courtesy visit of acknowledgement that next Saturday would see the traditional junketings in the traditional place. "Folk'll start to arrive around mid-morning to prepare, but we'll have everything cleared away not so long after tea. . . ."

That evening in The Scold's Bridle, Caleb relayed to an

astounded audience Montague's gape-mouthed response to this (surely harmless?) information, mimicking his town-bred accents with all the contempt of a countryman born.

"Why, Mr. Duckels," he said amid a chorus of laughter, "what do you mean to tell me—that you're letting all these strangers come wandering in and about my house with never so much as a by-your-leave?" He chuckled at the memory. "So what else should I say to him but that the Izods, rest his soul—and wishful to have *her* back again with us we surely are—*they* never made no complaint, but deemed it an honour to them as well as an obligement to us village folk—which is what it was, and is. So then he sees there's no point to argufy further, and just mutters a bit, and says nothing."

"Nothing?" demanded a disappointed chorus of villagers, upon whose imagination the sudden appearance in Redingote of Mr. Rowles "with all that money in his hand" had reacted like some fabulous yeast. They said he was a criminal, in hiding from the police; or a gunrunner, hiding from both sides of some obscure civil war to whom he had sold the same dubious weaponry. He was also a black-mailer, retired with his ill-gotten gains; a coiner (about to set up a plant in the ample cellars of The Stooks); or a Mafia hit man, gone into rural retreat for the sake of his health. Rumour could not agree upon what exactly he was or why he was there; but everybody agreed that he must be up to no good.

"But we're here now, and the fete set to run as usual," said Caleb to his fellow churchwarden, Joseph Norton, standing beside him on the lawn at The Stooks to observe with pride the tumult of parochial activity all about them. "It would hardly have looked well for the new parson to enter into his duties with discord and strife in the parish—"

"Saving the fete, of course." Joseph grinned. "Never a year goes by without some manner of upset, remember." Mrs. Smith wants to put the Fancy Goods where, last year, Mrs. Jones had her Secondhand Clothes; Mrs. Black feels put out that Mrs. White, and not herself, was asked to take

care of the Lucky Dip; the Mothers' Union and the Young
Wives bicker over who should arrange the Teas. . . .

"The man's been a parson long enough to understand
such ructions, Joe. I fancy there's no fear of him being
scared away before his cassock's properly warm—
leastways, that's my hope. After the way poor Old Parson
let things slide, some new blood will come as welcome aid
to you and me."

Joseph nodded. Redingote's lamented former incumbent
had drifted into a haphazard policy of parish rule which
burdened his churchwardens for many years with far more
than should rightly be required of such officers. His memory
was unreliable. He could never be sure whether he was to
conduct a funeral, a wedding, or a baptism: except, of
course, in May, when the preponderance of births resulting
from high jinks at the previous year's Harvest Home made
baptisms far outnumber any other ceremony. Even the day
of the week frequently escaped him, so that Caleb and Joe
had been forced to start calling upon their vicar the previous
Saturday night, or early Sunday morning, to ensure that
services were held at the appointed time.

And there were other inconveniences, not entirely due to
clerical amnesia. Old Parson's habit of procrastination
meant that the parish rooms, well-used for generations, were
now, through lack of maintenance, almost falling down; the
parish books, entrusted upon his arrival in Redingote to Mr.
Wilford, a local bank manager, were understood to be in a
state of confusion; and the very fabric of the church,
stalwart stone though its walls might be, was roof-riddled by
worm and deathwatch beetle.

"A rare old shambles we've bin left," said Joe, sighing.
"And the new parson too, of course."

"And his wife." Caleb stole a sideways look at his
friend, whose long, strong, and silent courtship of Mildred
Waskett, Caleb's widowed sister, was fondly supposed by
that shy bachelor to be known only to himself. "Oh, yes,"
mused Caleb, "it'll be a grand thing to have a parson's wife
about the place again, to check the tongues of the womenfolk in their gossip. . . . And, talking of womenfolk, Joe,

how about going to see how sister Mildred fares along of her Bottle Stall?'' He cast a withering eye over the tipsy little group elected to set up stalls and trestles, whose efforts in that direction were proving of decidedly limited success. ''They won't reach her in good time today, I'd reckon—and she in a rare old hurry to get home and prepare dinner for the new vicar and his lady.''

''Oh,'' said Joe, and blushed. ''Well, I'm always willing to oblige a friend, Caleb, as you know. . . .''

And, with a twinkle that agreed he most certainly did, Mr. Duckels led him away.

On the upper lawn, the merry crew whose antics had led to Caleb's disapproving comments were disporting themselves in a glorious turmoil of ropes, tent poles, and grey canvas. They were trying to erect the Flower Show marquee, and on such a hot day were taking their time over the task. Daisy Hollis, in whose charge the Flower Show had been for more than a decade, scowled as she stood watching them. Hovering nearby was Montague Rowles: who, having decided to make the best of what circumstance had brought, had offered his services in a gesture of manorial cooperation—and had been soundly rebuffed.

''Do this blindfold after so many years, they can, thanking you,'' he was told by Daisy: who added under her breath that it would help if they'd only sober themselves up a bit, and so early in the morning, what's more. She then turned her back on Mr. Rowles to shout at Ernie, her husband, who'd been coerced not only into the pre-fete stall building, but into supervising the Donkey Rides as well. Ernie had a morbid fear of donkeys, one having kicked him in a tender place as he passed through its field on a poaching expedition; and he was bolstering his courage for the ordeal to come by frequent recourse to a crate of beer brought by his fellow construction men, Ralph Stretch and Roy Urvine, who never needed any excuse for a drink. Ernie had been glad to follow their lead, with the result that he now felt happier about the Donkey Rides: but Daisy was far from happy with him.

''Ernie Hollis, you and your friends make a pretty bunch,

I must say. You just hurry up! There's more to do after this—and we're already running late!''

From within the boiling canvas porridge of the mangled marquee came a ribald chorus of complaint. Daisy couldn't make out the words, but their sense was clear. She flushed, and took a deep breath. ''Now listen to me, you three—''

''Are you quite sure,'' came a voice from just behind her, ''that you don't want any help?'' There stood Mr. Rowles, butting in on her again with the job barely begun and all in confusion on account of Ernie and his drunken friends! Her second rebuff was not as polite as her first.

''If you'd mind out my way, Mr. Rowles, we'd have room to work as we please—sorry, was that your foot? It's not so good an idea to stand about when folks is pushed for time and needing a bit of space. . . .''

Crushed in more ways than one, Montague limped a retreat to the top of the steps leading from the upper to the main lawn and stood hopefully on one leg to survey the organised commotion all about his garden. Things were starting to go, he thought, more smoothly: the marquee had lurched into some semblance of the upright, and the gang was busy now with tent pegs and mallets; the lower lawn was dotted with groups of people who seemed to know what they were doing, and how best to do it. It could just be that—

''Hoy!'' came a roar by his ear. He jumped. Cedric Ezard had just delivered his hamper of stolen fruit to Mrs. Millage at the Raffle and was therefore free to go on the rampage. ''Hoy, you, Daisy Hollis, what d'you think you're playing at—banging all them holes in my turf, and that blamed heavy pole scraping the surface away . . .''

He stormed up the steps, shaking his fist. Mrs. Hollis straightened herself, eyes flashing. Montague, fearing bloodshed, hurried over to them. Cedric was, after all, in his employ: it was up to him to keep the peace between members of his staff and these—albeit uninvited—guests.

''Ah, Ezard—perhaps, today—a special occasion . . .''

This was hardly the voice of command. Francis Izod, the late squire, would have shouted as loudly as Daisy and

Cedric combined, and achieved a perfect resolution—which Montague's diffidence also achieved, though for quite another reason. That this interloper should dare to break in on a private squabble annoyed Daisy and Cedric equally, and they fell silent at once, turning together to glare at poor Montague, who, startled, rocked back on his heels.

"Urgh . . . well," said Cedric, calmer now, preparing to depart, "just you be careful of my grass, that's all I've to say to you—worse than Allingham fairground after a bank holiday, so this is. Pah!" And he spat an unlovely dollop on the grass midway between Mr. Rowles's left foot and his right; scowled; and stalked away.

Whatever protest Montague might have made was drowned out by Daisy's shriller tones. "Now see here . . . sir . . . you've no cause to bother yourself with anything today, on account of we all know what's to be done, and just needful to let off steam, in a manner of speaking. Cedric Ezard, he takes such pains on account of being part Family, you understand, and liking all to go well. Gives the lawns an extra trim, sets young Barney to clip the maze and deadhead the roses, tying back such as have slipped from the trellis . . . work hard, they both do. As we all like to—if we're only left alone to get on with it, that is. Right?"

"Oh—ah, yes," mumbled Montague. "Yes, right. . . ." And he was about to drift away when Daisy's eyes lit up in a smile of welcome.

"Hello there, Mrs. Radlett, dearie! How nice to see you here good and early."

"I hope—not too early," came a low, husky voice, with a Scandinavian intonation which matched the speaker's cornflower blue eyes and glorious pale gold hair. This was Ingrid, wife to local doctor Oliver Radlett; and her face wore a smug expression as she swayed gracefully past Montague where he stood at the top of the steps. "Perhaps you would be kind enough to excuse me, Mr. Rowles?"

Montague jumped further out of her way than he needed, and his gaze followed her, despite himself. "I wish," she said, "to deliver my rose to you in safety, Mrs. Hollis. Here—you see it?"

In her slim, outstretched hand Ingrid held a diamond-cut crystal vase containing a single rose, over the beauty of which Daisy exclaimed. Ingrid smiled a slow smile of satisfaction, and relinquished her trophy with admonitions that Daisy should take the greatest care of it. "This is my entry for the Flower Show, Mrs. Hollis, and I think a fine bloom. I chose it myself, for it is important that I should make every effort, in the circumstances, is it not?"

Daisy promised that the vase would be guarded to the very best of her ability, and hurried away to the marquee, inviting Mrs. Radlett to follow in a few minutes to see for herself. Ingrid murmured something in reply, then turned her attention to Montague. She leaned closer to him, so that her nearness enveloped him in the sensuous perfume of her skin and hair. Her lips parted in a smile.

"I have come early, Mr. Rowles, so that there may be time enough for me to judge all the other entries—and I intended that my rose must be the first to arrive. But it seems that those who build the tent—is that the word?— work very slowly in such heat. . . ." She wafted the back of a languid white hand across her brow and sighed. "Yet who shall blame them? So now I must wait for the other entries—which cannot be too long in being displayed, I am sure, and then I may carry out my duties." She smiled. "Have you also a duty to perform on this busy occasion?"

Recalling the snubs administered by Daisy and her cronies, Montague scowled. "I fail to understand how, if you are judging the Show, you can enter it as well. Or"—maybe the owner of the house was, after all, to play some part in the festivities—"are they having other judges, too?"

Ingrid must have read his mind: her delight in puncturing his hopes was obvious. "Dear me, no, my rose is merely a token *pour encourager les autres*, as one might say—a sign that I take a proper interest in what goes on, you understand? It is so important for me—an outsider, a foreigner—to accommodate myself to the . . . the mood of my husband's home, as I am only a woman. . . ."

Mr. Rowles, who felt her honey breath on his cheek, was only too well aware that she was a woman, and took a swift step backwards.

"Oh dear—so very steep, that bank, is it not?" came Ingrid's sympathetic murmur. "It is far wiser, I would suppose, always to mount and descend by the steps—but perhaps I am more fearful than you, Mr. Rowles. And especially now that I have been given a greater part to play in the life of my husband's village, I must not allow myself to be injured or rendered incapable of my new duties. . . ."

With what cunning she could plant her little darts! Montague Rowles, the outsider able to play no part, whether small or great, gritted his teeth at this reminder of Ingrid Radlett's recent election to the presidency of the Redingote Ladies' League: a position which she, so very much more obviously than himself a foreigner—and in every sense of the word—must owe entirely to her marriage with the local doctor—whereas *he* had bought the manor house, and yet . . .

The woman was a tease—a tormentor—so blatant . . .

"Let me escort you, Mrs. Radlett," he found himself saying, to his great surprise. But Ingrid's personal enchantment had worked its spell on him as it must on every normal male with whom she spent more than a few minutes.

She dismissed his offer with a throaty laugh, and went tripping her triumphant way towards the Flower Show marquee. Ernie and his friends were pegging the final guy-ropes in place, and she paused to give them her most brilliant smile before passing inside, whither Daisy had already disappeared, having instructed that various stacked seed trays and boxes should be brought in after her. This had not yet been done, but as Ingrid swayed past them, the three men speeded up their hammering so that they would soon have an excuse to follow her.

Everyone had some part to play that morning—everyone except Montague Rowles. With a sigh, he wrenched his gaze from the marquee entrance through which Ingrid had vanished and turned his attention to the lower lawn. This fairly hummed with activity which to an onlooker must seem chaotic: but the participants knew it would come right in the end, as it had always done before.

About the perimeter of the lawn were dotted heaps of coloured timber that in time would be assembled into stalls. When Ernie, Roy, and Ralph had duly carried Daisy's flowers into the marquee, and had drunk the beer they saw as their reward, they had further tasks to perform on the upper lawn before they descended to struggle with the erection of the various sideshows. Only the black Raffle stall stood complete. This was due to the presence of Ian Millage, Redingote's resident do-it-yourself buff, whose wife Fiona had undertaken to run the Raffle, and co-opted him at the first available moment. Once the heavy work was done, she kept him firmly by her side, though he was one of the few able-bodied men present. Let the others wait their turn for the official assistance of Roy, Ralph, and Ernie! Fiona Millage wanted to have the most successful stall of the entire fete: having it the first assembled and the first set out would go a long way to achieving that goal.

It had been Ian who designed and supervised the building of the stalls during the past few months, adapting with reasonably faithful care a plan from one of his many handyman journals. If he couldn't put one together now without effort, Fiona had warned, there was little hope for anyone else. She had dragged him to The Stooks at an early hour to ensure the job was safely done, and ordered him to remain with her in case of accidents. At present, he was disembowelling the ancient loudspeaker system which lived for most of the year in a dusty box beneath the little stage of the creaking parish room, while Fiona gloated over the contents of Cedric Ezard's unauthorised prize hamper.

"Oh, we should do really well with all this, Ian. Even in summer, grapes and peaches aren't cheap—and figs, too! Only ten pence a ticket! I mean to sell every book—but oh, dear, just look at poor little Tibby with her precious Tombola. She hasn't even got it set up yet. What a shame there's nobody to help her!"

"Trust Bob not to get lumbered," came Ian's voice from under the table, where he was fiddling with two lengths of flex and some metal clips. "No flies on him, are there . . . bet he's in the pub right now. . . ."

"Whereas you," she reminded him, "are here, helping me!" It was more a command than a statement. "Helping me, and nobody else—we want to make more money than the rest of the fete together, don't forget."

Ian grunted. He knew what she really meant was that they must make more money than Maisie Tibb, who with her husband Robert was their nearest neighbour. When the Millages, at Fiona's urging, had moved to the country to be closer to Mother Nature, the Tibbs viewed them with suspicion and scorn. Fiona named the chickens Pertelot, Licken, and Len; the cockerel was Chanticleer; the pig was called Cranberry. His companion was Llama, a goat with an elastic neck and a catholic appetite. The Millages never seemed able to maintain their fences in good repair; the Tibb vegetable patch was the envy of Redingote . . .

Left to themselves, the two husbands might have made friends soon enough. In The Scold's Bridle they would nod, pass the time of day, and buy each other the occasional pint. But their wives took the feuding seriously. Great tact and cunning had therefore to be employed to avoid a major confrontation—a state for which parish fetes are all too renowned. . . .

Yet it was tradition alone, rather than a wish to avoid confrontation with anyone—Ingrid Radlett, for instance—which now found Gwendolyn Pasmore working for the fete at the opposite end of the manor grounds. In contrast to Ingrid's languid attitude in the Flower Show marquee, Gwendolyn was a tornado of energy. In the rose garden at the foot of the main lawn she and her friend Myra Wilford, wife to the bank manager, were setting out in their usual places the benches, trestles, and tables for the Teas. With the cunning of long experience, Gwendolyn had arranged for the urn to be positioned outside in the main drive, at some strategic point past which everybody must walk at least once that afternoon.

"Goodness," gasped Myra, pushing back tumbled hair from a perspiring forehead. "If this keeps up, we'll make a fortune. They'll all be parched!"

Gwendolyn eyed her in concern. "My dear, if you're so hot, let's stop for a while. Now that I look at you, you're quite pale. Shall we sit down?" She led the way to a tree of climbing aspect, beneath whose rose-laden boughs a short bench had been set to catch whatever scant shade there might be. "Why, you're exhausted!"

"Just a little tired." Myra sighed. "I suppose if I'd had the car—if I hadn't had to walk . . ."

"You walked? In this weather?" Gwendolyn's eyes went to Myra's feet. "Good heavens! Why didn't Silvester—"

"He was still asleep," Myra broke in, then blushed for her apparent rudeness. "You see, he had rather a late night—he seems to work all hours at the bank now. I shouldn't scold him for being conscientious, should I? He needs his rest so much—I hadn't the heart to wake him just to bring me here."

Not for the first time, Gwendolyn wondered whether Myra could truly be as ignorant of current gossip as she seemed. The village had strong suspicions of Silvester, and voiced them more loudly with each passing week; and few doubted Myra's devotion. Some years older than the husband who was popularly supposed to have married her for her money (which he delighted to spend at every opportunity), Myra treated him in that doting fashion peculiar to those women who, marrying late in life, have no children. Not even to her close friend Mrs. Pasmore had Myra ever breathed a word of dissatisfaction with her lot, though the unusual sexual requirements of the younger partner had been rumoured in Redingote for some time now. But the village liked and pitied Mrs. Wilford, and kept its counsel when she was near. Even so, Gwendolyn reflected, nothing ever remains a perfect secret in any small community; and she admired her friend's composure, her steadfast loyalty and silence.

"I agree," said Myra—by what train of thought, Gwendolyn could not guess—"that it was a clever idea of Ingrid

Radlett's to save money by building our own stalls—but how I wish she'd thought more carefully about who was to erect them! In the good old days we'd never have had to do everything like this, would we? Our own people always helped us, while the market men did the necessary on the main lawn.''

Gwendolyn nodded. "They'll be hours before they reach us, I'm afraid. I've only seen a couple of able-bodied men so far this morning, not counting Old Cedric, that is—and everyone seems to be drunk, in any case.''

"Then we'll have to press on regardless by ourselves.'' Myra rose to her feet with reluctance. "Oh, dear. . . .''

Gwendolyn picked up a small card table. "Where would you—oh, damn! Look, a ladder—and these were new today!'' She scowled at her stocking. "If *only* we didn't have to do all this—bother Ingrid Radlett and her interfering ways, making so much extra work and trouble for everyone!''

"I suppose,'' said Myra, with a sigh, "it might have been more sensible to wear trousers, but it's so hot—and Silvester doesn't really like me to, of course.''

"Ah, yes—Silvester. Isn't he meant to be bringing Edgar Hemingway along with him later? We'll conscript them both,'' said Gwendolyn, brightening at the thought.

"Well . . . I'm not sure when they'll be here. Silvester was so very tired, poor lamb—and you know what a fusspot Edgar is about his secondhand books. He's bound to ask Silvester to help him first. . . . I think we'd better resign ourselves to doing everything on our own, Gwen. But''— Myra tried to smile—"I feel cooler after the rest. . . .''

Gwendolyn bumped her knee against a chair leg, and muttered behind a well-bred hand. She caught Myra's eye and sighed. "Oh well, maybe I'll take a quick look on the main lawn, in case I can spot anyone at a loose end.''

"Like Old Cedric? You know he's devoted to you, and if he told Barney to help us, I'm sure he would.''

"I haven't seen Cedric for ages, and Barney not at all—though the grounds are large enough for them to be anywhere, of course, getting things ready for this afternoon. I'll go for a quick scout around. . . ."

When Gwendolyn returned, Myra was standing where she had left her, still and thoughtful. She roused herself to look a question at her friend, who pulled a face.

"They're still miles away at the Bowling for a Pig, and they have a crate of beer with them—I told you so! Only the marquee is ready, and the Raffle—Mrs. Brown's arrived to do her stall, but she doesn't count, of course." A cough and a sallow blush. "I saw Mr. Rowles watching it all, with great interest—but I suppose we could hardly ask him. . . ."

Preoccupied as she was, Myra nevertheless felt herself smiling. "I suppose not." Recent events had led to strong speculation that Gwendolyn Pasmore might be contemplating marriage with the manor, despite the dubious nature of its new owner. And who was Myra Wilford to warn her friend of the possible perils of an unequal partnership? "I suppose not—but if he should happen to come along, we could always ask him, couldn't we? Until then, though, we'd better get along by ourselves, if we want to be ready by—oh!"

"A ladder," sympathised Gwendolyn. "What a morning."

"And barely eleven o'clock," lamented Myra. "What a morning, indeed—you were so right, Gwen. Damn and damn and *damn* Ingrid Radlett, say I!"

Two

EDGAR HEMINGWAY PROFESSED to be a man of letters, but his looks and life-style were far removed from those of his namesake. He hung chintz curtains at every window of his thatched cottage, and was given to much violence of colour in the drooping bow ties he affected.

He was pacing now about his cluttered sitting room, the creases on his forehead portraying, to his own satisfaction at least, artistic uncertainty. With every few steps he had to hop nimbly to one side, for the room contained, among its myriad pieces of furniture, a bulky selection of cardboard boxes, which were piled high with the perennial bargains of never-purchased tomes whose prices Edgar always marked in pencil, for the convenience of index-linking the increases. Every year these books were brought out for the fete; every year he failed to dispose of more than one or two.

"But *nil desperandum* and *excelsior*," he was wont to say, clapping fluttery white hands together in an ecstasy of enthusiasm. "My books are sepulchres of thought— medicine for the soul—so cheaply bought, for thrice their weight in gold! Golden volumes! Richest treasures, objects of delicious pleasures! If only," and now he pouted, "Mr. Wilford would but hurry himself to collect them—and me. . . . Twice, nay, three times I have telephoned to remind him, with no reply! Can it be that he has already left—perchance has dallied on the way—or are his ears deaf to my summons?"

Edgar barked his shin against an unnoticed crate as he turned a corner of the Persian rug, and said something unartistic to alleviate his feelings.

The mishap decided him. "I shall await his arrival no longer! I shall this instant mount Shanks's Mare, and go to remind Mr. Wilford of his duty!'' He pranced into the hall, snatched a floppy felt hat of oppressive mauve from the table, and crammed it on his blond curls as he locked the front door. Then he began to mince delicately down the garden path and in the direction of Silvester Wilford's house, in search of the promised lift.

This had been Myra's covert attempt to redeem her husband in village opinion, though she had sense enough to trust Silvester with no more vital task than the transporting of Edgar Hemingway's much-mocked books from his cottage to the manor grounds. Failure to carry out so simple an act would gain far less censure than if he had caused the same inconvenience to one of the really popular stalls, such as the Raffle—or the Bottles.

Mildred Waskett wished to ensure her success with the Bottle Stall on this occasion of the new vicar's introduction to Redingote. She had welcomed the slow approach of her brother Caleb and his fellow churchwarden, and at once began to make them work for the pleasure of her company.

"If Mr. Millage can build his own stall, Caleb Duckels, then so can you," she said, with sisterly severity. "You too, Joe Norton—never mind standing there with that grin on your face! These bottles is all to be won, so you can keep your thieving hands off them, save for setting 'em out on the stall once you've put the thing together."

Joe, whose gaze had been fixed more on Mildred than on her prizes, turned red at the scolding she had only inflicted on him to cover her own embarrassment at his silent worship. Caleb spoke up to rescue them both from the predicament into which they'd brought themselves.

"Fair enough, Mildred, for us to help you set them out, but when you're away to the house getting dinner ready for the new parson and his lady, what's to stop us quenching our thirst with a drop or two of good ale?''

All three paused in their labours of stall construction to glance towards the Bowling for a Pig on the upper lawn, where the forms of Ralph, Roy, and Ernie were slumped in hot exhaustion about their crate. Mildred sniffed. "If you're desperate, you can share with those three pot-valiants—if there's any drink left by the end of the work! But you've both to leave my prize bottles alone, do you hear? And stop wasting time in nonsense—we've this stall yet to build.''

''I fancy,'' said her brother, ''that by next year, once we sort out the teething troubles with 'em, we could make us a bob or two renting these out to other fetes, eh?''

Mildred and Joe, labouring in energetic silence, nodded wisely. Caleb fastened the final bolt. The stall might be wavering a little, but it stood upright, and looked service-able enough to him. '''Twasn't such a bad idea of Mrs. Radlett's,'' he remarked, ''was it? Not just a pretty face. . . .''

''It don't look so bad,'' agreed Joe, surveying the result of their hard work with pride. ''What we'd have to do is ask what Allingham market charges, and charge a bit less. We'd make money hand over fist, so we would.''

''And spend it as fast,'' said Mildred, as she began to bustle about her stock of boxes and bottles. ''There's the lych-gates to pay for, don't forget—not to mention the parish rooms being painted. A powerful deal of money you'll need for all that, I reckon!'' Both churchwardens chuckled at this reminder of Redingote's most recent feud, but said nothing. Mildred frowned. ''And you'd need to keep proper accounts, too—time to stop the muddling along you've done since Mr. Wilford came to the village, him adding the interest and doing the sums as the mood takes him. With being a bank manager, he did ought to have been better at the job than ever the pair of you were . . . but it don't seem that way, does it?''

''Hard enough to keep track of the housekeeping, let alone balancing books when you're not trained to the task,'' said Caleb, recalling his own dismal state after the death of his wife, and how he had welcomed Mildred's offer to come home and take care of him. Bachelor Joseph nodded, but said nothing. ''So pleased we were that a man had come into the parish as was suited to the work, I suppose we never thought it all through proper. . . .''

''Only too glad, we were,'' confirmed Joe, ''to be rid of

the worry and confusion of it all, and not having to think of things save only once a year. . . .''

"Or when a new parson comes to take over," said Mildred. "You'll need it straightened out methodical before he comes, won't you?"

The three shared village doubts of Silvester's character and worth, but, sharing them, saw no reason to speak of them now. His strange treatment of his wife might be accepted as virtual fact, but the rest was, in Christian eyes, still conjecture. Until it had been proved, were they to condemn him without trial? And, if such trial found him guilty, were not others almost as much to blame? Which blame, once broadcast, could do only harm in so small a community: better to say as little on the matter as possible, even among trusted intimates.

"Coronation year, the parish rooms were last painted," reflected Joe, reverting to a safer topic.

"Lych-gates or parish rooms," said Mildred, briskly setting out her prizes, "we've money for neither till the fete is done. So let's be getting on with the job, eh?"

Had Mrs. Waskett been on the upper lawn to oversee the efforts of Roy, Ernie, and Ralph, they might have already completed the Bowling for a Pig and the Coconut Shy, and have moved down to the stalls on the main lawn. But Mildred wasn't in the right place to chivvy the workers, and neither was Daisy Hollis, whose powers of nagging were notorious. Daisy was still out of sight in the marquee with Ingrid; and the three men were gathered about their crate of beer, refreshing themselves more deeply than their labours so far seemed to justify.

"He's there again, staring at us," muttered Roy, with a backward jerk of his head. "That's to say Mr. Rowles, which I don't like it, not in a man—gawping and hovering like an old woman! It ain't natural for anyone to be so idle when there's honest work to be done."

"Stands to reason, though, since there's none among us'd want him to help them." Ralph Stretch hiccupped. "We don't take kindly to foreigners in these parts, do we, boys?"

Roy loudly agreed, but Ernie spotted the flaw. "It's the

man's own house, remember. Whatever letters I bring for
him, I bring here—and if a man's got no right to wander
about his own house and garden, well, what rights do any of
us have?'' Which bravado, from one whose wife bullied
him from dawn to dusk, rang hollow in the ears of his
friends.

"The sun's addled your brains, Ernie Hollis, to talk so
daft.'' Roy took a draught from his tankard, and his next
words were slurred. ''Many's the time haven't you said to
us—loud and clear you've said it—as this Rowles never
gets no letters! So how can you say now as you deliver 'em
for him, whether to this address, or no?''

"Ah, well . . .'' Ernie grinned. ''Not *letters*, I'll
agree—never gets none of them, he don't, but official
communications, that's a different story. Which is all he's
had since he come to live among us. Gas and telephone and
selectricals. . . .'' He frowned at the final word, burped,
and let it pass. ''Bills, anyway, all of 'em, which I brings to
his own front door. And so why shouldn't he walk about and
stand in his own garden, say I!''

"He's not one of us.'' Ralph Stretch summed up the
misfortune of Montague Rowles in five short syllables.
"That man don't belong here—and we don't like that, do
we?''

But, even as the others chorused over their beer that
indeed they didn't, within the Flower Show marquee Ingrid
Radlett, whose exotic presence at first sight belonged in
Redingote far less than did Mr. Rowles, had been working
with Daisy Hollis to play her part to the full. Still ignorant
of the seething undercurrents of village politics which had
brought her to prominence, Ingrid admired and pondered
many a choice bloom and ornate arrangement before pleading a sudden need for fresh air. Daisy observed her growing
pallor, agreed that the lush green richness inside the
dust-dancing canvas was sometimes a little too much, and
gave her permission to escape. Ingrid emerged thankfully on
to the upper lawn, and took several deep breaths to recover
herself.

She noticed Mr. Rowles, watching in wistful mood the

pre-fete frenzy on the lawn below. She made for the steps, and had to pass close by him; she thought she heard him sigh. When she addressed him in her husky tones, he jumped.

"You still wander with no work to do, Mr. Rowles? Those fellows over there"—she smiled and waved at Ralph and his cronies around their crate of beer—"take a long while over their task, do they not? How Mrs. Hollis will berate them when she appears at last from the marquee to find that her husband is not as hardworking as she would wish him!"

Montague glanced at his watch. "Two-thirty's coming closer all the time, but they haven't left the warming-up stage. If they didn't keep stopping for a drink every five minutes, of course, they'd be halfway done by now."

"But it is so very hot, do you not think? And with the afternoon to come even hotter, I fear." Ingrid's pallor had not completely disappeared, and she contrived to look frail. "The marquee was so stuffy I had to leave for a while—yet I must return before long, to complete the judging. All has to be ready for the new vicar and his wife." She smiled. "You must be a lover of fresh air, I think, Mr. Rowles, for you have been standing oh, so still, out here for so long—we must find some work for you, must we not? If even such as I, a foreigner, can be pressed into service . . ."

They exchanged few words more, for Montague found her teasing tolerable in only small doses. They parted company: he to stump grimly down the slope towards the left-hand side of the main lawn; Ingrid, calm as ever, though pale, gliding down the steps in the direction of the Raffle, and her good friends the Millages.

Fiona and Ian had been squabbling—or rather, Fiona had scolded while Ian endured in silence. Ingrid's curiosity pricked her. The stalls stood sufficiently close to one another for neighbours to overhear enough to whet the appetite and, by straining only a little, on occasion to hear far more. The ladies of the nearby Produce Stall listened avidly, without wishing to show it, but to Ingrid Radlett such subterfuge was unnecessary. She might torment with sideways words and looks, but she could be direct when the mood suited; so she drifted into the Millages' view, and waited with a patient smile on her lips for Fiona to fall silent.

It was the dawning of a sudden grateful light in Ian's eyes which alerted his wife to the appearance of Ingrid. Fiona glanced round, saw her friend's look of amusement as she listened, and flushed. She frowned, then decided to make the best of things.

"Oh, hello. Have you come to rescue Ian? He's lucky I don't thump him. He almost electrocuted me just now."

"I did tell you not to touch that loudspeaker wire . . ." But Ian was more interested in their audience. "I say, Ingrid, you're looking a bit peaky. You icy blondes from the frozen north aren't used to this sort of weather, are you? Come to think of it, neither are we."

Fiona was still annoyed with him. "It's so middle class to complain about the English weather, Ian. Remember, we moved to the real countryside to get away from that sort of artificiality."

"Good lord, the farmers round here are always going on about the weather, no matter what it does. *All* the locals love to moan about it—and they're never satisfied, so I'm in good comp—"

"Nonsense," snapped Fiona, throwing an apologetic look at Ingrid, married to a local man.

Mrs. Radlett could not miss the chance to sow a little discord. She sighed. "I myself also, Fiona dear, find it hot . . . Although," she added, judging nicely just how far she might push her luck, "that must be, I think, because I have been assisting Mrs. Hollis with the Flower Show. Inside the tent is very stuffy—and she was talking, always talking—and marking cards of entry with one of the pens which smell so of waterproof ink. . . ." She shuddered. "I was not able to concentrate at all upon my work—but you, how you have already been working! To make such a wonderful display—so many prizes—such fruit! It looks delicious!"

She reached out to stroke a peach with a gloating

slowness that brought Ian, standing near her, red-faced and confused, even closer. "I say, Ingrid," he warned, as she caressed the soft bloom again.

Fiona saw signs of danger. "Those are prizes, Ingrid, and you can't have one. But if you buy a ticket—buy a book, or two—these are our best selection, so for heaven's sake treat them gently. Don't—"

Ingrid had picked up the peach and was staring at it. "So sweet it looks, so very tasty—I cannot resist!" And, before the astonished Mrs. Millage could prevent her, with her sharp white teeth she bit into the skin, revelling in the luscious flavours and rich, sticky juice.

Even Ian looked shocked at such wilfulness, but Ingrid was equal to the occasion. Prettily contrite, she looked for a place to deposit the peach stone (Ian earned another scowl from Fiona when he produced a clean pocket handkerchief for the drying of Ingrid's juice-dampened fingers) and awarded Mrs. Millage a wide smile. "Oh, Fiona, it was one only, and so delicious! I promise I will buy many books of tickets this afternoon, to compensate—but for this morning, I brought with me nothing but my vase, with its single rose, walking in the heat of the sun." An exhausted sigh quivered softly on her lips. "Do please reassure me that I have not destroyed utterly your display. . . ."

Fiona rearranged the hamper's top layer, hoping not to appear less delicately sweet in her husband's eyes than her friend. "Oh, well," she said at last, "there's no real harm done, I suppose—but you'd better buy plenty of tickets, I give you fair warning. You have your position to maintain, remember—and besides, I'm determined to do better than poor old Tibby and her Tombola. If everyone keeps pinching the prizes, I won't be able to."

"I promise," said Ingrid, with a soulful smile for Ian's benefit. "Many, many tickets I shall buy—for it would not be well that Mrs. Tibb should present a fine total of money to the new vicar, while my dear friend Fiona does not."

"Here, I say," protested Fiona's husband. "The Tibbs are perfectly decent sorts, if you stay on the right side of them, and—well, neighbours—community spirit, and all that—and, uh, this is supposed to be a *Christian* church fete, isn't it?''

The look of utter astonishment with which the ladies, at once united, greeted this innocent remark turned Ian's ears an embarrassed pink. He mumbled something, and bent to fiddle again with the wires and workings of the temperamental loudspeakers.

"That's right," advised Fiona, "keep to what you know—or at least, leave me to get on with what *I* know." And she favoured Mrs. Radlett with an exasperated smile.

Ingrid smiled back. "You have achieved so much—the stall built, the prizes on display, and looking so fine. . . ." She was unable to resist another little dig. "Although now I see over there how Maisie Tibb has at last someone to help her. She may yet manage to catch you up."

Fiona looked quickly across the lawn, then relaxed. "Oh—your pal Rowles. He's been hanging about all morning asking daft questions and getting under everybody's feet." She smirked. "Tibby must be really desperate to have asked him—you know what the locals can be like," she reminded Ingrid with glee, "about strangers."

But Mrs. Radlett remained serene. "Am I not a stranger myself, Fiona? Yet made welcome in the village—if only as a wife?" Her smirk was less obvious. "And why do you refer to him as my friend? Poor Mr. Rowles, so abrupt, so uncomfortable—no wonder he is much suspected in Redingote. . . ."

The object of this suspicion was oblivious to it as he conversed now with Maisie Tibb in what he hoped was true lord-of-the-manor fashion. "There's really far too much for you to manage on your own, Mrs. Tibb. You must allow me to assist you," he said, looking upwards to the clutter where Roy, Ralph, and Ernie tried to make sense of the Bowling for a Pig and the Coconut Shy. "It is the least I can do, in the circumstances. Since Cedric Ezard and Barney seem nowhere to be found. . . ."

Maisie could see the beer crate, and the glasses wielded to such effect by the three men; she could also see, across the lawn, Fiona Millage—with time enough on her hands to

stand talking to Mrs. Radlett! Her stall built, her prizes
prepared . . . and herself with the Tombola still a heap of
planks on the grass, the boxes barely unpacked, the tickets
needing to be sorted. . . .

Maisie sighed. ''I'll say yes, thanking you, Mr. Rowles.''
And felt a flicker of guilt at the pleased look which lit
Montague's sallow face. Had it not been for her wish to
spite the Millages, there was no way she would have turned
traitor to Redingote opinion and invited him to help her—
some folk'd never fit into the village, not if they was to try
for a thousand years. . . .

Edgar Hemingway was another who had no idea of the
true general view of himself. Redingote had long since
dismissed him as a harmless, literary lunatic. His books and
poetry and posing did no harm, and were the source of rustic
witticisms of which he remained blissfully ignorant. He
considered himself a beacon of light in the darkness of
Allshire philistinism, and believed each year that the value
of his Book Stall must at last be recognised.

But this year, the books had yet to be united with their
stall: the late arrival of Silvester Wilford at Edgar's cottage
had distressed that gentleman—as had the blisters he felt
sure grew ever larger on his heels as he went tittupping the
final few yards along the road.

Turning in at the gateway, he stubbed his toe against a
raised paving-stone, and uttered a remark under his breath
on the topic of the parish council which would have
shattered his image, had anyone heard it. But it was
drowned out by a sudden shrieking whirr of missed gears
and false starts—a sound which suggested that Silvester had
at last remembered what he was supposed to be doing.

Edgar forgot his blisters and sped up the long curved path
in delight. He peeked round the corner of the house, and saw
a man, bleary of eye and disordered of dress, hunched over
the steering wheel of a car.

''I give you good day, Mr. Wilford,'' he piped. ''I
thought—that is, I began to fear our paths might cross and
confusion arise—your kindly promise to myself and my
precious volumes, you know—so I felt it better to come

straight to you.'' And he beamed upon Silvester with grateful goodwill.

The bank manager groaned, and buried his face in his hands. Edgar Hemingway summed up the situation with the experienced eye of one who, in his lost youth, has starved in garrets with the best. ''What you need, Mr. Wilford, is coffee—black as Hades and *superlatively* strong! Nobody with the least spark of compassion in his soul could expect you to drive a car until you have refreshed yourself!''

''Drive?'' Silvester shook his head. Evidently he had come out to the car on automatic pilot. ''Drive? Where the devil was I going, I wonder. . . .''

''Coffee!'' trilled Edgar, and shook a playful finger. ''I shall join you in a cup, if I may—before we *whistle* away to my little home to collect my cartons of books!''

''Books? Ugh!'' Silvester closed his eyes, then opened them slowly. ''Oh, yes, I believe Myra did mention . . .''

''And coffee would be so refreshing for *me*, after such a long walk, you know.'' Edgar tugged at Silvester's sleeve, and startled that sleepy heterosexual into a swift exit from the car. It seemed no time at all before they were in the Wilford kitchen, where Silvester slumped cautiously at the far end of the table, keeping a wary eye on what Edgar was doing with the percolator and the grinder.

Edgar sighed. ''Ah, what a blessing it must be, to be able to drive.'' He frowned at the bubbling percolator and raised his voice. ''Alas—the temperament must be suitable, in order to associate successfully with the infernal combustion engine. I fear that we artists . . .''

Silvester, with the immediate threat of Edgar's presence removed as he spooned sugar, muttered some reply which satisfied Mr. Hemingway while requiring no effort. For Mr. Wilford had begun to remember what he had been doing the previous night to have rendered him such a wreck: she had been so lively, so demanding, so inventive—but he was growing no younger, and, even though she had accommodated herself wonderfully to his wishes . . .

''Poor Mr. Wilford! So woeful a countenance!'' Edgar set a dainty cup on the table before his host. ''Drink up—all of it—and we can soon be on the road. Plenty more where that came from, should you wish it!'' He sipped his own coffee and chirrupped blithely on about unimportant matters to which Silvester listened with a heavy heart. If only he hadn't made such a fool of himself last night—the risk was too great—and did Myra know? Had she guessed? Would she understand? Everyone was different—had their own needs, their own desires. And if, for whatever reason, his usual partner was unwilling, then he must experiment elsewhere. . . .

He drained a second cup of coffee. How had that come to be full? He had no recollection of asking Edgar to give him more, welcome though it was: and the thought that Mr. Hemingway had been creeping about close to him without his knowledge made him jumpy. He began to urge his guest out of the kitchen and towards the car. Catholic though Silvester's tastes might be in some respects, he had no desire to remain for too long alone in the company of Edgar Hemingway.

''Ugh!'' In full daylight he noticed for the first time the colour of Edgar's shirt, his tie, and his hat.

Edgar misunderstood his distress. ''You feel poorly again, Mr. Wilford! Why not try sunglasses?''

''What? Oh, no—nothing like that. Come on, will you?'' And once more Silvester began struggling to set his car in motion—anything rather than have to look at that silky floral horror round Edgar's skinny neck. . . .

Bright colours were great favourites with Barmy Barney, gardener's boy at The Stooks. Barnabus Chilman, incestuous brother-son of Tabitha ''The Touched'', blessed like his sister-mother with one blue eye and one brown, had always found his fancy caught by extremes of sight and sound and perfume. They seemed to compensate in some way for what, in his half-witted fashion, he was occasionally aware that he lacked.

This morning, Cedric Ezard had set him to sort through the fete boxes, which were brought out each year for the great day. Barney's delighted rummaging had lasted until Cedric, with a kick and a curse, had returned to order him to make himself more useful than plain gawping over streamers and flags in the middle of the lawn. Whereupon, duly chastised, Barney had gone striding up to Miss Phoebe Barrie's White Elephant Stall with an overflowing fall of gaily-coloured bunting in his huge hands. "Pretty, Miss. Fetched 'em for you, I have." And with a broad grin he thrust the brilliant bouquet into the arms of his former schoolmistress. "Pretty, ain't they?"

"Very pretty, Barnabus, thank you. And . . ." Phoebe was tired of waiting under the weeping willow for Roy Urvine and his friends to reach her and her huddle of green planks: and she set herself to press Barney into service in the erection of the White Elephant Stall. He had the strength of two normal men in his huge body, and if properly supervised was able to follow basic instructions. Miss Barrie coaxed and coerced; Barney's muddled memories of school, once she had made cunning reference to Cedric's sure approval, wrought slow obedience in him; and the stall was built at last.

Miss Barrie's evident pleasure at his achievement made Barney stand on one leg to puzzle how he might please her further. "Pretty . . . string, Miss. Hang 'em up for you, shall I?" And he seized one of the flags at random.

"Barnabus, no—wait! They're still very tangled. We must unravel them before we can put them round the tree."

"I'd like to hang 'em round the tree, Miss. All green and yellow and blue and red . . . red . . ."

An unfocussed look came into his eyes, and Phoebe's long knowledge of the Chilmans prompted her to try changing the subject. "Where is your, ah, mother this morning, Barnabus? Barnabus!"

His wayward attention returned. He dropped the bunting back on its pile, and stood on one leg again as he strove for an answer to her question. "Oh . . . her's at home today, Miss. Brewing. . . ."

"Oh," said Phoebe. Tabitha Chilman, more cunning than her sibling-son, had long ago convinced superstitious Redingote that she (like Barney the product of illicit familial affection) was a witch. There was widespread belief in her ability to ill-wish livestock, addle eggs, curse the crops or bless them, as the mood took her. She and Barney lived a comfortable existence on the pacific oblations left by night on their doorstep, and bartered for extras with Tabitha's sorcerous remedies for those various rustic ailments deemed unfit to be entrusted even to the care of Dr. Oliver Radlett, son of the Old Doctor.

Oliver Radlett dismissed Redingote's attitude as likely, on the whole, to cause little harm. "If they will insist on medicine that tastes nasty, well—Tabitha's muck is as nasty as anything I could concoct!" For the village still preferred his home-dispensed bottles to the dangerously modern pills or injections other doctors might suggest. Redingote was conservative in such matters, and had been acutely suspicious of Oliver's recent removal to a new house, until he confirmed that his father's entire clinic would be accommodated on the premises, just as in the old building. And, he reminded them gently, there always remained Tabitha Chilman and her witch-bottles to comfort their prejudices. "She's done no harm that I know of," he would say, "and may even do some good. If people *believe* what they take really helps them to get better, that often does more for them than the best orthodox medicine money can buy!"

Phoebe, in her role as schoolmistress, could not encourage such scandalous and irresponsible opinions, striving to educate them from the minds of her young charges. Once, however, Redingote had left school and entered upon adult life, it reverted to type with a vengeance: Tabitha and her brewing were as much a part of village custom now as they had ever been.

"Sometimes," confided Barney, still fumbling among his collection of flags, "her lets me help when her's brewing. I do so like to pestle them berries, squish 'em flat with the juice dripping out—like blood. . . ."

Phoebe said quickly: "Aren't these flags pretty colours, Barnabus? Red, blue, yellow, green—but I wonder whether we have enough, you know. Perhaps we should count them as we go, just to make sure."

After a moment's thought, he nodded. "All right, Miss.

I'd like to count 'em for you. I remember. One, two—red, yellow . . . three, four, five—blue, purple, green . . . five, seven, eight . . ."

"Splendid, Barnabus, splendid." She wouldn't break his fragile train of thought in case it wandered back to those earlier, gruesome meditations. She hoped she had diverted him successfully: he probably had no idea of how unnerving his presence, even to one who knew him well, could be at certain times. A simple, routine task involving the easy repetition of basic facts was the best way anyone in Redingote knew to keep him under control. . . .

Suddenly, he stiffened, stopped counting, and pointed, like an enormous, ungainly gundog. Phoebe followed his gaze. Ingrid Radlett, having moved on from the Raffling Millages, was talking to the ladies of the Produce Stall. With a grunt, Barney dropped the flags and stood up, breathing heavily. He saw her—right near to him, if he took but a few long steps—

"Barnabus!" Miss Barrie spoke with the voice of old authority. "No slacking, now. Pay attention. We have the rest of the flags to sort out, as well as streamers to put round the tree—to make it pretty. . . ."

With a sigh, he allowed himself to be ordered away from staring at Ingrid, settling back to his mundane task with grudging obedience. His heart was no longer in what he was doing: he stopped gloating aloud over the colours, and did not number the flags any more as he worked. . . .

For which Phoebe felt mingled relief and guilt. Those references to blood had rattled her more than she might have expected. Barney had always been erratic, though his moods were usually kept in check by the fresh air and exercise prescribed by Dr. Radlett. Oliver had persuaded Cedric Ezard to take Barney as an apprentice when Tabitha's treatments started to lose their limited effect and he became a nuisance. Generally, the prescription worked.

But when the moon was full, it could take very little to unhinge Barnabus Chilman.

And Phoebe had remembered, with a sinking heart, that there was to be a full moon that night. . . .

───── Three ─────

BUT THE NIGHT was far off; the day would grow hotter before evening came at last. For Montague Rowles, struggling solitarily with Maisie Tibb's Tombola, it was already too warm. City life had not accustomed him to hay-making, rick-stacking, and the myriad other rural pursuits which tone the muscles. He hadn't gone far in his labours before he had to remove his jacket, revealing a brocade waistcoat which would have delighted Edgar Hemingway; and he paused frequently to mop his overly moist forehead with a bright silk handkerchief.

"This, er, isn't as easy as it looks, is it?" he said in breathless accents to Maisie. "I notice they've finally finished up there. Do you think they might come down to the main lawn next?"

"They will," said Maisie, "but they'll not come over here till the end. Clockwise round the lawn they always go—but, seeing as Mrs. Millage is ready on the Raffle, they'll start now on the Produce. It's all right for Fiona Millage. She's got her hubby to help—and he designed the stalls, what's more," she added with an envious glare in Fiona's direction. And poor Maisie, desperate to catch up with her rival, urged Mr. Rowles to ever more strenuous efforts.

At last, flushed and weary, though pleased to have completed his task, Montague turned to Maisie and smiled. "So what next, Mrs. Tibb?"

But now came the crunch. Maisie, forced by jealousy to employ an outsider's aid, scorned to give Fiona any further cause to sneer; and with brief thanks told Mr. Rowles she had no more need of him. At first, he was dismayed; then he was (secretly) relieved. He had made his first essay at fitting into village life, but today was really very hot. . . .

He decided that a squirearchical stroll would set him to rights, and moved away from the purple piles where Edgar Hemingway's Book Stall was to stand and the space left for the Candy Floss barrow. He arrived at the drooping shade of the willow tree, now festooned with yards of bunting by Barney and Phoebe, and moved gratefully out of the sunlight.

Miss Barrie welcomed her visitor (so much more in command of his wits than poor Barney, who was growing restless); and sped the gardener's boy on his way, aiming him in the direction of the rose garden, in case he might otherwise be tempted to accost Ingrid Radlett. Then she smiled at Mr. Rowles.

"I suppose you haven't come to offer your services, by any chance? I hesitated to entrust to poor Barnabus the unpacking and setting out of my goodies—putting the stall together was quite enough for him—so I wondered whether . . . You would? Why, how very kind of you."

With a silent groan, Montague again removed his jacket and set to work. Maybe it was better not to be in too much of a hurry to integrate into the community, after all. He thought Barney Chilman had been lucky. . . .

"Ah, Barnabus!" Down in the rose garden, Gwendolyn Pasmore saw the chance to ensnare another worker. "Are you doing anything special? Would you like to help Mrs. Wilford and myself arrange the tables and chairs for tea?" She and Myra had suffered enough splinters and bruises in the cause of charity, and Barney with his beef could achieve more in ten minutes, if carefully watched, than the pair of them in an hour.

"I've helped already," he informed her, with a quick look behind him up the steps. He was waiting for Ingrid to come down them, certain in his poor mad mind that she must walk that way to see him. "Flags I've put up, round the willow for Miss Barrie—three, four, five . . ."

"And very nice, too, I'm sure. Cedric told me"—in her most coaxing tones—"how pleased he is that you are being so helpful and making such a splendid contribution to the success of the fete.''

"Old Cedric said that?" Barney's bicoloured eyes brightened. He held his mentor in high regard, and Mr. Ezard's word was generally law where poor Mr. Chilman's daytime activities were concerned. Besides, everyone knew as Old Cedric had took a fancy to Mrs. Pasmore and wouldn't let nobody do nothing to upset her. He'd surely be pleased if somebody was to do his best to help her. . . .

"I don't mind," said Barney, "if Old Cedric says so."

"We want the rose garden to look smart and tidy for the Teas, don't we?" Mrs. Pasmore smothered her sigh of relief, and began to issue instructions. "What Mrs. Wilford and I were doing was—"

"Same like always. I know." Barney gave her one of his more intelligent looks, and she decided to count her blessings and let him carry on with the work in his own way. It was too hot to argue.

Heat or no heat, the ladies of the Produce Stall were arguing. They stood in a critical huddle to watch what was being incoherently achieved by the little band of Ralph and his friends, now finally descended from the upper lawn to start the next stage of their duties. Since they'd already drunk more than half the contents of their crate, they were making hard work of assembling the stall, even though Fiona Millage—who could hardly avoid hearing all the grumbles—had taken pity on their plight and hurried across from the Raffle to see what advice she could offer.

"You," said fat Hermione Plenty, "had your good man to help you, and a pity he's not still here, Mrs. Millage." Her several chins vibrated as she sighed. "A *great* pity, say I. Many hands make light work, eh?"

"And too many cooks," retorted Elsie Lilleker, "does no good at all, as everyone knows!" She glared at the three befuddled workers puzzling over the various unconnected sections of the stall. "One of 'em sober," she said, "can do more good in half the time than three of 'em drunk—"

"So who're you saying's drunk?" demanded Ralph

Stretch, slurring his words and swaying. "Thirsty work, so this is, and nobody'll deny it. . . ."

Elsie had stationed herself in front of the beer crate, and continued to glare. "Not another drop do you rumbunctuous sots deserve, not till my Produce Stall is up and in one piece, I tell you straight. So just you get on with it!"

"Ian went off somewhere to find something to fix the loudspeakers," apologised Fiona, as by some strange village telepathy everyone turned towards her. "I could go and look for him, if you like—"

"What's the use of that?" demanded Elsie, waving Roy and the rest back to work. "They has to learn for theirselves sometime, so now's as good as any other. But"—she did not trouble to lower her voice—"though these fancy new stalls may well save money in the long run, there's no saving us time, and that's a fact!"

Ingrid Radlett, talking at the next stall with Mildred Waskett and her helpers, did not appear to notice what Elsie said, though an awkward pause ensued. Fiona hurried to fill it. "What super fruit," she exclaimed. "What a marvellous display your stall's going to have—"

"When it's built," snapped Elsie. Hermione wobbled in sympathy, but said nothing. Ralph Stretch glanced their way, but changed his mind about arguing further when he saw the expression on Mrs. Lilleker's face.

"When it's built," Fiona agreed. "It will look splendid—the peaches and things are almost as good as the ones Cedric Ezard gave us for the Raffle—"

"Which so they should," retorted Elsie, "seeing as how he brought these here to us, too, not an hour since, and never mind Mr. Rowles giving permission or no. Charity, it's for, ain't it?"

Fiona was surprised. "You mean Mr. Rowles didn't want to—but surely he can't have minded! When the fete is in the grounds of his house—and, well, look." She indicated Montague's labouring form over by the White Elephant Stall.

Mrs. Millage hadn't integrated as well as she thought, for she had no idea of Montague's earlier refusal to Caleb

Duckels concerning the fete's customary location. Hermione chose to enlighten her—a little.

"He's no lord of the manor, that one, for all he might wish to follow the Izods." She chuckled richly. "Not that there ain't some as would like to help him aspire to the position, mark my words—if you can't buy breeding you can allus think of wedding with it, eh? You can be sure of what you're getting!" And the garland of chins beneath her moist mouth quivered as she leered, and laughed.

Elsie Lilleker frowned. "Wedding may be all well and good when folks *can* be sure of what they're getting, but Mrs. Pasmore ain't such a fool. Ladies like her only weds with gentlemen born, you mark *my* words—"

Hermione's shriek of glee interrupted her. "Lancelot Pasmore," she crowed, "weren't so much of the gentleman born, was he? For all his mannerly ways and fine talk!"

Fiona pricked up her ears, but Elsie cut in with a sharp reminder to her loquacious friend—and to Ralph and his cronies, who were chortling lewdly as they toiled—that it was all a long time ago now. "Best not to rake up old memories," she said, and Hermione subsided, though gurgles of mirth shook her frame for some minutes yet.

Fiona tried not to feel snubbed at being excluded from the scandal, and said again that the box of fruit looked splendid. A sudden thought came to her. "Any chance you could spare me just one peach? To make up the numbers in my hamper, you see."

Elsie gave her a knowing look. "Mrs. Radlett played her tricks with you too, eh?"

"Well—tricks, I hardly . . . that is . . ."

"Stops to pass the time of day, then whips a peach from our basket without so much as a by-your-leave! Said as how it weren't really so sweet as she'd wanted, but she'd settle up this afternoon when she'd got her money with her—which I'll not," said Elsie, raising her voice for the benefit of the Bottle Stall, "be forgetting, neither!"

Hermione made sympathetic noises. "A cruel thirsty day, so it is, and no doubt will get hotter as time goes on. Hard on everyone, such weather is, and not just them of my

size—though there's still no excuse for sneaking peaches,''
she added.

"Talking of thirsty . . ." Ralph, Roy, and Ernie had
come to the end of their labours, and were making for the
beer. Since Elsie could see no further reason to stop them,
she shrugged, and left them to it. Ernie Hollis beamed as his
eyes fell on the crate.

"And the Bottle Stall afterwards," he gloated: which
gave Elsie her parting shot.

"You sottish slowpoke, can't you see as they've done it
for theirselves, hours back? Tired of waiting for the whole
drunken pack of you, and I don't blame 'em, indeed I don't!
Be off and bother someone else, can't you?" And she glared
at them in scorn until, sheepish yet cheerful, they picked up
the crate and staggered away.

Elsie drew a deep breath. "Now we can get on.
Hermione—stir yourself, do, and let's start arranging the
goods—jams at the back, cakes and biscuits at the
front . . ."

They began to unpack boxes and baskets, while Fiona
hovered in helpful fashion nearby. She knew enough of
village custom not to offer assistance too soon: this had
been, she realised, Montague's mistake. Redingote wanted
to assimilate newcomers slowly, cautiously; they were
happy enough to unload such jobs as nobody local wanted
onto strangers keen to be accepted into the community,
flattered to be asked—but there had to be the right sort of
hints dropped, and she had not noticed them now. She stood
watching with interest, saying nothing.

"This lemon curds looks funny to me." Elsie stared at a
sinister and bilious jar with a greaseproof top. "Maybe we
hadn't ought to risk it—might poison someone, wouldn't
you think, Mrs. Millage?" Fiona had cleared another of
Redingote's numerous social hurdles.

"It isn't quite what I would have expected," she agreed,
while Hermione pursed her lips and looked wise. "Sort
of—sloshy, isn't it?"

"Tabitha made it, most like," opined Mrs. Lilleker,
looking quickly over her shoulder in case the witch should

be able to hear. "It's her style, no doubt of that—I really don't care to throw it away, but . . ."

"I'll drop it for you," Fiona volunteered. "If the jar is smashed, nobody could expect you to sell it—and I'll put the money in, of course. Tabitha doesn't bother me," she stated in decided tones. She was surprised that postmistress Elsie so clearly credited Tabitha Chilman with the ability to ill-wish the Royal Mail. "Shall I break it?"

Hermione's face creased with worry. "Best make sure as Barney ain't nowhere about to tell tales to her afterwards. Specially with it being full moon tonight. . . ." And behind her back she made the sign of the horns, to fend off evil.

All this was making Fiona nervous. "Well, look—give it to me, and I'll pay you for it and get rid of it at home, shall I? Then nobody will know about it except us three." She pocketed the lemon curd with only slight hesitation, and in her turn looked round for any sign of Barney or his mother. "But I'm afraid I don't quite understand—I mean, I thought the Chilmans were meant to be, well, harmless. Why, Barney wanders about the place all day—"

"And all night, too," broke in Hermione, restored to her normal good humour now the threat of Tabitha's wrath had been transferred to an incomer. "When it's full moon, that is. Brings out the courting couples, and Barmy Barney with 'em! Really takes an interest, does Barney," Hermione said, and her eyes disappeared into laughing slits.

"Full moon's tonight," said Elsie, like her friend maliciously relieved that the problem had passed to another. "Tonight as ever is. . . ."

"Oh. Oh, dear." Fiona slept in the nude, and sometimes went barefoot in the dew to feel close to nature. "I hadn't realised . . ." Her hand tapped nervously on her pocket, and she wondered whether she had acted wisely.

Someone else who was wondering whether recent actions had been altogether wise was Montague Rowles. He had said good-bye to Phoebe Barrie at the White Elephants before he was exhausted, and had strolled off towards the Teas in the rose garden—a move which must be seen as

coincidence, for a newcomer could not have known that
Gwendolyn Pasmore would be there manoeuvring furniture
with Myra and Barney. Who, on seeing his employer,
exhibited signs of agitation, fearing that Mr. Rowles was
checking up on him. Old Cedric might be his nominal boss,
but even Barney's weak wits knew who paid him; and the
look on Montague's face as he stood at the top of the steps
staring down made young Mr. Chilman freeze in his tracks,
too nervous to fidget.

Gwendolyn, far wiser, recognised physical weariness
when she saw it. "Poor Mr. Rowles! You look worn out.
Why not join us for a while, and take a seat in the shade of
your beautiful roses? Barnabus has been most helpful in
setting out the chairs and tables—you shall be our first
visitor."

Myra Wilford hid a smile for her friend's quick thinking.
Marriage with the manor, even if Montague Rowles was an
unknown quantity, seemed likely to be what Gwendolyn
wanted; and Myra wouldn't stand in Mrs. Pasmore's way.
"I wonder," she said, "why Silvester's so long coming
with Mr. Hemingway and the books? I'll just slip up to see
if they have arrived—he promised he'd come along to help
us here after the Book Stall was ready, but he may have
forgotten. And I'm sure Cedric"—she turned to Barney—
"will have some more jobs for you, Barnabus, now the
tables are nearly all set out. . . ."

Her stare was so pointed and penetrating that even
Barney, who had been shuffling from one huge foot to the
other, could sense that it was time to be gone. "Old
Cedric'll be wanting me," he agreed, with a pleading look
at Mr. Rowles. "Never told me to set out tables and chairs,
he didn't; make myself useful, he said. Twenty tables I've
carried today, twenty—counted 'em myself. And four times
twenty chairs, what's more."

"Which is quite enough, on such a hot day." Myra
nodded to Gwendolyn, beckoned to Barney, and headed
briskly for the main lawn: so briskly that she did not see
how Barney, fired by some unspoken impulse, ambled

instead towards the drive, leaving Montague alone with Mrs. Pasmore.

Myra found no sign of life at Edgar Hemingway's purple Book Stall, which seemed to be the only one as yet unbuilt. Everyone else, observing the slow progress of Ralph, Ernie, and Roy, had assembled his or her own stall themselves, and was busy arranging goods and prizes in full display. Ralph and the rest had dumped their crate in the middle of the main lawn, and were refreshing themselves yet again from its contents, relieved their work was done. Myra looked round for something useful to do. She had no wish to play gooseberry among the roses; she realised Barney hadn't followed her, and was therefore out in the drive—and she had no wish to be alone with him; there were only two ladies working by themselves, and she did not care for Phoebe Barrie. Slowly, she walked towards Mrs. Margaret Brown.

Mrs. Brown's Prize Every Time was her totally autonomous and invariably successful contribution to the annual parish fete. She arranged and ran it entirely by herself: providing all the prizes, supplying her own float of small change, and even building it herself out of decorating tables, light enough for one short woman to carry instead of the usual heavy stall, which did not suit her system so well. She had five hundred prizes to set out in numerical order for ease of location once they had been won, and great concentration was required in the setting. As Myra approached, Margaret looked up quickly, smiled what was obviously no more than a polite greeting, then bent her head to work on with busy hands which clearly needed no assistance.

But Ingrid Radlett was talking to the churchwardens on the Bottle Stall—the Produce and the Raffle seemed well ahead with whatever needed doing—Phoebe Barrie's White Elephants were depressing. . . . So Myra hovered by the Prize Every Time, ready to offer help if asked, but otherwise at a loose end.

She would have been gratified to learn that her generous strategem was paying off. In the rose garden, Montague, reluctant to seem feeble in Gwendolyn's eyes, had removed his jacket for the third time, preparing yet again to assist a lady in distress. "I've already obliged Mrs. Tibb on the Tombola, and Miss Barrie, so you see—"

"I see that's how you've torn a button loose!" Gwendolyn clicked her tongue as she drew closer, ignoring the waistcoat's deplorable design and concentrating on the damage suffered by the jacket. "You'll lose it altogether if you're not careful, and I should think it would be difficult to match. Unless you already have a spare, that is."

Mr. Rowles stared briefly at the button, then wrenched it off. "Difficult to match—yes, you're right, Mrs. Pasmore, as ever. Very good of you to mention it. . . ." He placed the button carefully in his pocket, then favoured her with a shy smile. "Do you suppose I could persuade you to fix it for me later—once we've finished here? One good turn deserves another, they say." He had made up his mind: he knew breeding and influence when he saw them, and Gwendolyn Pasmore personified both. His hopes for a prosperous and successful future in Redingote were rising by the minute—particularly as Mrs. Pasmore gave him a pleasantly flustered reply in the affirmative to his suggestion. It had, he reflected, been a long time ago, and since then he had changed his name—what harm could it do . . .

There were those at The Stooks that morning who needed more encouragement to set about their courting. On the Bottle Stall, Caleb and Joe had watched Ingrid Radlett drift elegantly away, and returned their attention to helping Mildred Waskett. Mildred had completed most of the setting-out by herself, and was inclined to be brisk.

"Parish business or no, Caleb Duckels, there's a time and a place for everything," she reminded her brother. "I suppose you've forgot as the new parson and his lady are to eat their dinner at our house today in time to open the fete—and me having the meal to prepare as well as do here. . . ."

"You leave all that to me and Joe," said Caleb firmly. "You've no need to fret yourself—we'll do what's needful here while you get the dinner ready. But hey, now," and his eyes twinkled, "what about fitting in an extra mouth once we're through with the Bottles, eh? A fair exchange that would be—right, Joe?"

Mr. Norton caught Mildred's eloquent eye, and turned a pleasing shade of Courtship Crimson as she smiled the invitation she had hesitated to offer on her own account. Then in her turn she pinkened with a Bridal Blush, muttered something, and hurried away down the lawn and round the side of the house.

Joseph Norton's gaze followed her. He sighed. "A fine woman, your sister, Caleb. . . ."

Mr. Duckels was pleased to misunderstand. "A fine cook, certainly, and a housekeeper to beat all. We'll eat well today, us and the new parson, and his wife . . . ah now, what did that remind me of?"

Joe looked puzzled. "What did what remind you of?"

"Wife, Joe Norton, that's what!" Caleb chuckled, and Joe turned even redder. His fellow churchwarden suddenly reached over and thumped him on the shoulder with a friendly fist. "Joe, we've known each other years, man and boy—all our lives, near enough—and with my sister being that few years younger nor us, I reckon you've known her a lifetime and more, right?"

"Right," mumbled Joe, looking at his boots and blushing.

"And after a lifetime—or two—such as this, what call have you to haver and hedge so about putting the question to her? If you carry on in such a fashion, there'll come somebody more forrard as'll snap her up from under your nose, Joe—and serve you right, say I."

Joe opened his mouth, coughed, and shut it again. Caleb laughed aloud. "For pity's sake, man, ask her, and put us all out of our misery! What are you waiting for?"

"Well, now . . . what about you, Caleb? She'd be leaving you to fend for yourself if she was to—to wed with anyone, whether 'twas me or another. . . ."

"So how d'you reckon I managed all the years after my Susan was took, before Mildred's good man died? Get away? You've no call to trouble yourself over Caleb Duckels this way, Joe—no call whatsoever.''

Mr. Norton's eyes brightened at the reassurance. "Could make a fine welcome for the new parson, to have a wedding so soon after he's settled . . . and it's a grand day for thinking of getting wed, no mistake about that." He gazed into the sun-bleached sky above, and smiled. "Swallows raising their second brood, if I'm not seeing things. . . ."

"It's an omen, Joe. A good omen, for both of you."

There was some moments' silence, heavy with thought. At last, Joe straightened his shoulders. "I'll do it, and this very afternoon, what's more—once the fete's quietened down a bit and she'll fancy a break. I'll ask her to take a walk with me through the maze and into the middle—to sit on the bench near that statue . . . what's bin good enough for Doctor Oliver is surely good enough for Mildred and me."

Caleb heartily approved this suggestion, adding that it had been on just such a hot day that Doctor Oliver had asked Mrs. Radlett (as of course she'd not been then) to marry him. "That old maze could tell a few tales if it wanted—and the statues most of all! Maybe it's lucky they can't talk, some of the goings-on there must have bin over the years. . . ."

"We were all young and foolish once, Caleb Duckels, but it was a long time ago. There'll be no such nonsense for Mildred and me, at our age—although," and Joe's eyes began to twinkle, "it's a grand place to go courting, indeed. . . ."

"Then you be sure that's where you go and what you do, Joe Norton, this very afternoon!" Caleb seized one of his sister's bottles with a laugh, ripping off its ticket. "And here's a drop of champagne for drinking your good health in, brother-in-law!"

Joe looked properly shocked. "You can't do that! Your sister's as particular as Mrs. Radlett, with her systems and tickets—right angry she'll be, if you go messing things up out of order. Put it back, do!''

Caleb grinned. "Nothing like a spot of Dutch courage to spur a man on, Joe. Just one drink of this, and—"

"Drink?" came a voice, rather slurred, from behind them. "Now, that's a word to cheer a man's heart on such a day!"

Ralph Stretch had abandoned his cronies (and the crate) to stagger across to the Bottle Stall, whose contents he surveyed with a wistful eye. He leaned against one of the uprights, which wobbled. He pushed himself away, gazed at the stall in wonder, and said: "Done our job for us, so you have—but not so good, seemingly." He shook a fuddled head, and leaned on the other upright to balance himself.

"Catch him, quick!" Caleb grabbed Ralph's arm, and shook him. "He's not to go tumbling about and breaking all Mildred's bottles. . . ."

"Bottles enough of our own," came another voice, as Roy Urvine appeared, walking with great care, to find out what was happening. "Powerful hot day it is, too. . . ." He looked from Ralph, reeling in Caleb's grasp, back to Ernie, still sitting by the crate. "Ernie! Any beer left, eh?"

"I reckon," Mr. Hollis called back blurrily, after a long pause. "A few bottles, maybe. . . ."

"And the work all done for us," observed Roy. "Good!"

Churchwarden Caleb was displeased. "*Good* it certainly is not, and not *all* done, neither, with the Book Stall yet to build, and Mr. Wilford due any minute with Mr. Hemingway in his car—and never mind what use it is, the new parson won't think so highly of us if we aren't ready for him when he comes. Joe, you and I had best help Ralph and Roy fix Mr. Hemingway's stall, and"—raising his voice—"you, Ernie Hollis, get along to the meadow and fix up the Donkey Rides. And leave that crate behind! You won't need that to hammer in a couple of stakes. . . ."

"Would do him no harm to stick his head in the beast's bucket of water, neither," muttered Joe Norton, as Ernie set off erratically round the opposite side of the house from that towards which Myra Wilford, murmuring of Silvester, had gone when Mrs. Radlett had joined her near Mrs. Brown's Prize Every Time. All about the grounds of The Stooks people were busy with their own affairs: there were various disputes and heated discussions, some of which mattered more than others. Most would be over and forgotten by the time the fete was open, though some would fester and annoy for a long while to come.

Amongst all the confusion and tumult, any late arrivals went unnoticed. Mr. Wilford and Mr. Hemingway might appear with the latter's books, but once the stall was duly erected nobody would have cared when—or indeed if—this happened. Anyone organising a parish fete is far too preoccupied with their own worries to pay attention to the comings and goings of anyone else, no matter who they are.

Which (understandable) lack of general observation was to contribute much to the difficulties encountered by the police when, later that day, they were trying to solve the first of the Redingote murders. With hindsight, of course, the problem would never have arisen—with foresight, it would have been easy to remain watchful. . . .

And then there need have been no mystery at all.

───── Four ─────

TIME MOVED ON as it always does: slowly for some, quickly for others. People began to go home, for a bustling midday meal and an early return. Cedric Ezard, who had kicked Barney out of the drive and set him to watch Olive Yetts of the Candy Floss, excused his henchman from guard duty once Mrs. Yetts went home, and permitted him to join himself and Ernie Hollis at the entrance to the maze. There they ate bread and cheese, and finished the remains of the crate of beer which Ralph and Roy had abandoned on the lawn, and to which Ernie, returning from the rough-grassed meadow where he had struggled with the Donkey Rides, had laid claim. Apart from these three, the grounds of The Stooks were almost deserted. The sun passed its zenith, to begin its slow, scorching decline. The heat made the whole world lazy. Even the bees, normally so busy among the nearby roses, seemed barely able to buzz. The swallows wheeled weary spirals in the air, and whatever breeze there might have been flickered, and faded away.

Then people started to reappear: stall-holders, hangers-on, customers. Cars crunched along the gravel, to be directed into the lower field, well away from the Donkey Rides. Somebody took up a position by the gate and began to demand money from each new arrival: walkers, motorists, and even a pair of cheerful young punks with a motorbike handed over without argument the sum required.

The public address system was as efficient as ever. ". . . cackle . . . in a few minutes . . . zzzzz, whiiine . . ."

Ian Millage was in despair. He had gone home alone to consult his reference books, and returned to The Stooks with confidence and a tool-kit—but to no avail. Fortunately, most people knew from long experience what he was saying.

"Not much longer, then," remarked postmistress Elsie Lilleker on Produce to fat Hermione Plenty. Hermione nodded, and sighed, and fanned herself wearily with her drooping cotton hat. Elsie, less affected by hot weather through wiriness of frame, sensed a furtive movement behind her, and quickly turned.

"Now then, Tabitha, you can't buy nothing yet. Didn't you hear just now as they told us to be in our places ready for the new parson's wife to Open? We can't take no money till then—it wouldn't be fitting."

Tabitha Chilman's eyes—one blue, one brown—brimmed with tears of frustration, for her fancy had been caught by the bright scarlet of strawberries. As Elsie hesitated to remove the punnet from the witch's reach, Tabitha drew in her breath and fixed Mrs. Lilleker with the unblinking gaze that rarely failed to achieve its object.

Elsie froze, her hand hovering above the punnet, and it was Hermione who spoke as soothingly as she could, torn between the demands of parish etiquette and the risk of having her chickens cursed with fowl pest. "See here, Tabitha my dear, just so soon as New Parson's wife has Opened, you can buy as much as you like, and welcome. But we wouldn't wish to start selling too soon, now would we? Hardly polite to the poor lady, is it?"

Cedric Ezard was being far less hesitant in his refusal to begin his particular part of the proceedings. Outside the maze stood Ethel Maggs with her impatient grandchildren, Damian and Dawn, arguing. The Gibbins twins were trying to behave well, since Gran's moods were dreadful now she'd had that quarrel with Auntie Elsie at the post office and come to live in their house—but it was hot, and they were restless, and their promised treat seemed a long way off.

"Gran's going to take us right into the middle," Damian explained, in a petulant squeak that penetrated even the wilfully deaf ears of Cedric Ezard. "We might even have a race, on the way back—then we can go round all the other stalls, and—''

"I want candy floss," interposed Dawn, not knowing this was the remark most calculated to inflame Mr. Ezard's temper. He had disputed hotly with Olive Yetts over the risk to his lawn from her Candy Floss barrow, but had an unhappy suspicion that he'd lost. As Ethel Maggs added her protests to those of her grandchildren, he folded his arms, and glowered at everyone in sight.

"Not till we're Open," he said, and turned to where Barney stood guard at the entrance. "You hear me, boy? Only when we hear the parson's lady say we're Open does anyone get into this maze—money or no," he added, for Ethel's benefit. She had already tried what he saw as bribery, offering to pay extra if he'd only let her and the kiddies in quick, so she could take the weight off her poor feet for a spell once they got to the centre. . . .

"Money or no," he insisted, "nobody goes into my maze till we're Open!"

"Come on, let the kiddies in," urged young Mrs. Gibbins, who with her husband had heard the complaints of her family borne on the summer air, and had come at once to find out what the matter might be. "Their gran promised she'd look after them—they'll do no harm to your precious maze, if that's what's bothering you."

"Take 'em in ourselves, if you like," volunteered her spouse, with a reminiscent gleam in his eye. He nudged his wife, and winked. "Be like old times, going back in there, eh, girl?" And she giggled.

"No," said Cedric. "Not till we're Open."

Ethel had gained her second wind now reinforcements had arrived. "There's nobody to notice whether we go in or not, nor to care, neither—and me with my poor feet. Stop all this talk and let us in, do!"

"Well there is so," said Barney, who had listened to the discussion with an alert expression on his normally vacant face. "Somebody to notice—I seen 'em. Two more, waiting round the back—a wench, and a spark from the town, leather jackets and orange hair—orange hair . . .'' He gurgled with sudden laughter, his blue eye glittering, his brown eye gleaming. It was obvious from his leer what he was thinking of, and Cedric's reply was sharp.

"Keep a clean tongue in your head, boy, and a clean mind as well. Whoever they are, and whatever they want, orange hair or green, it's all the same to me—rules is rules. We ain't Open yet. . . ."

Among the ruins of the loudspeaker system on the main lawn, Ian Millage struggled again with the wiring, watched by an exasperated Fiona.

"For heaven's sake leave that alone! I don't know why you bother—it hasn't worked properly for years, and nobody listens, anyway. She'll just have to say her piece without mechanical aid—which is so much more rural and authentic, in any case. And it will be over that much sooner, because we'll be spared a long speech, thank goodness."

Ian nodded. "They say she isn't one to rabbit on interminably, any more than his sermons last for hours—whether there's a loudspeaker or not." A faint sigh escaped him. "They sound a nice, sensible, ordinary couple. . . ."

Fiona glared at him again, then switched on a smile as someone rushed up with a message. Ian nodded again, leaned forward to seize the ancient silver-meshed microphone, then yelped. A small cloud of blue-grey smoke, speckled with red sparks, danced its way upwards from the Raffle Stall to disperse with a low, loud buzz, the passing of some giant swarm of electrical wasps or hornets. As the sound faded, Ian was left wringing his hands.

"Just as well," remarked Fiona, "they haven't arrived yet. If the new vicar had heard what you said—"

"He'd have said exactly the same," he replied, through gritted teeth. "So would anyone who's been electrocuted! But it's really kaput now. There's nothing I can do—she must just yell a simple blessing on the afternoon, and get everyone spending. We'll need to make even more money now, with new loudspeakers to buy."

Fiona was not listening. "They're coming—at least, I assume this is them. The dog-collar . . . so watch your language in front of them, please!"

Ian and Fiona were not the first parishioners to catch a glimpse of their new vicar and his wife: the gatekeepers had an unbeatable claim to that honour, though they were closely seconded by Gwendolyn Pasmore and Myra Wilford, stationed in the drive beside the Tea Stall. Gwendolyn and Myra had been discreet, though interested, observers of the triumphant arrival at The Stooks of the Reverend David and Mrs. Gregory, escorted by Mildred Waskett and the churchwardens. Cherry Gregory was suffering a mild attack of indigestion from having bolted her lunch, but urged the others not to tarry on her behalf, insisting that the Opening must be delayed no longer than necessary.

"They seem a pleasant young couple," murmured Myra, as the cavalcade vanished round the corner of the house. "Mind you, she looks as if she won't stand any nonsense—which is likely to surprise quite a few people in Redingote, after fifty years without a vicar's wife to its name."

"She might even," said Gwendolyn, "persuade Mrs. Radlett to curb this sudden enthusiasm for parish affairs—after three years of couldn't-care-less, the last twelve months smack of hypocrisy to me." She looked sideways at her friend to see whether Myra might be tempted to make some comment; but Mrs. Wilford's reply was noncommittal.

"You can't deny she's had some good ideas." She rattled the vacuum flask filled with crushed ice. "Selling the fruit squash really cold for once is going to be a splendid gimmick on a day like this."

"Then it's a pity she didn't think to suggest that we had a bigger tea urn, as well—although, if you ask me, her interest in the Teas is of a rather . . . haphazard nature, to say the least."

Myra followed Gwendolyn's gaze as it scanned the groaning table. "Yes, that was funny about the butterfly cakes, wasn't it? Do you think—"

"I'd rather not! Today's not the day for thinking much about anything—it's far too hot. Let's just put it down to one of those moods, shall we? Or the heat, or something. And let's forget about it."

"If you say so, Gwen." Myra frowned. "All the same, it does seem funny . . ."

"Funny they've not started yet," said the mother of a tot waiting outside the Flower Show. The tot was anxious to learn if its Six Wild Flowers (Sunday School Members Only) had won a prize, but the doors of the musty marquee were still lapped firmly across. Daisy Hollis wanted no sneak previews until the Opening: partly out of politeness to New Parson's wife, and partly from her own desire for time to recover herself. The judging had only just been completed. When Ingrid Radlett broke her promise to return once the fresh air had revived her, Daisy had been forced to swallow her pride and hurry to the cottage of Caleb Duckels, knowing she must eat humble pie—and, in such an emergency, trying not to grudge the eating, though she was now, like Cherry Gregory, suffering acutely with indigestion.

Ian Millage, at the Raffle, was also eating humble pie, as he explained to the Gregorys what had gone wrong with the loudspeakers. The Reverend David regarded his breathless wife with amusement.

"Three cheers for the loudspeakers, that's what I say— throw away your notes, darling, and just tell everyone to start spending. Short and sweet and exactly to the point. Perfect! I hate preaching long sermons—and listening to them, too." He turned to Caleb before Cherry had time to think of some withering reply. "Mr. Duckels, could you do the introductions?"

Caleb cleared his throat with a rumble, and stepped forward with his cupped hands raised in a megaphone. "Good day to one and all!" he boomed in the bass which made him a worthy member of the choir. "Now then, seemingly we've had a mishap with the speakers—but not to worry," as poor Ian's ears turned scarlet. "There's few enough words needed saying on such an occasion, goodness knows. And all you'll hear from me is that this lady here is Mrs. Cherry Gregory, and her husband our new parson, the Reverend David Gregory, and both of 'em's come to

Redingote fete today as Mrs. Gregory's kind enough to Open for us. Mrs. Gregory!''

He bobbed his head and stepped back, as Cherry stepped forward. Everyone strained their ears to make out what she said, which was sensible and succinct, culminating in an almost siren shriek that the Summer Fete of the Parish of Saint Swythun and Saint Jude was well and truly Open. Those nearest heard most of her speech, but the general import was clear to all; everyone on the lawn emitted a spatter of applause which circled out from the Raffle Stall and rippled round to meet, mingle, and fade by the far willow tree; then people began to open purses or delve into pockets, and to exchange words with the servers behind the stalls; and the money came rolling in.

Caleb now introduced David and Cherry more fully to Ian, as Fiona was busy selling yet more raffle tickets and could only smile. Mr. Duckels explained that they had Mr. Millage to thank for the grand array of homebuilt stalls around the main lawn. . . .

''Though of course 'twas Mrs. Radlett, that's our young doctor's lady, she had the first idea, being an accountant by trade. She took it into her head last winter to work out how much we spent on hiring ever year from Allingham market—very methodical, she is. Even suggested we should paint 'em different colours, so they could be sorted more easily when we took 'em out of storage.''

David looked suitably impressed. ''A useful member of the parish, then. I look forward to meeting her when she's feeling better—the rest of my new congregation as well, of course—but first I think we must buy some raffle tick—''

A loud wail from the Flower Show drowned him out, as on the lawn above, the tot discovered that it had failed to win even a Highly Commended. There came the sound of frantic shushings, and a sharp slap; then a small, plump shape hurtled tearfully from the main marquee entrance and, yelling, headed for the Candy Floss, pursued by its red-faced mother.

Olive Yetts on the Candy Floss, Roy Urvine (now almost sober) at the Bowling for a Pig, Ralph Stretch (not quite so sober) with his Coconut Shy were all doing brisk business; Mildred Waskett on the Bottle Stall, assisted by a quietly adoring Joe Norton, was having her share of excitement as the customers flocked to spend. "Any lucky number wins a bottle—twenty pence a time—oh my goodness, no!"

Joe turned to blink at her. "What's wrong?"

"Whisky! And only a kiddie, too—you put that back, my dear, and take something else. We'll change the tickets so there's no muddle to the system, but I'll not have a youngster walk away from my stall to tell all and sundry as I gave a bottle of whisky for a prize. With the new parson here—and me the sister of a churchwarden, too. Whatever next?"

The unhappy winner had gathered the import of Mildred's words before she'd finished the first sentence, and began to back away, wide-eyed and wary. "Yar—smine! I wunnit, so I did, and I wanna keepit!"

Joe felt he should act before things got out of hand. He leaned across the stall, to smile in avuncular fashion. "Now see here, son—"

"Me name's Julie."

Joe flushed. Why did modern parents insist on unisex dungarees and pudding-basin haircuts for their offspring? "Julie, then. Now you listen like a good girl to your Uncle Joe. It ain't fitting for a little maid like you to drink spirits—but there's no need to take on," he added hastily, as Julie opened her mouth to emit a howl of rage.

"You ain't my uncle—you're nasty! And I hate you!"

"What d'you think you're doing, upsetting my girl this way?" Julie's father came rushing to the rescue. "What's going on?"

"We just didn't—didn't want her taking such a thing as a prize," mumbled Joe, with Mildred's eyes upon him. "Not with being such a young kiddie, you see. . . ."

"What!" Julie's father had recognised the bottle she clutched to her chest, and had a sudden awful vision of what would have happened had he not appeared. "You mean—good God, what a way to treat a little girl!" He turned to his daughter and smiled a rapacious smile. "Now then, Julie

love, tell you what your old Dad'll do—suppose I give you
a pound for this here bottle you've got, then you can have
a few more goes on some different stalls, maybe win
yourself something you'd like better. What d'you say?''

"Two pounds," proposed Julie, after a tense and
thoughtful pause during which her father tried to suppress
any display of emotion. Now he sighed with relief, and
completed the transaction before she could change her
mind. Mildred and Joe watched as the child scampered off,
the possessor of riches, then looked at each other as her
father strode away with the whisky cradled in his arms.

"What a way to treat a little girl, indeed!" exclaimed
Mildred, and Joe nodded; but before he could comment
there came a sudden rush of customers, and the moment was
lost.

At the Teas, Myra and Gwendolyn were consulting their
watches in some perplexity.

"We must surely be Open by now," Myra said, frowning
for the third time. Gwendolyn nodded.

"There was that bang, of course—probably the loudspeakers gone again. Oh dear, there seems to be no end to
what we need to spend money on, does there?''

"We'd better mention it to Ingrid Radlett—if she ever
condescends to appear, that is. I suppose she might just
come up with another of her brilliant schemes. . . ."

"We must be Open," Gwendolyn announced a few
moments later. "Here comes someone carrying something," and Julie's father hurried up to the Tea Stall.

"Have you got a cup?"

Please, supplied Gwendolyn silently, while aloud she
enquired: "Tea or coffee—with or without sugar?''

"A cup—an *empty* cup—or a glass, or a tumbler—just
make sure it has a hole in the top. All right?''

In silence, Mrs. Pasmore tipped the just-poured milk back
into its jug. "Five pence, please," she said firmly. Since the
fete was Open, he must be a paying customer: and so very
forceful was her look that Julie's father handed over a ten
pence piece and did not ask for change, but made straight
for the rose garden, gloating.

In this general region, the Open question was still being debated with vigour. The lowest-lying areas of the grounds were concealed from the main lawn of The Stooks by a brick wall, mellow and creeper-covered; the demise of the loudspeakers had left many distant places incommunicado, including this. Cedric Ezard and his henchman Barney were standing strong against a swelling tide of discontent, as people insisted that the time for Opening was, according to their watches, long past.

"We don't sell no tickets till this fete's officially Open," insisted Cedric for the umpteenth time, "because till it *is* Open this here maze ain't Open, neither. You'll have to wait, the lot of you."

The male half of the courting teenage couple which had so roused Barney Chilman pointed firmly to his wrist. "See this, Grandad? See them figures? It's way after half past, near enough twenty to three, it is! Look!"

Cedric glanced at the digital timepiece, snarled, and glowered. "This here maze ain't Open till I say so, boy, and I ain't said so yet. And a bit less of the *Grandad*, you and your imperence!"

Before he could say more, the pretty young girl with the orange hair decided to try persuasion instead of argument. "Oh, won't you let us in? We're going to get engaged when we get to the middle—read up about it in a book, my Gary has, and we're going straight there so's he can give me the ring official. Oh, please. . . ."

"Stop your sniggering, boy! And keep your eyes to yourself!" Cedric was more bothered by the behaviour of Barney Chilman than by the betrothal plans of strangers.

But the two young punks did not protest alone. Ethel Maggs, about whose bulk the Gibbins twins frisked in heated impatience, waddled up to peer into Cedric's stubborn face. "Plenty past the time it is, like the lad says, and you know it." She scowled. "It'll be real cool and comfortable when we can get to the middle and have a nice sit-down under the willow tree—my poor feet. . . ."

The Gibbins parents had retreated to the shade of the brick wall, but now came forward to add their voices to the general disaffection. Cedric began to feel threatened. In grudging slow motion, he drew from his pocket a large gold hunter; opened it; and stared long and hard at its face.

"Well," he said at last. "Well now—I dunno . . ."

"It's close on quarter to three now," the youth Gary informed him. The others nodded, and drew ever nearer.

The realisation came to Cedric that even he could hold out no longer. With a sigh and a curse, he spat once on the grass to prevent advancing feet trespassing still further, then took three ponderous steps back to his official chair, behind his official table, and settled himself to check once more the small change of his float tin. As everyone watched and muttered, he riffled through the printed instruction sheets without which nobody was expected to find their way to freedom from the centre of the maze. Another of Ingrid Radlett's innovations, these sheets had been produced with Cedric's particular assistance. He had been highly flattered by the attention she paid to his advice during their compilation, dictating them slowly, enjoying every moment of his self-importance.

He had not been so flattered at the suggestion that he must henceforth issue tickets from a roll. If folk were daring to doubt his honesty, after so many years . . . Ingrid used her most coaxing tones, and smiled her most seductive smile. Cedric could no more resist her wiles than any other man, though he held out rather longer before capitulating. Very well. If Ernie Hollis on the Donkey Rides was to have tickets, Cedric supposed as how it made sense for the maze as well, knowing himself better suited to modern methods than a drunk like Ernie, who'd most like not understand 'em even when he was sober. . . .

Out in the donkey field, Ernie was proving Cedric's very point, to the amusement of his customers. He seemed unable to grasp that issuing tickets in order from a roll must ensure that those who had bought them could wait in similar order, and nobody would be cheated of their turn. Like Cedric, Ernie had wanted everyone to wait, as he had not heard the official Opening; his reasons, however, were caused not so much by misanthropy as insobriety. The aftereffects of uncounted bottles of beer made him prefer to slumber peacefully for a few hours rather than lead a donkey up and down a field. He was so drowsy, and his wits so fuddled, that it was easy for his impatient clientele to persuade him to open for business; and as soon as he had hiccupped, and made the announcement that the Rides were now ready, he was swiftly overwhelmed as the crowd closed in.

There was also a fine crowd about Margaret Brown's Prize Every Time. In the shelter of the rose garden wall, grey hair tossed by the speed of her movements, Mrs. Brown tried to do fifty things at once, and did not observe that the clerical party on its grand tour had finally reached her.

"We'd better come back when it's quietened down a bit," suggested the Reverend David, while Cherry Gregory stood admiring the stall with its bright array of multi-coloured shapes, its variety of prizes large and small.

"Does it all by herself," whispered Caleb. "A marvel how she can, with her daughter wed and away from home—always used to help her mother, she did. Between 'em they'd sell the lot inside of an hour. Now she's on her own, it'll likely take longer."

"Then we'll come back after an hour," David decided; and at this exact moment Margaret looked up for a breather. She caught his eye, and smiled vaguely.

"She's seen us," said Cherry. "We'd better explain why we're dashing off so rudely—shall I give her a shout?"

But the shout they now all heard came from nowhere near the yellow Prize Every Time Stall; nor did it sound like the normal joyous shouts of a summer day, a happy gathering. . . .

"Help! Someone, quick—help!"

Cherry clutched her husband's arm. "David—listen—"

"Help, for God's sake! Somebody come quick—please!"

"The rose garden," said Margaret Brown, pulling herself together in the startled silence.

"More likely the maze." Caleb frowned. "Though mebbe it's no more than some youngsters fooling . . ."

"Get us out, please! There's a dead body here!"

"It doesn't sound as if they're fooling," said David.

Caleb, looking grim, nodded; then brightened as Joe Norton came hurrying across from the neighbouring Bottle Stall, and said quietly that they'd best take a look down there.

"Reckon we had, Joe," came Caleb's reply, above repeated cries from below which degenerated into a confused, horrified babble of shrieks. "What say Parson and I go to see what's what? And Joe, you stay here—keep 'em, away, just in case there's really summat the matter—"

"I rather fear there is," said David; for a third voice, banshee-like in its wailing, sounded sudden, but sincere:

"Hurry up—get us out of here! Somebody, come! Help!"

And everyone who heard those cries knew that they came, with all their pleading horror, from the middle of the maze.

———— Five ————

THE SHOCK-STUNNED VILLAGERS broke suddenly from their trance and surged towards the lower steps of the lawn, but Caleb Duckels was there before them. Turning, he faced the inquisitive throng with his hands upraised.

"Right then, everyone, keep back, and let's have no fuss while Parson and I see what's to do. Joe—keep an eye on things here, will you?"

The cries and sobs from below had erupted once more, and some of the shrieking was so clearly of the feminine gender that Cherry, anxious to be of help, had to be restrained by Joe in his capacity as guard.

"No, ma'am, you'd better stay here with the rest. If there's bin mischief done, that'll be no place for the likes of you."

"But there's a girl—in trouble—listen. . . ."

Caleb and David paused briefly at the entrance to the maze and also listened to the tumult from within— the tumult whose clamour and volume lent power to the argument now entered into with Barnabus Chilman. Barney, obedient to the trust laid upon him, was trying to prevent the passage of any person through the high green gateway. Old Cedric, at the first intimation of trouble, had left his assistant in charge, with strict instructions to let nobody pass, while he himself made his way to the centre; and Barney, who had twice already allowed himself to be elbowed to one side, was suffering pangs of guilt over his neglect of duty.

"Don't talk so soft, Barney!" The churchwarden spoke with the double authority lent by age and long acquaintance. "Do use your common sense, boy, if you can—it's gawpers and time-wasters as are to be kept out, not folk as might be of some use! This here's the new parson, and he'll tell you the same—won't you, sir?''

At David Gregory's affirmation and support, Barney was forced to acknowledge the sense of Caleb's argument; and, though his conscience still troubled him, mumbling and looking miserable he nevertheless let the two men by.

The sobs and cries for help had been augmented now by the wailing panic of a child, and the robust quarrelling tones of older voices. When Caleb and David—the latter's head whirling with twisted yew paths and piercing sound—came at last, breathless, to the middle of the maze, they stood in silence to survey the scene before them.

Near an oak settle, stretched beneath the kindly willow shade, lay the body of a woman. Beside her, crumpled in misery and clutching her hand, knelt a man. A broken garden statue nearby hinted at the manner of death's calling. As far from it as possible stood an ashen-faced youth absently patting a girl whose orange head was buried on his shoulder. Close to them a fat elderly woman, flushed and trembling, confronted an even older, weather-beaten man with a bright and glittering eye—even in such tragic circumstances, the clashing personalities of Cedric Ezard and Ethel Maggs could make themselves felt. Supporting Ethel, though silent, were a married couple who each by the hand held a child of the opposite sex to themselves.

Cedric, recognising reinforcements, stopped glaring at Ethel Maggs and stumped over to the newcomers. ''Thank the Lord—sorry, Parson—for someone with sense right now. Them fools''—he spat automatically, then scowled as he recalled the circumstances—''won't shift theirselves, and that Maggs female accused me of harming them pesky brats of hers too, when all I want is to clear the lot of 'em away and send for Ben Davers. Bodies ain't none of my business!'' He seemed about to spit again, then recollected himself, and angrily indicated the distant body of the dead woman.

''Yet they might well be considered mine,'' said the vicar softly. ''Although . . . are you absolutely sure she . . .''

''She's dead, right enough.'' Cedric's eyes glittered.

"And whoever he is, he wanted to do the job proper. Smashed that statue to smithereens over her head, so he did—a fine thing for the poor doctor to find, when he hears that wench caterwauling and comes along to help, and it's his own wife the cause of it all—dead!"

"Doctor Oliver," breathed Caleb, gazing more closely at the kneeling form beside the body. "It's Doctor Oliver—the poor Mrs. Radlett, dead—"

"Not so loud, you fool!" warned Cedric. "If that young Barney was to hear you, well . . ."

"Her husband, you say?" David Gregory looked again at the little tableau of grief by the settle. All the others were moving now towards the entrance, and rescue; but Oliver Radlett remained, holding his wife's white hand. "I must be of comfort to him, if I can."

Caleb turned to Cedric. Seldom had the two patriarchs agreed so completely, and so quickly, on any topic. "We'd best get Ben Davers—and fast. If we hustle 'em all outside—Parson can stay here with Doctor Oliver till help comes. . . ."

And, with the voice of quiet authority, comforting in crisis, he and Cedric set about removing everyone from the centre of the maze—everyone except the vicar, the victim, and the victim's mourning spouse.

The police cars arrived, their sirens screaming, and swept up the drive with a flurry of gravel. Detective Superintendent Trewley, his window fully open, caught a speck of sand in his eye, and sat back with a muffled curse.

"Steady on, girl—no need to scorch about the place like a mad thing. It's hot enough today without that!"

Those who met Superintendent Trewley for the first time were always unable to make up their minds whether he resembled a bulldog more than a bloodhound in appearance. He was a large and heavily built man of late middle age, with dark brown, mournful eyes, set in a face so lined with folds and wrinkles that mischievous members of the Allshire constabulary, when safely out of earshot, had been known to refer to him as the Plainclothes Prune.

"Sorry, sir." Detective Sergeant Stone—his sidekick, driver, and intermittent irritant—slowed the car to a more decorous pace. "But might I just point out that it was done for your benefit? I was only trying to create a through-draught. . . ." For it was well-known in Allingham that Trewley was thoroughly miserable when the temperature rose much beyond seventy; and the police station's air-conditioning had broken down only that morning.

Trewley replaced the handkerchief in his trouser pocket and then, with a sigh, drew it out again to mop his heated brow. The creases of his face glistened with perspiration, and his brown eyes were dull with weariness. "What I wouldn't give for a couple of hours' rain. . . ."

"And the thunder to go with it? Ugh." Thunder was one of the few things Stone really disliked. "Not while we're working, thanks. Hey!" She stiffened in her seat. "Look—over there, to the left! See him, sir?"

Trewley was leaning forward. "No, missed him. What did he look like? And where's he gone?"

"Wherever it is, he won't get far. The whole place will be swarming with bluebottles before another five minutes is up—and when a copper finds anyone skulking about in the bushes, he's bound to have his suspicions and haul the chap in. Care to take a bet, sir, on what he was doing, and why he bolted like that?"

"Guilty conscience, girl. When there's a murder, the red herrings multiply like rabbits, as you should know very well after all this time."

The car drew up past the now-deserted Tea table, at a discreet distance from the house. Upon the steps Cedric Ezard was waiting. Every inch of him proclaimed disdain and disapproval for the occurrence which had brought the police in such numbers to his ancestral domain: he scowled in reply to the official greeting, nodded abruptly when Trewley acknowledged Stone by name and waved behind him to the rest of the team as they emerged from their car; and fretted with impatience as the superintendent issued a few swift instructions before asking to be shown the scene of the crime.

The crowd on the main lawn fell silent as the little procession passed. None could doubt that Trewley, his face lined by years of grim experience, was the man in charge; but some surprise was expressed on seeing Stone, so clearly his second-in-command. She was small and slight. Her looks did not proclaim her either the black belt in judo that she was, or the student of medicine she had once been. (She had found that the sight of blood disturbed her even more than the sound of thunder. Her greatest fear since joining the police had been that she might one day be called upon to deliver an emergency baby.)

Behind the leading pair came men with cameras; men with notebooks and other, less recognisable apparatus; men with expressions of silent efficiency. And before them all, the personification of truculence, stumped Old Cedric Ezard.

Having led them down the steps to the entrance of the maze, there he stopped. "I'll go no further," he announced. "And I'll thank you to get off my chair, Ethel Maggs!" The fat woman, defiantly seated, bridled, but said nothing. "You, Barney—your place is here by me, boy!" And Cedric turned to Trewley, keeping Mrs. Maggs in his peripheral view as he went on:

"There's Caleb Duckels as can take you in, for I'm not wishful to see that sight again. Nor am I wishful"—and he spun round to glower—"to see my authority . . . besmirched in this fashion, woman! You can shift your backside right away, Ethel Maggs, off of my official chair!"

"I did tell her, so I did," gabbled Barney, quailing as his superior's glower reached him. "Told her as it was your chair—said you'd soon be back and how it weren't no place for her, but—"

"Seats enough in the rose garden," growled Cedric. He jerked his head towards the Teas, and spat. "Be off with you, woman, away from my official chair this instant!" And he advanced upon her with menace in every step.

The fat woman glared up at him. "I've had a shock," she

protested. "Me with my poor feet, coming upon her like that—I need to sit down—"

"Then do it somewhere else!" He turned to Barney again, just as the Gibbins parents, hearing above the quiet hysterics of their offspring the argument between the gardener and the grandmother, came across to join in on Ethel's behalf.

"Barney"—Cedric took no notice of anyone else—"tip her off my chair, boy, seeing she'll not shift herself of her own choosing!" And without hesitation the obedient hands of Barnabus Chilman reached out, seized the back of the folding chair, and rocked it violently until Ethel, clinging in desperation to no avail, tumbled heavily to the ground.

"Why, you bullying old badger!" cried Ethel's horrified daughter. "What have you done to my ma? Setting him on to do your own dirty work for you. . . ."

Her husband was helping his mother-in-law to her feet. "Always does as he's bid, does Barney," he said, regarding Cedric with a sneer. "Must make a change—for you, eh?" And he began to brush Ethel down with a brisk hand.

"After your Abigail," added his wife. "Well, stands to reason it does!"

Trewley and Stone had been watching the little fracas with interest, in case it seemed about to get out of hand—which, at this mention of the mysterious Abigail, suddenly seemed probable. Cedric had ignored fat Ethel's struggle up from the grass, and her family's complaint, and was settling himself smugly back on his chair; but on hearing the name he turned anger-white beneath his tan, his eyes blazing with a fury that seemed set to choke him as he gasped and spluttered for a suitable response.

The superintendent hurried into the breach. "Didn't I hear some talk just now of a cup of tea? Must have been a shock for all of you, I'm sure. See here, Stone . . ." He caught his sergeant's eloquent eye; hesitated; then grinned. She was not one of the most assertively liberated ladies of his acquaintance, but she had fought her battle—and beaten him—early in their working relationship. This, however, had never stopped him teasing her when the chance presented itself: and on this occasion she was glad of the teasing, as an indication that the heat had not as yet completely overcome him.

"Get one of the others to organise something, will you? And we'll go straight to the maze," he concluded, as Stone met his twinkling gaze calmly. "And tell 'em to save a cup for us, too!" He mopped his forehead once more, loosening his tie. With an effort, he turned back to Cedric. "You were saying we'd need someone to guide us to the centre. . . ."

A throat was cleared behind him. "Caleb Duckels is the name, sir—know this maze like the back of my hand, I do, so if you'd care to follow me. . . . By rights," he confided, "it did ought to be Old Cedric as takes you in, being the man in charge like he is, but he's that young Barney to see to, understanding him as well as most, working together as they do. . . ."

Trewley and Stone looked at each other in mystified silence, but no further explanation was forthcoming. They made mental notes to ask about it later, and continued to follow Mr. Duckels as he threaded his way through the verdant complexities of the old yew maze. The forensic team trailed close behind.

Sometimes he walked directly towards the tall willow in the centre, sometimes he diverted to right or left; sometimes he even turned back on himself. He walked swiftly, without hesitation: his boast that he knew the maze well had been no idle one. Trewley and Stone kept up with him, the sergeant's lighter frame more easily than her superior's bulk; she cast several anxious glances at him as they sped on their way, but was wise enough not to ask that Caleb, so much older than the superintendent, should slacken his pace.

"There's Ben Davers." Mr. Duckels paused at the entrance to the centre. "He'll see to you now. And I'll go on out, if that's agreeable to you?"

The sorry tableau now revealed to the detectives was being intently observed by a shirtsleeved giant in regulation boots. Dr. Radlett still knelt quietly holding his wife's dead hand; close to him, murmuring clerical consolation, was David Gregory. Neither paid any attention to the arrival of

Trewley and Stone, but the burly sentinel spied them with relief, and came hurrying over, sketching a salute as he did so.

"Police Constable Ben Davers, sir," he said, his eyes more on Stone than on Trewley. It was a phenomenon to which both detectives were by now accustomed, and the superintendent took no notice as he nodded for PC Davers to continue.

"Local bobby, sir—been here since I was first called to the scene," and he stood to attention. Then he became conscious of the informality of his attire, and struggled to be unobtrusive in the rolling down of his shirtsleeves: but without success.

Trewley shook his head, grinned, and unbuttoned his own cuffs in sympathy. "Easy, Davers. As you were. How about telling us the tale? Who raised the alarm—what did you do when you got here? The usual thing."

PC Davers shuffled his large feet into a parade-ground stance, and clasped his hands behind his back. He raised his head to stare into the recent past, and recited a careful monotone of previously rehearsed statement.

"At approximately two-fifty-five this afternoon, sir, I was summoned by Barnabus Chilman, under-gardener at The Stooks, to the maze on the said property, where I discovered several persons in an excitable state, and was informed by the head gardener, Cedric Ezard, as the maze contained the dead body of a woman. I therefore proceeded at once to the middle—"

Trewley held up a hand. "At once? How?"

Davers took only a moment to work out what he meant. "Why, that's easy enough, sir. We all know the ways of this place hereabouts—whenever there's junketing in the village it's open to everyone, besides folk doing their bit of courting. . . ." He coughed, blushed, muttered something, and cleared his throat before continuing:

"Upon my arrival at the centre of the maze, I found the dead woman, known to me as Mrs. Ingrid Radlett, with her husband, Doctor Oliver Radlett; our new vicar, the Reverend David Gregory; and Caleb Duckels, a churchwarden. I sent a message by Mr. Duckels for someone to telephone at once for assistance after I had ascertained as Mrs. Radlett was beyond all human aid—the doctor himself being able to assure me of that, sir. But I made no attempt to clear the maze of the other two persons. . . ." Davers looked with pleading eyes at the superintendent. "Him being her husband, sir, well, I didn't rightly like . . . "

Trewley grunted. "Awkward, yes, I can see that. You've not let them touch anything?"

"I'd take my oath they didn't, sir, always excepting what went on before I arrived. The doctor was holding her hand like he was when you got here, and the reverend was—was praying with him, like you saw. Though he'd no doubt be able to tell you more of that himself—or Cedric Ezard, and the rest as was first on the scene with him."

"Umph. I'd say you've done well enough, Davers, considering the difficulties. Not the normal sort of case for you, is it?"

Davers permitted himself the ghost of a grin. "Tell the truth, sir, round here it's mostly poaching—which isn't seen as a crime anyhow. And the last proper murder in Redingote was near enough a hundred years ago—always barring what can't be proved, of course."

Stone smiled. "But today's your parish fete, isn't it? I'm always amazed there's never wholesale slaughter on occasions like this!"

"Hear, hear," Trewley seconded her: his wife belonged to the Women's Institute. "But never mind all this old-time business—we've a murder to deal with today. . . ."

He allowed Stone, with her superior understanding of shock and its treatment, to coax Dr. Radlett from his wife's side. David Gregory, still murmuring, accompanied him; the stricken widower ignored the official huddle which parted to let them through, but David nodded acknowledgement of their presence. The two men disappeared from view, and the team were free to set about the ritual of investigation.

While the routine matters were being attended to, Trewley turned with an afterthought to Davers. "Her

husband—local man, is he? No problem finding his way out
of here? The poor bloke's had quite a shock.''

"Redingote born and bred, sir. The vicar, now, he's
new—neither inducted to the parish yet nor in residence, but
Doctor Oliver knows his way as well as any, I reckon.''

"An unfortunate start to the poor man's ministry," Stone
said. "If it's over a hundred years since the last murder,
what rotten luck to have this happen. . . ."

PC Davers looked towards Trewley, and for the superintendent's benefit elected to expand on his brief mention of
the village's previous claim to homicidal notoriety. That
victim, too, had been a young woman, though she hadn't
been, as he put it, bashed over the head. "Found drowned,
so she was," he said with relish. "In Doom's Deep, as
ever is.''

"In what?" demanded Trewley and Stone.

"Doom's Deep, sir. That's the bottomless pond down by
the village green, where in times past they used to deal with
nagging women by—ducking 'em, sir." His eye flicked
towards the sergeant, then quickly away. "Haunted, it is, by
a maid what was killed by her lover when she fell in the
family way, and him unable to give her an honest name
along of how he was already wed. Then, when suspicion lit
on him, and her ghost come to torment him into confessing,
before justice caught up with him he drowned himself too,
sir, in the very selfsame place.''

Stone was intrigued. "Would history be likely to repeat
itself? I mean, would anyone local prefer to drown his
victim, rather than do her in on dry land?''

Davers glanced at Trewley, as if to enquire whether this
question merited a reply. Stone scowled, and elaborated.

"Well, look—if old habits die hard, wouldn't it suggest
that it was a stranger who killed her here, instead of—oh.
Oh, yes.''

"Oh yes indeed, Detective Sergeant Stone," said Trewley, who was apt to address her by her full title only when
he felt he'd scored. Stone shrugged, and grinned.

"Of course," she said. "It would take local knowledge to
get into and out of the middle of this maze, so, unless she

brought him with her . . .'' She regarded Davers with a look of challenge. "She *was* local, wasn't she? Would she have been able to find her way in here with him?"

After a moment, Davers explained as how Ingrid had come from foreign parts—Norway or Sweden, he reckoned—and had not been long married to the doctor: three or four years at most. He doubted whether she'd ever been in the maze by herself in her life. There weren't so many as bothered to come that far just to sit on a bench under a willow tree and look at all the statues, though it was a favourite spot for courting couples. In fact, Doctor Oliver had taken her into the maze the very day he proposed to her. . . .

Davers found himself drifting to an uncomfortable halt as he glanced in the direction of the body, and the shattered stucco by its head. Trewley and Stone followed his gaze. Stone shuddered, and was the first to look away.

"All clear here, sir—over to you now!" The cry came from the forensic team, packing their equipment into boxes and bags. A strange voice called out in reply from behind the superintendent's back.

"Good, good. I'll take a look, shall I?" Trewley and Stone, recognising the voice, glanced round. At the side of Caleb Duckels—who had evidently assumed the role of guide and materialised again in the middle of the maze—was a tall, stooping, bushy-bearded figure with eager spectacles, brandishing a sinister black bag. This was the police surgeon, who rejoiced in the surname of Watson and was liable to throw things when new acquaintances made the inevitable jokes. He said a quick hello to Trewley, nodded to Stone, and went briskly about his business.

"Another question for you, Davers." The two detectives knew how much Dr. Watson disliked having people breathe over his shoulder as he worked, for which reason Trewley now led the constable further from the body. "Would you say they were a very . . . superstitious lot around here?"

"Folk don't care to go near Doom's Deep when the ghosts may be abroad, sir, if that's what you mean."

"Umph." The superintendent rubbed his chin in thought.

"I was thinking more of, well, odd religions—witchcraft, maybe, or something of the sort. Because, if you only look at the woman—well . . ."

PC Davers scratched his head. "There's Mr. Hemingway, of course. He's supposed to be a writer. . . ." Trewley muttered something Stone could not catch. "All books and poems, he is. Never eats meat, they say, and gets up early to look at the sunrise."

Trewley rolled his eyes, resembling a lugubrious bloodhound more than ever. "Doesn't sound likely, though we'll bear him in mind. Anyone else?"

Davers appeared unhappy, trying not to peer over his shoulder as he replied, after another pause: "There's . . . Tabitha Chilman, sir. Tabby the Touched as we—they—call her. Some folk hereabouts say she's a witch, sir."

"Do they, indeed? Hocus-pocus and cauldron bubble?"

"So they say, sir. Some folk, that is."

Stone was quick to raise an objection. "If a witch wanted to get rid of anyone, she wouldn't bash them over the head, you know. All she'd have to do is curse them with the evil eye."

"Ah, but Mrs. Radlett wasn't a local," Trewley reminded her. "So she wouldn't believe in the evil eye. Perhaps this Tabitha made sure her curse would work by, well, using the statue as insurance."

Stone shook her head. "She'd believe it would work on anyone, local or not, if you ask me, sir. Call it women's intuition, if you must"—she ignored his smothered chuckle—"but I bet that's how this Tabitha thinks." And so decided did she sound that PC Davers was observed to stare at her as if she possessed her own unorthodox powers.

"It wasn't," said Trewley, "a large statue, or particularly heavy, if the others dotted about are anything to go by. A woman could have picked it up, I reckon. Perhaps, Sergeant, you'd be kind enough to oblige us with a demonstration?"

Stone's eyes narrowed briefly, then she lifted from its ornamental base the statue farthest from Ingrid's body, brandished it, set it down again, and nodded. "Easy enough to do, sir, I'd have to agree with you—perhaps without really meaning to do it, what's more. And it's concrete or something of the sort," she added with a sigh. "No chance of decent prints off the bits that are left. . . ."

Trewley grimaced, and mopped his brow. Davers shuffled his feet, and continued to look unhappy. The superintendent said:

"Go on telling us about Tabitha, Davers. Does she . . . er, work—if that's the word—alone?"

The constable's eyes once more flicked towards Stone, and he blushed. "There's her son Barney—Barmy Barney, he's known as. Her son, he is . . . and her brother as well, so they say, on account of his father was also *her* father, and going right back through the family, too. All of 'em witches, and a bit—a bit funny-like, sir. And Barney, he likes to help her with her brewing. . . ."

"How funny is funny?" Trewley wanted to know, just as Stone asked: "Are they both crazy?" Davers, flustered and hot, shuffled his feet again, and dropped his gaze.

"Depends what you mean by the word, sir. She—they—talk a lot of nonsense sometimes, making out as it's spells—but it's nonsense, sir," and he forced himself to meet the superintendent's gaze, and to give every appearance of one who did not believe in nonsense. "Barney, now," he went on, rather more boldly, "Barney's inclined to have . . . to have *turns*, as you might say—especially when the moon's full. Like it's going to be tonight. . . ."

"A genuine lunatic," exclaimed Stone, delighted.

"Dangerous?" demanded Trewley. Davers shook his head.

"Not so far's I know, sir. Just goes prowling through the woods and peering in at windows, not that anybody's made any official complaint about it, mind you. And I've not managed to catch him at it, being as he's mighty thick with the local poacher, and skilled in woodland ways. . . . But you can be sure Barney'd never harm Mrs. Radlett, sir. Certain sure, so you can."

"Oh, I can, can I?"

"Oh yes, sir. Barney adored her, see. Thought she was an angel, or the fairy off the Christmas tree, what with her blue eyes and golden hair. . . ." All three turned to look at Ingrid's still shape in the shade of the willow, then looked quickly away. "She first came to live in the village at Yuletide, sir, and Barney, he sort of got things confused. Followed her around, he did, used to sing under her window at night and all—carols, and songs too—but worshipfully, you understand. Never so much as laid a finger on her—but it unnerved the poor soul, not being so used to his ways as others in Redingote, sir. That's how she and Doctor Oliver first come to be so very friendly, with her trying to get him to have Barney put away on account of being dangerous, and the doctor knowing full well as he wasn't. He might not be right in the head, you see, but it wouldn't do him or anyone else harm to go wandering about the place. . . ."

"Umph. So the doctor certified this Barney as being . . . well, safe to have around?"

"That he did, sir, rather than have him took into a Home—found him this job as under-gardener here, to keep his mind off everything. Exercise regular and plenty of fresh air, and Cedric Ezard better able to control the lad than—than Tabitha, the more he grew so big and she so small, and simple with it. Worked a treat, it did. Kept him peaceful, as you might say—and just so soon as the doctor and Mrs. Radlett was wed, he never went near her again, being another man's wife, you see. Only looked at her from a distance, he did, and much given to doing so—but he'd never have harmed her, sir! Most like, once he knows what's happened to the poor soul, he'll be wanting to harm him as done it."

Trewley was about to comment on this remarkable tale when Dr. Watson summoned him and his sergeant to join him at his post. "She's dead," he informed them, as he was duty bound to do. "Hit on the head with that statue, at a guess. One tremendous wallop which, from what I can tell, did for her at once and didn't do the statue much good, either."

"How long ago?"

Dr. Watson shrugged. "This hot weather . . . well, some time today, and morning rather than afternoon, probably. Say between tennish and—when was she found? Between ten and half an hour ago, then, for starters. Once I've had a proper look, I might know more—find out what she last ate and when, for instance. But . . ."

"You'll have fun and games getting her out of here." As Trewley gazed at the high screen hedge all about them, a sigh escaped him. His handkerchief was still in his hand, and he dabbed the back of his neck gloomily. Stone looked at him, and resolved to keep him in the shade of the willow for as long as possible, though as the sun crossed the sky the shadow moved with it. . . .

The doctor was frowning towards the entrance, for Caleb Duckels had once more withdrawn from the centre of the maze. "Never mind that—how am *I* going to get out? I've other calls on my time, you know. I can't hang about for hours while the pair of you detect all over the place."

Stone's eyes danced with sudden mischief. "PC Davers might be able to help you there, I imagine." Again the sergeant's tone was very decided, and it was Trewley's turn to stare; then he caught her meaning, grinned, and beckoned the constable across to join them.

Almost before he had finished explaining the problem, Davers had whipped out his notebook and begun to scribble. "Here, sir." He tore out the sheet and handed it to Dr. Watson, who peered at it through his spectacles.

"First right, first left, second left . . . splendid! If you're quite sure this is correct, Constable."

"Oh yes, sir." He blushed again, and Stone, still annoyed by that male obstinacy which had made him address Trewley throughout most of their interview, informed the doctor brightly that Davers was able to be so sure of his facts because this was the local spooning spot. "There isn't a soul in Redingote," she said, with a chuckle, "who couldn't find his—or her—way in or out of here blindfolded, I gather."

Dr. Watson did not share her amusement. "It's getting *her* out that's going to be the problem—reverence for the dead, and so on. Can't be helped, though. . . ."

Paper in hand, he was gone, leaving the constabulary trio

thoughtful about the body. The forensic team had withdrawn in Dr. Watson's wake; the centre of the maze seemed
far larger with their going.

Trewley was the first to break the silence. "Any idea why
I asked about witchcraft? Stone?"

For all her two years' medical training, the sergeant had
never grown used to the reality of some aspects of her
substitute profession. She had been relieved to observe that
the dead woman's eyes were closed, and that, though there
was plenty on the ground, very little blood from the broken
skull had stained Ingrid's face. . . .

"Almost as if she's been, well, tidied up," she murmured
thoughtfully. "Laid out with her hands folded—assuming it
wasn't the vicar who did that, of course, which seems highly
unlikely—and . . ."

She bent to examine the slip of green which Dr. Watson
had replaced in the folded hands. "A sprig of yew—freshly
picked, what's more. Enough of it around to choose from,
of course." She frowned. "Grows a lot in churchyards,
doesn't it? To stop the cattle eating it—and to let it grow
large enough to make six-foot longbows out of, in the old
days—and to line graves with as well, I think, sir. But"—as
a dutiful sidekick, she remembered her cue—"I bet none of
those is what you meant, is it?"

"All of those reasons are true, as far as I recall," said the
superintendent, whose schooling had been of the old-
fashioned sort which required a broad base of general
knowledge. "But there's yet another reason, Stone—the
most important here, maybe. The yew is a symbol of
immortality—left over from an older belief in the need to,
er, pacify the spirits of the dead. Especially anyone who's
died by violence."

"Of course, sir! The yews somehow stop the spirit
haunting the killer, don't they?"

"Somehow," he agreed. "Not that I can say exactly how
they do it—but I reckon anyone local could, to the last
detail. So don't try to tell me, Davers, it wasn't a local who
set that twig in her folded hands. . . ."

PC Davers was emboldened to make a suggestion.

"Maybe the doctor himself, sir, or"—he glanced at Stone—"the vicar—"

She interrupted him with scorn. "No modern clergyman's going to lend himself to a pagan superstition, surely! And as for her husband—I take it you weren't referring to Dr. Watson—well, I'd have expected him to *want* her ghost to torment the person who killed her, if he believed in that kind of thing. He'd want them punished, just as your hundred-year-old seducing suicide was."

Since Trewley nodded in silent support of this argument, Davers was forced to agree that she might, after all, be correct in her assumption. "Which really leaves us, sir," he said, "with near enough anyone from Redingote as could've done such a deed, knowing how it would stop her coming after 'em. Redingote keeps to the old ways, sure enough. What with . . . with Tabitha, not to mention that son of hers, more than one has a knife blade under the mat, accidental-like, on the night of the full moon."

"Might the night itself be significant?" For all his general knowledge on the matter of yew, Trewley was happy to consult Davers, the expert on local variations of beliefs and superstitions. "From a ritual point of view, I mean. Right in the middle of the maze, a woman dead—Midsummer Day, or something. . . ."

"But, sir, it isn't," Stone reminded him. Davers, on being appealed to, coughed, and turned red once more.

"She was—she was married, sir," he said, and as Stone caught his eye turned almost purple. She chuckled.

"You mean a sacrifice would have to be a virgin? That's one theory exploded, then—but you'll never convince me she was a mother figure instead. Nobody who looks and dresses in clothes like that could possibly be the maternal type." The sergeant had a very practical nature, wearing slacks rather than skirts for most of her working life; she disapproved of anyone who was purely decorative, whether male or female. "Oh, no, not maternal—but a goddess, an ideal, I'd believe that, all right. Especially with this Barney—but that's quite a different matter. You don't ritually slaughter your tame goddess, do you? Wouldn't it be rather dangerous?''

Trewley suddenly realised where his first remarks had brought them. "Look, this must be a mistake—witchcraft and ritual killing. There can't be anything in it. . . ."

Stone looked straight at Davers. "The full moon, you said? What have you got under *your* doormat tonight, Constable?'' And his fiery blush was answer enough.

Trewley felt some sympathy for his fellow male, and shot his female sergeant a quelling look, even while he admitted that there was some strength in her argument. "All right, we'll say definite local knowledge, then. Now—if Mrs. Radlett didn't know the way in, the chap she was with must have done, mustn't he? And after she was dead, he laid her out in that special way. . . ."

"Unless," suggested Stone, "a stranger came in here with her—maybe she knew the way after all—and he killed her, and then someone local found her and laid the body out. . . ."

"Umph." Trewley rubbed his chin; then shook his head. "If he was a stranger, how did the killer find his way out of the maze, Detective Sergeant Stone? You could lose yourself for hours in that long green rigmarole if there wasn't anyone to show you the way. And I'm not going to believe''—as she drew breath to speak—"there were two of them on the job. Talk about overkill. No, Davers has told us she didn't know the route, so . . ."

"She might," suggested Davers, with a shy look at the superintendent, "have been killed somewhere else." He had started to warm to the detective way of life. "Killed somewhere else, and brought here after—oh."

"Oh, no," said Stone. "The same argument has to apply in that case, too. It still requires someone with local knowledge—quite apart from the practicalities of carrying a corpse on a day like this right through the maze—but we must certainly check," she added kindly, "for broken twigs and crushed leaves, on the way out. Just in case." Perhaps she'd been rather hard on him; from Trewley's expression she probably had. "Anyway, never mind that now. You must have known her—maybe not well, but certainly better than either of us,'' and she stared about her at the drooping fronds of the willow, the central urn with its surrounding statues. One of which was missing. . . .

"A romantic sort of place," she concluded, while Trewley watched her with interest. "An assignation, maybe?"

Davers was shocked. "Here? Why, it was here as Doctor Oliver asked her to marry him! On just such a blazing hot day as this, and a garden party in full swing—so he brings her in here to pop the question, and comes out ten minutes later looking pleased as Punch she's said yes."

It took only a moment to divine his meaning. "And it wouldn't be fitting for her to come with a man not her husband to the traditional courting place? But"—as Davers nodded, surprised the question needed to be asked—"what about some man she wouldn't necessarily see in that sort of way? Someone like this Barmy Barney of yours—or someone old enough to be her father, say." Trewley growled inaudibly at her side, but she ignored him. "Do you think the same . . . inhibitions would still apply?"

Davers was just about to ask what she meant when a sudden yell burst forth from outside the yew-walled labyrinth. "No—no, it ain't true! No! No!" And this high-pitched, frantic denial was followed by an excited hubbub.

"You blabbermouthing fool to open your trap. . . . Hold the boy steady, now. . . . Where's his mother? . . . Someone fetch Tabitha here, quick. . . . Quiet, for heaven's sake be quiet!"

Trewley looked at Stone, who looked back at him before they both turned to Davers. The constable frowned. "That's Barney, seemingly—he's found out what's happened to Mrs. Radlett, and he's took it hard, like I said he would. And especially tonight, of course. . . ."

Trewley was thoughtful, listening to the sounds of poor Barney's moon-crazed grief as they began to die away. "Not the most obvious candidate for Suspect Number One, judging by that performance—although . . . Anyway, we may or may not have a man to look for. Davers, *was* there a man? I don't mean Barney. Someone else? I know you don't like to think she'd make an assignation here—and you could well be right—but we have to start somewhere.''

Davers scratched his head. "Folk don't say too much to me, viewing me as a foreigner like they do, even though my mother, her family comes from these parts—but she was a fine-looking woman, sir, Mrs. Radlett.''

Everyone's gaze turned to the still, silent form on the ground close by, and there was a thoughtful silence. Davers cleared his throat.

"Yes, sir, many were the men as admired her, and envied Doctor Oliver his good fortune in winning her to wife. . . .'' Stone muttered something; the superintendent rolled his eyes. Davers turned pink. "Well, sir, there *has* been a bit of talk, but among those as gossip the most, so I can't be sure of the truth of it. About how she only wed him for a work permit, and was getting a bit bored of the man now. . . .''

Trewley had proposed to his wife out of affection, and hoped her motive in accepting him had been the same. Stone, though unmarried, had a close personal friend of some years' standing, a member of Allingham constabulary's Traffic Division, with whom a relationship had been based on happy compatibility. She and the superintendent looked suitably startled by the revelations of PC Davers.

"Mind you," acknowledged Trewley, after a pause, "a work permit . . . could be something in it. Gets her British nationality settled, then she can afford to start playing around. . . . Davers, how recent are these rumors? Would you say it was a—a successful marriage before they began?''

The constable stared at his boots once more, his blush more pronounced than ever. "Folk'll always gossip, sir, in a village—and, as for the other, I'd find it hard to tell. Being a bachelor, that is, and not even courting. . . .''

Stone smothered a grin as the unhappy Davers continued:

"There are those as say she, well, resented the way he sort of—sort of bamboozled her into saying yes, sir, with it being such a hot day, and her coming from northern parts as she did, her wits all topsy-turvy from the heat. He was crazy about her, right to the end—anyone could see that, sir, couldn't they? And she was a lovely creature, to anyone's mind. She really was. . . .''

Even in death, some of Ingrid's Scandinavian beauty remained: the fine bones, the glorious hair, the pale skin, the slim, graceful shape. But there was nothing left of the spirit, the character, the soul: and Davers seemed unable to tell his colleagues what she had really been like.

"Exotic," murmured Trewley, after another pause. "Glamorous. How on earth did someone so . . . unusual fit into a place like Redingote? You say they aren't keen on strangers—and I suppose she spoke with an accent, too.''

PC Davers was not only a bachelor, he was an old-fashioned one. "Why, sir, she was wife to the doctor, and he was born here. Most of 'em would've took to her well enough for his sake, sir, even if not for hers.''

Stone snorted, but said nothing. Trewley winked at her before enquiring: "So, apart from the murderer, you can't think of anyone who . . . actively disliked her?''

Davers cast an apologetic look in Stone's direction, and muttered something about the usual women's squabbles; adding in some haste, as her eyes glittered, that he didn't feel he could rightly comment on that. Trewley, who had sensed his sergeant's surge of irritation, was torn between amusement at her attitude and annoyance that, because of it, Davers might have been deterred from speaking his mind.

"Go on," he prompted, as the constable yet again found the condition of his boots a matter for concern; and Stone's struggle with herself was pitiful to see.

"Well, sir," Davers brought out at last, "like I said, they don't talk to me all that much, being only three years resident in the place—it takes time for 'em to get on with incomers, and more so if there's nothing they're wishful to palm off on 'em by way of village dirty work, sir, as nobody else would want to undertake. There's nothing of the sort they could do to me, so they've left me pretty much alone . . . nor they don't care for it if someone tries too hard to fit in—which is what they've felt about this Mr. Rowles as owns the house here and the grounds. There's been much said to me concerning *him*, sir. And proper odd he sounds, too.''

When Trewley and Stone together demanded the details of the proper oddness of Montague Rowles, Davers set about a recitation of everything Redingote suspected of the man, then threw in a few ideas of his own for good measure. Leaving the detectives wishing they could talk to the owner of The Stooks—soon.

''But he's not here, is he?'' said Stone, as she jotted the final shorthand squiggles in her notebook. ''And there must be lots of other people to talk to. . . .''

''Then we'd better start, girl, hadn't we?'' said Trewley.

So they started.

Six

OUTSIDE THE MAZE, they came upon what should have been a soothing sight: a tall, tweeded lady with a cup-laden tea tray. Yet something about this particular Hebe did not seem as soothing as they might have expected. Gwendolyn Pasmore—for with a murmured reply to Stone's enquiry she had so identified herself—carried the tray in hands that shook slightly. Every saucer contained a dark brown liquid ring around the base of a cup that, careful though she was, clattered and clinked as Gwendolyn moved.

Trewley took a cup with thanks, and Stone nodded her approval. As he drank, the superintendent pulled a face.

"Sugar," he muttered in dismay. Gwendolyn did not hear him, though Stone did.

"Good for shock," she hissed, and went up to Mrs. Pasmore again. "Would you be able," she asked, "to spare a second cup—or will it be less confusing if you could bring us a couple later on? This hot weather doesn't agree with Mr. Trewley, you see. If I don't keep a close eye on him, he sometimes forgets to maintain his liquid intake."

"Why yes, of course. Two more cups of tea—certainly." And Mrs. Pasmore almost managed to meet Stone's gaze as she replied—almost, but not quite.

Stone gave her an encouraging smile before hurrying back to Trewley, who saw her coming and pointedly drank more tea.

"You're fussing over me again, girl," he growled, though with less than his normal astringency: it really was a very hot day. "Second cup, indeed! And this one full of sugar, what's more—when if anyone knows I have to watch my weight it ought to be you. Sugar! We're investigating death by blunt instrument, not poison."

"You'll live, sir—especially," and she began to lead him away, "if you come over into the shade. . . ."

The superintendent realised that she was manoeuvring him out of earshot. Cedric, Ethel, and the rest seemed far too interested in the way he was letting a slip of a girl order him about. Though their opinion did not bother him, it was in a brisk tone that he demanded to know what on earth Stone thought she was playing at.

"Come on, sir, we both know how much you dislike the heat—but it made a good excuse, didn't it? Mrs. Pasmore," she explained quickly, as he glared at her. "I'd say she's rattled," the sergeant told him, a gleam in her eye. "When I took my cup, she gave me . . . I hate to say it, but a meaningful look. Honestly, sir, that's the way it seemed," as he snorted. "My guess is that there's something she's not quite sure whether to tell us—or how to, if she decides she will. So I thought I'd provide her with a reason to come back later."

"Umph. So, if she doesn't take advantage of your kind offer, you'll be able to say she lost her nerve, and ask her about it point-blank. . . ." He gulped another mouthful of tea, and pulled a face. "Could be you were wrong in the first place, of course. The woman's conscience might be as clear as yours. Meaningful looks, indeed. . . ." But Stone regarded him with a faint grin on her face, and it wasn't long before Trewley grinned back.

"All right, girl. For the sake of peace and quiet, I'll agree Mrs. Pasmore's attitude may have been a little odd, and could be worth looking into. Later," as Stone seemed rather too pleased with herself for her weary superior's liking. "We'll see what she's got to tell us when she's had time to pickle—*if* there's anything to tell. If there is, though—could be she's the type to prefer spilling the beans to a woman rather than to a man—and I have to admit your . . . feminine intuition has come in handy in the past—once or twice." When Detective Sergeant Stone, with her university education, was first posted to Trewley's team, he had been astounded. Now, though he would never encourage her by admitting it, he didn't care to think of doing without her.

"Feminine intuition," he muttered, draining the last of the tea. Stone chuckled, saying that it would do him no harm to have another cup in any case.

The truth of which, as he mopped his brow, the superintendent had to acknowledge. "Mrs. Pasmore'll have to wait her turn, though," he said, his gaze returning to their not-so-distant audience. "We've any number of people to interview before we talk to her—everyone from the maze, for a start. But first, I'd like to know what caused all that rumpus we heard a few minutes ago. It might have been the old lady after the miserable bloke's chair again, but . . ."

"Davers told us," she reminded him, "that it was Barney, having a fit of some sort, and I'd guess he was right. They were all shouting to fetch somebody's mother, weren't they? And—assuming Barney was that young giant with the vacant face who was goggling at us when we arrived—he isn't here now, so I expect his mother or whoever took him away to look after him. . . ."

Stone's assumption was confirmed. Barnabus Chilman (an excited chorus informed the two detectives) had erupted into hysterics more violent and uncontrolled even than those of the youngsters who had discovered Mrs. Radlett's body. Tabitha had been sent for—had slapped and shaken and shrieked him into a calmer state—had taken him home with her to complete the healing process.

"And you'll get no sense from the lad, not for a day or more you won't," Cedric informed them, in a tone which suggested he cared nothing if they never got any. "Like a soul in torment, so he was—ranting and raving in his sorrow—and all thanks to this fool here!" He jerked a contemptuous thumb in the direction of Ethel Maggs. "After I'd took such pains to keep it from the lad, that daft great lump of lard lets it out right in front of him—the fool!"

Ethel bristled with indignation. "It was a mistake—as anyone could've made in the shock of the moment—but then, we all knows how well *you* understand the youngsters, Cedric Ezard. Youngsters like your Abigail. . . .''

Cedric came leaping from his chair with such a roar of rage that everyone was startled. Then Trewley shouted at him, and Stone darted forward; but PC Davers was before them both. He moved his perspiring bulk steadfastly between the two combatants, and addressed them both sternly.

"This ain't the time for brangling, Cedric Ezard, nor yet the place. With Mrs. Radlett still lying dead and cold in there. . . . A shameful scene the pair of you are making— and with folk from Allingham to witness it, too! Let's have peace, and respect, and—and no more argufying this afternoon, do you hear me?'' And he stood with his arms folded, frowning from Cedric to Ethel and back, reminding them that village matters should remain village matters, and private—especially in front of townspeople. . . .

"Nor ain't it the weather for hanging around in the sun, neither.'' The young man who stood with his protective arm about the shoulders of the pretty orange-haired punk spoke up firmly. "My girl and me, we've had a shock—we found her, see? And we'd like to get off home so's we can have a couple of stiff drinks and forget about it.''

The girl nodded repeatedly as he said this, the stunned rhythmic reaction of one who is on automatic pilot after some traumatic experience. Stone looked thoughtfully at her, then addressed her boyfriend.

"Have you both had a cup of tea? It would be better for you both than alcohol, right now.''

The youth laughed, though not rudely. "No, we haven't, though a double scotch would suit me better, but with the bike to drive I've got to keep off the hard stuff till we get home. And that'll be soon, I hope. We didn't do her in—we never saw nothing—we don't know nothing, true's I'm standing here. Can't we go?''

Stone glanced at Trewley. "We'll be as quick,'' she promised, "as we can, and we'll only ask you a very few questions—we can follow them up later, if we need to, once you are over the worst of it. But suppose we have a chat and a sit-down for just a few minutes now? How about in the rose garden? From what we've heard it's bound to be cooler there, and you'll feel more comfortable for talking about it—honestly, you will.'' She looked at the girl again. Despite her leather jacket, she was shivering. ''Come along now—a quick chat, that's all. . . .''.

The boy did the talking for both of them. Their names were Gary King and Debra Jarvis; they had been going steady for more than two years. ''Wanted to pop the question official, see, in the middle of the maze,'' Gary explained, at which Debra managed a feeble smile. ''Only—when we got to the middle, we—we—she . . .''

''Suppose you hadn't found the middle?'' Trewley was curious about the courtship rituals of the younger generation. His three daughters were just approaching the dangerous age. Gary, grinning, tapped the side of his nose.

''Learned it by heart, I did. Got a book from the library, about the wonders of—of tope-aye-arey.'' With a scowl, he defied anyone to laugh at his pronunciation. ''Wonders,'' he said again. ''Old Grandad, he made us take one of his bits of paper with instructions printed on, but I never needed to look at it, not once I didn't.''

''So that's how you came to be first into the centre.'' The hint of doubt in Trewley's tone was enough for Gary. He proceeded to recite the clue to the maze, both inwards and out, without faltering. He might, the detectives supposed, be making it up—but it sounded convincing. . . .

''A book,'' prompted Stone. ''You were there first . . .''

''You bet we were! Mind you, them kids wasn't all that far behind—having a race, summat daft like that, and their gran yelling at them not to get too far ahead—wanting to see what they was up to all the time, I reckon—but they was too quick for her, and come in pretty soon after us. And saw—and saw—what we'd already seen. . . .''

Gary broke off, and Debra shuddered as she took up the tale. ''She was lying there, just like on a tombstone—like one of them marble statues in a church—he'd put her hands across her chest, and—and I screamed, I couldn't help it—and then that little girl, she was screaming too—and—and nobody came to help us. . . .''

Her face crumpled. Gary gave her a hug. "You've forgot fat old grandma, Debbie love. Remember how she come roaring in after the kids, and started yelling at the old man when he tried to turf them out? And he was yelling right back at her—same like they was carrying on just now, remember? Better than a cat fight, it was!"

She shook her head; her voice trembled. "I don't remember—and I don't want to, really I don't." She buried her face in her hands, sobbing. Even the jaunty orange spikes on her head drooped in distress. Stone, after catching Trewley's eye, addressed Gary again.

"Do you remember anything else at all? Who sent for us, or who took you out of there? Anything?"

But he was shaking his head, sure that he did not; and he was as sure that poor Debra couldn't help, either. It had all been so noisy and muddled; after fat Ethel's fight with Cedric they had noticed nothing . . .

"Except the look on her face, when she saw who it was all the fuss was about," he added suddenly. "Real mean, she looked. I reckon *she* wasn't sorry."

"Who wasn't—the little girl? Surely not!"

At such a ridiculous notion, even Debra emerged from her trance to scoff, her memory shocked into further slow revival. "The fat woman, he means—and didn't she look pleased! Almost—well, gloating, like, sort of evil—and you can ask the vicar, if you don't believe us," as Trewley and Stone looked shocked. "He'll tell you!"

Stone wondered how much of this was genuine memory, and how much was hindsight. "How did you know," she enquired, "that he was a vicar?"

Once more the ridiculous nature of her remark made them stare. "Wearing a dog-collar, weren't he? Don't need to be much of a detective to know that!" And Debra added:

"Ever so nice, he was. Real considerate—though of course there was her poor hubby, I think they said, to look after, when he come in to see what all the fuss was about and said he was a doctor, and the old man was trying to make him go away, only—only then he saw who she was, and . . ."

She started to sob again, overwhelmed. Gary, hugging her, glared at Stone: who returned his angry look with her kindest smile.

"That's enough for now, I think." She exchanged glances with Trewley, and added: "I'm sure they aren't going to run away, sir—they'll be our most important witnesses. But I do think that Debbie should go home now, to rest, and to let Gary take care of her."

As Gary preened himself, Trewley nodded. He knew that in such matters, his sergeant was more knowledgeable than he; besides, the youngsters hadn't had anything to do with the crime, he was sure. The boy had told them the key to the maze was readily available to the public—which could mean anything, or nothing—there was that twig of yew to take into account. . . .

He nodded again, and spoke to Gary. "You be off now, and find yourselves a nice place to pop the question. We'll have to get in touch with you later—but try not to think about it too much before then. Off you go, and the best of luck—oh, and congratulations. . . ."

"She'll get over it—they both will," said Stone, when the soon-to-be-engaged youngsters had thankfully departed. "I can't believe they had anything to do with it—and the girl was all in, sir. It didn't seem fair to—"

"No need for excuses, Stone. I agree with you. Come to that, I'm starting to feel all in myself—for a different reason, mind you," and he mopped his brow for the umpteenth time. "But there's a job to be done. . . . Let's have a word with someone who's not such a bundle of nerves. Even if you're up to coping with the hysterical types, I'm not."

"How do you feel about the bad-tempered types, sir? The gardener or the old lady, I mean. To separate them before they can start rowing again—they seem to do a lot of that, and Davers can't stand on guard for ever."

"Oh, the gardener. He was the first person we met in connection with the case, after all. . . ."

Cedric had been polite, according to his own lights, at their first meeting; but his second altercation with Ethel had soured his always uncertain temper. It was consequently hard at first to persuade him to part with the smallest morsel of information: he grudged each syllable even before it had been spoken.

He'd heard a load of caterwauling from a young wench, and suspected some daft prank, and—seeing there was no call for that sort of nonsense in the middle of his maze—had gone straight in to put a stop to it. Only—well, it had turned out not to be nonsense, after all.

"And lucky I never took young Barney in with me, you're sure. Why did I leave him outside? Stands to reason I'd leave him—to stop any more fools following me in to gawp at everything. Doing his job, he was—and good enough at it, he is, though inclined to be a bit wanting sometimes, and like to be set going for any foolish reason. . . ."

Before he could start reviling Ethel Maggs again, Stone persuaded him to agree that *getting going* exactly described Barney's behavior on finally learning the news of Ingrid's death. Which, he added, was no more than he'd feared for the lad, once he'd seen for himself as the caterwauling weren't the nonsense he'd thought it. And if the police was to trouble theirselves to remember, they'd know he'd refused to let Barney guide them into the maze when they'd first appeared on the scene. . . .

"Nor was I so blamed foolish," he continued, while Stone wondered how to stem the flow now it had at last begun, "as to tell him she was dead, doting on Mrs. Radlett like we all know he did—whether she was a fit female for such worship, or no. But that danged Maggs woman opened her daft great mouth at sight of the poor doctor a-coming out—crying and snivelling she was, in that fool way of hers, letting everyone know as didn't have no business knowing. . . .

"And how could *I* tell you why Doctor Oliver was so long a time leaving the maze? It ain't none of my business! You'd best ask him, or the new parson—or that fuzzy-faced bloke as come after 'em. A nasty piece of work he looked, as well, with his face all hid by that great black beard. . . .''

Trewley made a mental, Stone a pencil note to have a transcript made of this part of the interview, and sent to Dr. Watson. It might amuse the bewhiskered medico to be Suspect Number One.

The superintendent put the next question. Could Cedric go back to when he first reached the centre of the maze? He'd gone straight there, Trewley assumed. So what had he seen when he arrived?

Cedric shrugged. ''Not much as made sense, to begin with—and I'd like to know,'' he added, scowling, ''how a body's supposed to think straight in such a racket? Proper bedlam, it were, with all the caterwauling—that young wench screeching, and them Gibbins brats running plaguey riot all over—and Ethel Maggs''—another scowl—''trying to say as I'm bullying the little beggars, when I only wanted to turn 'em out of there, being a sight not fit for young eyes—as any but a fool like her'd understand. And then, having to hold back the doctor when he come along to help—and the parents interfering, as did oughter've known better. . . .'' He rolled his eyes, scowled, and spat on the grass. ''Believe me or not as you choose, right glad I was for the sight of Caleb Duckels and the new parson!''

''Oh, we do.'' Trewley chose to ignore the expectoratory habits of the witness, as Stone's shorthand seemed slow to keep up. ''In your place, I think I'd have been grateful for almost any reinforcem—''

''Bodies,'' broke in the old man, ''ain't none of my business—always excepting pigeons, and magpies, and suchlike garden scavengers. 'Send for Ben Davers' is what I said, and that's what was done, once me and Caleb Duckels had cleared 'em all away—barring the poor doctor, and the new parson. Which give me time to warn 'em to say nothing in front of Barney, being so fond of her as he was.''

Trewley, with a quick look at Stone, took over the questioning completely now that the conversational ice had been broken. ''How could you be so sure that the body was

Mrs. Radlett's? Did you touch her—get close enough to see her properly—disturb anything?''

He certainly had not! Knew his duty as a law-abiding citizen as well as any, so he did, though it didn't take no policeman to see she was dead, laid out that way on the ground with her hands folded like a corpus. And of course he knew well enough who it was! Hadn't he seen her flaunt herself in that same dress only that morning? Ever one to clothe herself for the admiration of men, she was—which meant she might not be so worthy of his regard as he'd every right to expect of his wife, poor Doctor Oliver. As fine a man as any, like his father before him.

''Didn't rightly know what he was taking on when he wed with her, the flighty piece, with her smiling and flattery—shameless, sometimes, so she was—and far worse, besides! Poked that pretty nose of hers in where nobody wanted it, interfered with other folks's business— tried to say as I'd bin cheating on the money, after all these years—tickets and bits of paper and clever, town-bred, organising ways—and much good it did her,'' concluded Cedric, in tones of decided satisfaction. ''Much! A judge- ment on her, some might say. . . .'' And the old man nodded, glowered, and prepared to spit once more.

This sounded promising; but promise had somehow to be metamorphosed to (presumably) profitable fact. Cedric was giving the appearance of one who had said all he was going to say; a slight change of subject could be the way to concentrate his mind again. . . .

''By the way,'' enquired Trewley, the personification of afterthought, ''who is Abigail? Because—''

Cedric, who had been about to rise from his chair, came leaping to his feet with a roar of rage, and clenched beneath the superintendent's startled nose a gnarled and powerful fist. Sergeant Stone dropped her notebook, and prepared to come to the rescue.

Trewley, motioning her to remain where she was, stared up at the fuming Cedric with all the severity he could at such short notice command. ''Sit down, Mr. Ezard! There's no need—''

"Aye, and there's no need for you to bandy names about, mentioning that baggage who's as good as dead to me—and has been for these several years past! What's it to you who she might be? A curse on all gossiping tongues, say I!"

He thumped his fist on the rustic table, spat once, and without another word, stalked away from the official presence with a ramrod back and his ears bright red. Trewley and Stone regarded each other wordlessly for a moment.

"You had a lucky escape there, sir," said Stone at last, picking up her pencil and notebook from the grass. "What do you suppose all that was about?"

He grinned, and shrugged. "Something interesting, one way or another. Not quite what I was aiming for, though— I wanted to catch him on the hop—hoped it would make him a bit more forthcoming about Mrs. Radlett's . . . flirtations."

Stone coughed gently. "Yes, well, it backfired on you, sir. Not so much forthcoming, you might say, as, er, out going," and her eyes followed the fast-disappearing figure of the irate head gardener as it stumped up the steps to the upper lawn. "Abigail, whoever she was—or is—came up in that argument with the fat woman, didn't she? We'll ask Mrs. Maggs, instead—and after that little display, I'll bet you it's something really juicy when we finally find out!"

"No takers." Her weary superior was mopping his forehead again. "And, even if you're right, I'm not sure my nerves could stand the excitement just yet." He sighed. The comparative coolness of the rose garden was not enough, it seemed, to spare him the worst of the heat; he had long ago removed his tie, but Stone was starting to worry. She studied him without being obvious about it, wondering where Gwendolyn Pasmore might be with the second round of tea.

"How about," she suggested, "having a word with those youngsters and their parents, sir? If you're up to it, that is," she couldn't help adding. He muttered something, and thrust his handkerchief back in his pocket.

"We'll see them. Don't fuss over me—you're as bad as

my wife, girl!'' And Stone snapped her notebook shut, rising to go in search of the Gibbins family without another word.

The twins were clearly under the influence of excess television, for the first demand of young Damian was to be taken to the police station and given the third degree.

"I thought," he complained, "that you'd let us talk into a tape recorder with a video running, and a clock to show you weren't tampering with the evidence—not just sitting in a garden to ask a lot of boring questions!"

Detective Sergeant Stone had already taken his measure on the journey back from the maze. Before the superintendent could reply, she narrowed her eyes into slits and leaned forward, menace in her every movement.

"So, young Damian—you don't care for gardens! Then what were you doing in the maze this afternoon? And be very careful with your answer. We'll know at once if you aren't telling the truth."

"Perjury," gasped Damian, turning pale with horrified delight. He missed the quick wink Stone directed towards his parents, and began shaking in his shoes. "We—we'd got a bet on—we were going to have a race, only Gran said it was too hot for her to keep up with us, so that silly pair got there first, and the girl started to scream, and we wanted to find out what was happening, and Dawn made Gran let go our hands—"

"It was your idea!" broke in his twin, squirming, with a wary eye on Stone's pencil as it noted all this down. "You said 'come on and let's find out'—you made me go with you—I wanted to stay with my Gran! And then, it was—it was horrible, what we saw!"

What they saw had been much the same as Gary and Debra, so far as Stone could coax them to tell: but all had been confusion, noise, and fright. "Most distressing for everyone involved," Damian informed her gravely: it seemed he'd been listening to the adults. Stone smiled at his parents.

"You'd agree with what the children say? You can't tell me anything that happened different?"

They both shook their heads, though Mrs. Gibbins, after a moment's thought, added: "When Ma never come out with the twins, we guessed it must be something bad—all that fuss and commotion, you see. But it was such a rush—"

"Once we got in there," said her husband sourly. "That fool Barney refused to let us in, saying how Cedric had left him on the gate, and he wasn't letting nobody past! Barmy or not, I put it to him straight. I told him, 'There's my kids in there, not to mention their gran, so out they'll come,' I said, 'and it's not for the likes of you to stop me. . . .'"

"Well, I didn't waste no time arguing," said his wife. "I pushed him out of the road and went right on in and called for Ma and the kids all the way. Only, they weren't nowhere to be found, not till—till we got to the middle . . ."

All four Gibbinses agreed that, once the centre of the maze had been reached, they could remember little. Old Cedric had barged in and started to throw his weight around—cleared out everyone except Parson and the doctor—said how he was going to get someone to ring for the police, and how nobody must say a word to upset Barney.

"Which Gran didn't mean to do," said Dawn, her eyes darting from side to side with worry. "She didn't know as he could hear her—"

"He's barmy," said Damian with scorn. "Stark, staring bonkers! You don't want to take no notice of Barney!" And he tossed his head, while his parents exchanged glances. Such bravado was all very well in broad daylight, and in the company of others; but there were times when it was wise to maintain as discreet a silence about Barnabus Chilman as about his mother, Tabitha, the witch.

Dawn was still sniffling, her brother's bold reassurance carrying little weight. Stone patted her on the shoulder. "You needn't worry about your gran, I promise. We only want to ask her a few questions. . . ."

"Not bad at all, girl." As the Gibbins contingent moved out of earshot, Trewley paid tribute. "You've got quite a way with the youngsters, haven't you? Wouldn't mind betting you'll make a good mother, one of these days!''

Stone, well aware that her superior knew she saw herself, for some time to come, as wedded to her career, refused to rise to the bait. She was, however, pleased to note his returning sense of humor. The temperature must be falling. Nevertheless, to ensure that this slight improvement continued, she would insist that Gwendolyn Pasmore was interviewed before much longer.

"Who next, sir? I suppose—"

"Mrs. Maggs, of course—might as well talk to the whole tribe before we start on anyone else." He chuckled. "Don't try to push me, girl—you'll find out soon enough why that woman was giving you meaningful looks. . . ."

Ethel Maggs made a great fuss about having her chair placed exactly level, and in the deepest shadow, since her poor feet had treated her cruel all day and the final straw had been the shock she'd just suffered. Well, not so long back, anyway. Bodies in mazes with their heads smashed in wasn't hardly what she was used to. . . .

"You didn't like Mrs. Radlett?" They'd guessed it, from what young Gary King had said; and she was confirming that guess by the disapproving, rather than distressed, face she assumed as she came to describe her part in the tragedy.

She tossed her head. "I speak the truth without fear or favour, let me tell you! Like the woman I could not, coming here with her slick city ways to interfere in Redingote affairs—told us how the lych-gate did oughter be repaired before the new parson comes, when there's the parish rooms needing a decent coat of paint, not to mention new windows, and not enough money to pay for both—and what's it to do with outsiders, I should like to know? But there were plenty as was fooled by her, oh, yes! Poor Doctor Oliver, for one—led him by the nose, so she did, so quiet and shy as he was before she made her play for him—dazzled him, she did, him as had bin dedicated to Redingote like his father before him—blinded him, so's he never could see her for what she really was—worshipped her, poor man, as crazy in his way as that Barney Chilman. But that,'' said Ethel, ''is menfolk for you, ain't it? No sense!''

She tossed her head again, and looked sharply at Stone. ''They either treats you like dirt, or they lets you walk all over them!'' Mrs. Maggs had been widowed very early in life, and rejoiced in her freedom—and in the insurance policy which had helped to make that freedom so comfortable. ''Walk all over them,'' she repeated, with emphasis; and pursed her lips, and looked wise.

''Well,'' acknowledged Stone, suppressing the twinkle in her eye, ''I suppose, sometimes . . .''

Her apparent doubt prompted Ethel to expand on her theme with such enthusiasm that Trewley was tempted to applaud his sergeant's manipulative skills, until he found himself wondering whether it had in fact been Mrs. Maggs who was the manipulator. Her eyes were bright with excitement. It was all too clear she intended to spill whatever beans she considered worth the effort after only a token hesitation.

''Course, I'd not care to say so right out, not even to the police—not with it being libel . . .''

''Slander,'' interposed Stone automatically, though Ethel paid scant attention.

''Seeing as it's an official matter, though, I don't mind telling you there's bin . . . something . . . going on in this village, of recent months—the sort of something as takes two, if you know what I mean,'' and she nodded, and frowned, and looked portentous. ''Something going on, indeed—and poor Doctor Oliver knowing nothing about it, and that—that wicked woman taking advantage of his good nature! Doted on her, the poor man always did, long before the day they was wed—which made a new man of him, anyone could see, for all she was never worthy of him, not by a long chalk she wasn't, if you ask me. *Him*, now . . . you'll not find a soul in Redingote to speak against the young doctor—and I've no doubt there'll be plenty,'' Ethel Maggs informed Detective Sergeant Stone firmly, ''as think he's well rid of her. Not that you'll get *him* to see it, I'm sure—bound to be proper cut up about it all, and no mistake. The poor man.''

For the first time, there was a suggestion of sorrow in Ethel's reaction to Ingrid Radlett's death, a glint of tears in her beady eyes. But not for the death itself, the detective realised at once: she was more bothered by the distress Ingrid's husband would feel at having lost her. Might the killer, Trewley wondered suddenly, have killed to strike more at Ingrid's husband than at herself? Was Redingote's own ''Doctor Oliver'' perhaps not as universally popular as Ethel Maggs had led the police to believe?

''Did Mrs. Radlett,'' he broke in, after an exchange of glances with Stone, ''have any enemies?'' Useless to ask if her husband had: Ethel's views on that topic had already been made plain. ''Can you think of anyone who might have wanted her dead?''

''Stands to reason it'll be the man she was deceiving him with. Poor Doctor Oliver. Right sorry I'll be for him to have his marriage flaunted about for all to make mockery of, in the newspapers and such—for, mark my words, that's who killed her, and to my mind the hussy deserved it!''

Hussy. A bell rang in Trewley's memory: and, as Ethel seemed prepared to carry on in similar vein all afternoon without adding anything constructive to the investigation, he enquired:

''By the way—before you go—perhaps you wouldn't mind telling us who, er, Abigail is? We couldn't help noticing Mr. Ezard's reaction when—''

''And no wonder!'' Ethel's smirk was of momentous proportions as she gloated over the memory of Cedric's discomfiture, and thought how, once she'd told what she knew, his hash would be settled once and for all in the opinion of the detectives from town.

It was a tale going back some time. Redingote's Harvest Home, the annual excess of September jollification leading invariably to a bumper crop of subsequent midsummer babies, had been attended one year by Lancelot Pasmore: husband to Gwendolyn but not, on this occasion, her escort, she having succumbed to a severe and unseasonal attack of influenza. Pitying his solitary state, Abigail Ezard (who since her early teens had delightedly deflowered every available village male of sufficient indiscretion) had been discovered acrobatically disporting with Lancelot in a pile of hay at the far end of the barn; whereupon her irate father Cedric, pitchfork in hand, had attempted to disembowel her.

Some snobbish realism in Old Cedric caused him to hold Lancelot blameless in the affair, more or less; but with his pitchfork and his furious glare he presented so formidable a sight that Lancelot promptly had a heart attack. (Many villagers held that this had rather been brought about by the demands of Abigail's athletic and imaginative contortions; but the result was the same in either case). Abigail ran away to walk the city streets; Lancelot faded away in hospital; and Gwendolyn Pasmore was left alone to face the whispers and prurient giggles of a gleeful Redingote.

"Yes," concluded Ethel, after a grudging pause, "Cedric Ezard won't hear a word against poor Mrs. Pasmore. . . ." She had no wish to pay the head gardener even the least of compliments, but she supposed she must tell the truth. "Speaks up for her, fair and square, he always does—a proper lady, so she is, being such a close friend to the Izods as lately owned the manor, and him gardener here, man and boy. He'll do anything for Mrs. Pasmore, he will—and precious few folk can say *that* of him, the old grumbleguts! You saw how he set that Barney to throw me off the chair—always does what Cedric tells him, does Barney. And to attack a helpless widow in such a fashion, well . . ."

"I promise you we'll be having a word or two with him later," said Trewley, taking care not to specify the nature of those words. And when Mrs. Maggs, limping and remembering to rub her bruised rear end, had departed, he gazed thoughtfully at Sergeant Stone.

"That Mrs. Pasmore of yours, girl. She does keep cropping up in all this, one way and another, doesn't she?"

"Let's see her next, sir. And find out what she wanted to tell us—I'm sure there was *something*," said Stone.

"Umph." The superintendent considered that humouring

her to excess would be bad for her; on the other hand, he had
to admit that he was now as interested as she to talk to
Gwendolyn. "Anyone that old cuss Ezard genuinely ap-
proves of must be quite something, I should say. If Mrs.
Maggs was right about how he feels towards Mrs.
Pasmore. . . ."

"I bet she was, sir. You could see she simply loathed
having to admit he had any good points at all, but she did
tell us that, didn't she?"

Gwendolyn Pasmore, in that first brief acquaintance, had
seemed just another tall, tweeded, country personage of
efficient manner and well-bred speech. But if what they'd
heard about her was even partly true, it was probable that
she had . . . "Hidden depths," muttered Trewley.

"Still waters, don't you mean, sir? And everyone knows
about *them*. About how they need investigating, I mean,"
and Stone jumped to her feet before he could change his
mind, to head off in search of Gwendolyn. But she did not
need to go far to find her. Mrs. Pasmore was hovering in the
shade of a nearby rose tree, the tea tray in her hands.

"Is that for us, Mrs. Pasmore? Splendid—exactly what
we need! Taking statements is thirsty work. Would you
mind bringing it over now? Then Superintendent Trewley
can ask you a few questions—killing two birds, as you
might say, with one stone."

The sergeant pulled a whimsical face at the final word,
but Gwendolyn did not react to the little joke in the way
Stone would have expected from one of her class: the silly
pun passed her completely by. At the mention of *taking
statements* she had stiffened—the hands which held the tray
trembled—her brow clouded with anxiety. Clearly, she was
preoccupied with other matters than common courtesy—
other matters which must be probed. . . .

They arrived rather too soon for Gwendolyn's liking at the
table Trewley had chosen as his operational base. "Your
sergeant said . . . I made you some more . . . there's no
sugar, I'm afraid—I forgot—but perhaps, just this once . . . ."

"Neither of us takes it in the usual way, thanks." Such
disjointed speech was far from normal to Gwendolyn

Pasmore and her ilk. Why had her normal country calm deserted her? The superintendent wanted to know—and know quickly, before she had time to recover herself, to reinstate that chilly shield of self-confidence which would, he knew, be almost impossible to penetrate. Once this chance of taking advantage of her momentary weakness was lost, it might be hard to find another.

"No sugar, thanks—but I won't say this tea's not welcome." Trewley reached for the mug Mrs. Pasmore had set with a too-steady hand on the table in front of him. With a visible effort, she took the seat opposite. He nodded genially. "A very hot day, Mrs. Pasmore. And my sergeant likes to make sure I don't talk myself dry, with all the interviewing I have to do—isn't that right, Sergeant Stone?"

"That's right, sir. This is such a marvellous setting for interviews that we've both, well, been rather carried away, and lost track of just how long everything has taken. Down at the station . . ." and Mrs. Pasmore went absolutely white. Stone smiled. "At the station, we're generally done in half the time, aren't we, sir?" She looked in triumph at the superintendent. Now it was up to him to add the final touches—he'd observed, as clearly as she had, Gwendolyn's reaction to the threat of more official action. . . .

"Half the time, easily," he agreed, watching the grey eyes of Mrs. Pasmore dart from his face to Stone's, then down to her lap where her hands were clasped tightly together. "Oh, yes, I'd far rather do my talking here in the open than in one of the rooms at the station—those little windows, the locked doors, air that's been breathed by fifty other people already—"

"Oh, please!" Gwendolyn shuddered. Her voice shook. "It—it sounds so very . . . you make it so hard for . . . oh, dear . . ." She unclasped her shaking hands to take a small, neat cotton handkerchief from her pocket, and dabbed her overbright eyes, and tried not to sniff. Stone looked with approval at her plain gold wedding band and unobtrusive solitaire diamond. For a woman so reserved to act this much out of character suggested, at the very least, an overactive conscience.

"I'm—I'm sorry, Superintendent." Gwendolyn gulped, and blew her nose. She replaced the handkerchief, and sat up straight. "This has all been—been the most dreadful shock. . . ."

"You and Mrs. Radlett were . . . close friends?" But Trewley knew, before he finished speaking, that this was not so: the opposite, if anything. Even in her anxiety, Gwendolyn's face had hardened on hearing the dead woman's name—had briefly, but definitely, hardened—with mingled annoyance and resentment, he thought. And then he watched her recall the circumstances of Ingrid's death, saw her struggle to soften her features to show that polite hypocrisy preferred—and expected—by society. Investigating officers, however, prefer the truth. . . .

And Gwendolyn had been brought up to tell the truth. She took a deep breath. "Not really," she said, in a low voice. "No, we weren't—not close—and you must be wondering, I imagine, why I—I seem so upset." She swallowed, and sat up again. "Just the shock, I expect."

"Well now, I'm inclined to think there's a bit more to it than that, Mrs. Pasmore. Shock—as my sergeant here will agree, I don't doubt—affects different people in different ways, but . . ." Trewley frowned, the bulldog creases of his face contorting alarmingly. He leaned forward to gaze at Gwendolyn, who seemed almost to quail as he said, slowly:

"No, I don't think it's just the shock, Mrs. Pasmore. It isn't so much that you weren't close to Mrs. Radlett, is it? If you're honest, you'll admit that really, you didn't like her at all. Did you? And that's why you're so upset."

Seven

GWENDOLYN'S EYES WIDENED, her mouth opened in surprise; she slumped in her chair with relief, almost losing the composure she had striven so hard to maintain. "You—you understand that? But—how did you know?"

He shot a speaking look at his sergeant. "Call it . . . call it intuition, Mrs. Pasmore," and he saw Stone grimace, even as she prepared to take down the notes which might, in due course, contain that which Gwendolyn had so far kept hidden.

"Intuition," repeated Mrs. Pasmore gravely. "Was it so very obvious? Because it was hardly—it wasn't *violent*, do please believe me. I—we—there was a . . . a disagreement this morning, between myself and Mrs. Radlett—we quarrelled—but not violently," she said again, insisting. Too much insistence, perhaps? She gave Stone an apologetic smile, her lips pale. "It was—oh, a petty women's thing—you'd call it nonsense, I know. It blew up out of almost nothing—but I'd already been feeling so very . . . so very angry at her, even before she turned up here and . . ."

"Here?" Trewley waved about him at the roses. "You mean in this garden—or just here at The Stooks?"

"In this garden, Superintendent. We were—we had to arrange the tables for the Teas—they're always set out in the rose garden because of the shade, and it's not too far to walk from the drive when you're carrying a tray. . . ."

"More than one of you," prompted Trewley, as she drifted into a thoughtful silence, her head bowed.

Her head jerked up. "Mrs. Wilford was helping me—practically the only help I was offered throughout the entire morning! The men who should have been here were drunk on the upper lawn, though that's nothing new—but it was

such a very long time"—her tone was almost plaintive—
"before anyone came our way. . . ." She lost her voice
again. "Myra—Mrs. Wilford—and I blamed it all on Mrs.
Radlett, you know. Oh, it sounds foolish, even as I say it,
but . . ."

Gwendolyn went on to explain briefly how Ingrid's new
scheme of stall ownership was supposed to save Redingote
parish the cost of annual renting from Allingham market;
and how the novelty of the design made those who normally
completed the heavy work on fete day slower than usual—
even, Gwendolyn added in more robust tones, without
taking the drink into consideration.

Trewley had to chuckle. He would, in other circumstances, have laughed out loud at the remainder of her story
as she pressed on with it. She was right to fear that he would
find it foolish: he did. New stalls, furniture shifting, hot and
heavy work, laddered stockings—the two friends grumbling
together . . .

"It wasn't until we'd almost finished," she said, with a
sigh, "that we had any help at all. And even then it was only
Barnabus Chilman—oh, he's willing enough, if you can
persuade him to do something, but he certainly isn't bright.
We spent as much time telling him what to do as he spent
in trying to do it. And then . . ."

A delicate pink crept across her sallow cheeks. "Then,
well, he didn't stay very long. . . ."

Trewley thought he knew why she had blushed. "Then
Mrs. Radlett turned up to scare him away? Which gave you
the chance to have your . . . disagreement?"

"Why, no." Gwendolyn's surprise seemed genuine.
"No, it wasn't Mrs. Radlett. It was—it was Mr. Rowles
who came along . . . and offered to help. . . ."

Trewley nodded. "Of course, the owner of The Stooks.
We haven't met the gentleman yet. Somewhere about the
grounds still, I suppose, and doesn't realize what's happened."

"Mr. Rowles"—Gwendolyn blushed even more—"is a
newcomer to Redingote, Superintendent. He, ah, hasn't
lived here six months yet—and he's finding it hard to learn

the ropes. I, ah, suspect he may be a little shy—especially with the villagers making it so very plain that they regard him as a—a usurper. The Izods go back generations, you see. And even . . . Mrs. Radlett . . . when she came into the rose garden, and found, ah, the two of us—resting, having a little chat, no more . . .''

"The two of you? I know you said Barnabus had already gone, but what happened to Mrs. Wilford?"

"Oh, she—she left, at about the same time as Barnabus. She was expecting her husband, you see, and went up to look for him—there were only a few tables left to set out, so it didn't really matter . . . and then''—Gwendolyn's eyes glittered—"along came Mrs. Radlett, drooping and drifting in that infuriating way she had—I could tell it was annoying Mr. Rowles every bit as much as it annoyed me. 'We meet again,' she said, or something like that—but it was all too easy to see he wasn't pleased. I, ah, suppose he might have thought she was, ah, pursuing him. . . .''

Trewley took pity on her blushes, even as he admired the effort with which she attempted to suppress them. Gwendolyn Pasmore had hidden depths, all right: reserves of character, strength of will . . . sufficient strength of will to murder?

"Yes, well," he said, "we've gathered that Mrs. Radlett had a bit of a reputation for—shall we say enjoying the company of the opposite sex?"

Gwendolyn sighed, and frowned, and looked down at her restless hands, delaying her reply as long as she dared. Even now, she struggled to be true to the custom of speaking as little ill of the dead as possible; and she shook her head, and sighed again.

"Not everyone," she said slowly, "saw her the same way—people misunderstand, you know. Mr. Rowles is a—a retiring person, and was glad, I think, of the excuse to, ah, leave us when he heard the argument on the main lawn—his position to keep up, you see. It was Cedric Ezard making trouble for Olive Yetts over the Candy Floss, I believe. The same thing happens every year, and I'm sure they both enjoy it, judging by the volume of the shouting. Cedric sees it as his duty, you see, to protect his ancestral property, grass and all.'' Her smile was thin, and forced. ''He's a tetchy character, but I rather admire him, you know, for sticking to what he feels are his principles.'' And she digressed briefly, explaining Mr. Ezard's dubious claim to family ties with the departed, and lamented, Izods.

Diverting though this sidelight on village history might be, Trewley wasn't about to let himself be too far diverted from the main purpose of the interview. ''So you and Mrs. Radlett had your . . . disagreement after Mr. Rowles had gone to intervene in the Candy Floss quarrel?''

Gwendolyn bit her lip, and once more dropped her eyes. There was a pause. She raised her head, and drew a deep breath. ''Mrs. Radlett claimed to feel a little faint—said she needed to sit down for a while. That was when Mr. Rowles left us . . . but it wasn't long before she evidently felt better—if she'd ever,'' waspishly, ''been off-colour in the first place. She started teasing, sniping in that clever way she had . . . why didn't we set out the chairs in a different order—and next year we really must see about getting some properly organised help in plenty of time to avoid having to rush the job. . . . You can imagine the sort of thing, I'm sure—the artful, annoying 'helpfulness' that makes you madder than ever when you're on the receiving end of it—and, oh, didn't she just know it, too!''

Then she went white with the realisation of how she'd allowed her guard to slip; and Trewley, taking pity on her again, remarked: ''Don't think we don't know, Mrs. Pasmore. Too many members of the public spend hours telling us how easy it would be to catch villains if we only did so-and-so . . . oh, yes, we know exactly what you mean! Make a habit of this sort of behaviour, did she?''

Gwendolyn hesitated. ''Well, yes—but . . . to be fair, it was more, I suppose, mischievous, rather than malicious—and not with everyone. Not usually with men, that is,'' in her driest tones. ''She preferred *them* to be kept—interested . . . but with a few of us women, and one or two of the men . . . we seemed to bring out some—impish—side to her nature that delighted to watch you squirm at her teasing. While she, of course, remained absolutely cool and composed—such a very pointed, clever contrast. . . ."

"Well now, isn't that the point of teasing people? To watch the victim lose his head . . . or hers," said Trewley. He had to lean forward to catch Gwendolyn's reply.

"Or hers. Yes . . . Somehow, this morning, she managed to get right under my skin—I was so hot, and tired, irritable about everything, not simply with her—and when she turned up the way she did, looking so calm, so fresh . . . and then she pretended to feel faint—just to have an excuse for sitting down with Mr. Rowles, I'm sure. . . ."

"Only she scared the man away instead of, er, fascinating him? So she decided to wind you up instead, by criticising all your hard work. And you—naturally enough, some might say—responded by letting fly at her."

Gwendolyn's fingers writhed on her lap, and her voice was so very low that Trewley was tempted to ask her to speak up. "I'm sorry to say . . . it just all . . . came boiling out of me. I—I snapped at her—and she said something back—and I snapped a bit more. . . . " She swallowed, and blinked. "But I—I didn't kill her, Mr. Trewley, believe me. I might have been sorely tempted to hit her over the head with one of the chairs she wanted me to move, but I—I never laid a finger on her. . . ."

"Hit her over the head," repeated Trewley, without emphasis. But Stone, too, had spotted Gwendolyn's unfortunate turn of phrase. Coincidence? Or did she already know how Ingrid Radlett had met her death in the middle of the maze—and, if so, just how had she known it?

Gwendolyn sensed the detectives' heightened awareness, though not knowing why, and was quick to protest her innocence. Ingrid had been alive and well when she left her to go out into the drive—quite in the opposite direction, she pointed out, from the maze. "And—yes! Myra—Mrs. Wilford—was looking for her husband. She might have seen her, or Barnabus could have done. They would confirm my story. . . ."

"Story? I thought you were telling us the truth, Mrs.

Pasmore? The whole truth"—Gwendolyn's eyes shifted under Trewley's interested gaze—"and, or so I understood it, nothing but the truth. Story?"

He waited, passing a fretful hand over his face, the heavy afternoon heat overpowering even the shadows cast by the roses; and realised that the moment was lost. If Gwendolyn had been on the point of saying anything, she swallowed it firmly. And it was in her usual authoritative tones that she remarked:

"Your cup of tea doesn't appear to have refreshed you much, Mr. Trewley. Do you really intend to conduct all your interviews out here? Why not go indoors, where it's so much cooler?"

He frowned. What had he missed, by letting her seize on the change of subject? Still, whatever it might have been, it was gone; and she had a point—his wits were certainly slowing as the weary afternoon wore on. From the look on Stone's face, she thought so, too.

And so, if he was honest, did he. "It's a very hot day, Mrs. Pasmore, yes—but it's hardly good policy for us to . . . to take over someone's house without asking. We're still looking for Mr. Rowles, you know."

The former friend of Diana Izod hesitated only briefly. "Nobody could possibly object to your using any of the rooms on the ground floor, I'm sure. I'll show you—we go in by the French windows, overlooking the lawn."

Stone stirred. Trewley looked at her. She smiled. "If it's French windows, sir—well, they don't have quite the same break-and-enter feel about them, do they? And we could square it with Mr. Rowles just as soon as he's found." She frowned at her dithering superior. "French windows, sir—a splendid idea. To get in out of the heat. . . ."

Her voice was the voice of a temptress. Trewley, tempted, before too long—as she had hoped—succumbed. "A very good idea, Mrs. Pasmore," he said with a sigh, and rose to his feet. "To the French windows, then!"

As she led the way to the house, Gwendolyn seemed more in control of herself, and was almost chatty. "There's one thing more, Superintendent—it's probably nothing, and

I'm not sure it's worth mentioning, but—it may have been simply spite, of course, only—I can't understand why Mrs. Radlett pulled off all the butterfly wings like that! Assuming,'' she added, as both detectives turned to stare at her, ''that she was the one who did it. . . .''

When she had left them, Trewley and Stone regarded each other in a thoughtful silence, unbroken until the former, having requested that his sergeant should read through her notes, remarked when she had done so:

''Strewth! *Petty women's problems*, all right—don't you ever try that sort of trick on me, girl, or I'll have you back in the uniformed branch before you can blink! Butterfly wings, indeed! Butterfly brains, more like.''

Stone nodded. ''I can't seriously credit it as a motive myself, sir. One plate of fairy cakes with the tops chopped off by person, or persons, unknown, but believed to be Mrs. Ingrid Radlett. It's crazy! Still,'' with a quick look at the superintendent, ''in this heat . . . it isn't only you who suffers the same way, you know. She was Scandinavian, after all. The frozen north, and so on—I'll bet her blood just couldn't cope with the sort of weather we're having today, and . . .''

''Stop measuring me for my coffin, girl! I haven't quite given up the ghost, remember—you're not in charge of this investigation yet.'' He mopped his forehead, then responded to her apologetic grin with a chuckle. ''Come on, let's have somebody else along. We've seen everyone from the maze. . . . How about this Wilford woman, to see what she can tell us about her friend Mrs. Pasmore and the deceased. . . .''

When Myra appeared, she was making as much of an effort to seem calm under the threat of police questioning as Gwendolyn had made. Her shoulders were held firmly back, her head unnaturally high; her eyes were bright, and darted from side to side. As she replied to the opening question, they were the only part of her which moved: the rest of her was under control as strict as any the detectives had seen.

''What do you mean, did I overhear anything this morning? It is not my habit, Superintendent, to eavesdrop—

not even for the sake of helping the police with their enquiries!''

Had she indeed heard the quarrel, and considered it more serious than Gwendolyn had led them to believe—or had she heard none of it, supposing now that by silence alone she could protect her friend? Surely that air of being affronted beneath the superintendent's questions was assumed, was forced? And, if so—why?

''I do not know,'' said Myra, ''why you suggest I must have been one of the last people to—to see her alive. At what time is she thought to . . . to have . . . to have died?''

Trewley's smile was thin, his eyes narrow, the wrinkles on his brow menacing in their complexity. ''I can't tell you that, Mrs. Wilford—and only partly because we've no idea ourselves until the doctor produces his final report. Only partly,'' he repeated. ''So now, then—we believe Mrs. Radlett went out to the drive once she and Mrs. Pasmore had finished their little . . . disagreement—and you were wandering about the place looking for your husband, weren't you? Did you see her at all—maybe talk to her? Or,'' he added, ''anyone else?''

Although she was frowning, Myra seemed rather more at her ease than before as she replied. ''Barnabus Chilman had gone out to the drive—have you been told about Barnabus? Well, then, you understand why nobody would wish to spend too long by themselves in his company, especially at the full moon. And Barnabus was in a most uncertain mood this morning. Cedric Ezard had worried him over the fete preparations—not that he would have harmed Mrs. Radlett, because he'd never dream of such a thing—but if she'd spotted him, she wouldn't have stayed around for long. Yet she must''—Myra frowned again—''have been there for a while—the butterfly cakes—did Gwendolyn . . . ?'' And, at Trewley's nod, she continued:

''But Barnabus might have gone off somewhere to do something else. . . . I assure you, Superintendent, that I never saw her there—I never went that way at all, in fact.''

"Then where," he demanded, "did you go, Mrs. Wilford?"

"I . . . she was still alive when I last saw her, up on the main lawn . . . when I was with Mrs. Brown at her Prize Every Time. . . . Mrs. Radlett came over to join us, but I was still wondering about . . . my husband—he still hadn't come—I looked quickly into the drive, and saw Barnabus there, so I—I didn't want to go back. I was . . . tired. So I—I came into the house to rest for a while."

"You avoided having to speak to Barney by coming in here instead of going back to help with the stalls on the main lawn? Why not go back to the rose garden? Was it"—the superintendent's gaze was penetrating—"because you knew that was where Mrs. Radlett had gone next, and you were trying to avoid her?"

"Oh, no." Was her denial too quick to be natural—too assured to be spontaneous? "Oh, no—I knew that Mr. Rowles was there, you see. Helping Gwendolyn—Mrs. Pasmore. So they wouldn't," she explained hastily, "have needed a third person. . . . Besides, I was so tired, and hot. I told myself I deserved a rest, after so many of those terrible tables and chairs! It's always delightfully cool in this sitting room, and there's an excellent view of the lawn. I would have been able to spot . . . my husband, the moment he arrived with Mr. Hemingway at the Book Stall—far more pleasant, you know, than waiting about in the drive, with the risk of Barnabus Chilman building up to one of his—his moods. . . ."

Trewley leaned back in his chair, then forwards, narrowing his eyes once more as he judged for himself the view through the French windows. He grunted. "With that creeper hanging down, you don't see the lawn clearly, by any means. Is this where you were sitting?"

"Your sergeant is in the chair I used, Superintendent." Myra's voice was cold. "And I am not accustomed"—it grew even colder, as he raised a questioning eyebrow in Stone's direction—"to having my word doubted. . . ."

Stone glanced through the window, observed the purple

edifice which was Edgar Hemingway's Book Stall, and nodded, adding to her notes as she did so. Trewley, having watched his sergeant for a moment, nodded in his turn, and said:

"So you sat in here, nice and quiet and cool"—he was tempted to mop his bulldog brow in sympathy, but restrained himself—"and saw nothing further of Mrs. Radlett—and you didn't"—in a tone of disbelief—"hear anything of her quarrel with Mrs. Pasmore? You'd need to be nearer the rose garden, I suppose, to be able to tell me about that."

Myra managed a little laugh. "I hope she hasn't given you the impression it was serious, Mr. Trewley! It was no more than a—a little squabble. If that! Ingrid Radlett was like a—like a gadfly, you know, with her teasing ways—I've no doubt Gwen felt tempted to bop her one, knowing how infuriating the woman could be. And I've no doubts at all that she didn't. She told me all about it later—she was perfectly calm, and needn't have said anything about it anyway, because nobody knew—and besides," as Trewley and Stone showed plainly that this argument carried singularly little weight with them, "I hardly think she would have been able to—to carry the . . . to take her into the maze, any more than I could have done. That is hardly, Superintendent, the work of a woman."

Trewley risked a quick look at Stone, whose pencil had scratched its final shorthand outline with such vigour that the lead broke. She did not meet his eyes as she felt in her pocket for a replacement.

He cleared his throat. "You mean, because of the weight of the body? Well, there are such things as wheelbarrows, Mrs. Wilford—but," as she opened her mouth to speak, "just at the moment, we aren't prepared to say anything about exactly what did hap—"

"You mean Old Cedric? That's ridiculous! He'd never agree to such a thing, not even for Gwendolyn's sake—and I'm sure she wouldn't. I'm sure. . . ."

But both Trewley and Stone longed to know why Myra had so thankfully seized on this new idea, and turned it to her advantage by suggesting to them what had not, in fact, been directly suggested to her. With friends like Myra Wilford, enemies might not, it seemed, be necessary. . . .

Time, Trewley decided, would reveal more about Myra's devious double game than further questioning now would do; and he decided to let her depart, watching those defiant shoulders, that determined spine remain rigid until their owner passed out of his sight. He leaned back in his chair with a sigh, and brooded over what he had so far heard; Stone, still without meeting his gaze, took her penknife key-ring from her pocket and sharpened the broken pencil into a convenient ashtray. She read through her notes, and studied the plan of the fete which PC Davers had produced at her request.

She coughed. Trewley looked up, met her gaze, and nodded for her to speak. "This Mrs. Brown, sir. Her stall's right at the bottom of the garden, close to the Teas. I bet *she* could have heard something of the row between Pasmore and Radlett—or she might be able to confirm whether or not Mrs. Wilford really did head in the opposite direction when Mrs. Radlett went down into the rose garden. . . ."

Trewley chuckled wearily. "If that's what your woman's intuition suggests, girl, then we'd better have Mrs. Brown in next. After all''—hastily, as she seemed about to protest— "apart from Barney Chilman, remember, Mrs. Brown's is the only name Mrs. Wilford could come up with as any sort of witness to her own movements. Sitting in the house having a rest, for heaven's sake!''

Stone raised her eyebrows. "A matter of her health, no doubt,'' she murmured. "The heat. . . .'' And Trewley chuckled again as he sent his sergeant on her way.

Margaret Brown was a brisk, plump, greying woman with alert eyes of a deep hue that complemented her surname. She regarded the detectives with some curiosity, but—in contrast to Myra and Gwendolyn—seemed unconcerned by their interest in herself.

"Oh, yes, of course I knew her. In a place as small as Redingote, everyone knows everyone else—though she wasn't a particular friend, let me add. We spoke when we met, but that was about it. . . . People who disliked her? Oh, I've no doubt they existed—don't they always? . . . No, from what little I saw of her, nothing out of the ordinary at all.''

"What—little—dealings did you have with Mrs. Radlett this morning, Mrs. Brown?"

"I'd hardly say *dealings*, Superintendent, because that would suggest I'd paid her some attention, which I didn't. She came floating along as full of herself as she generally was, and took it into her head to hang around, making suggestions and getting in my way when I was busy arranging my stall. I suppose she meant to be helpful, but as far as I was concerned she wasn't. I've run my stall in exactly the way I want for over twenty years, Mr. Trewley. The one person I've ever trusted to help me is my daughter Jill, but now she's married and moved away I infinitely prefer to be left to my own devices. Especially''—she smothered a smile—"when much of the help I'm offered is from people rather the worse for drink.''

Trewley sat up. "Are you talking about Mrs. Radlett?"

Margaret seemed surprised, rather than shocked, at the idea. "I wouldn't have said . . . though, come to think of it, she *was* rather pale and interesting . . . but I was referring to Ralph Stretch and his friends, who were supposed to put the stalls together for everyone else. I'm lucky enough not to need their help, but I can assure you that there were some very impatient people about the place earlier today!"

In response to her twinkle, Trewley frowned. "So you had someone to help you put up your stall, did you? But I understood you to say . . .''

"Oh, no. Didn't I explain that I never have any help? I arrange everything exactly as I want it, always. I was in the Wrens during the war, Mr. Trewley. What the Navy can't teach you about organisation isn't worth knowing! I provide my own stall—decorating tables, light enough for me to manage by myself—I painted them yellow to match the others this year—my own float—prizes—even a plastic sheet, in case it rains. So I hope you understand why I wasn't too happy having Mrs. Radlett chatter on about systems and tickets and her different plans to improve things. I was doing my best to concentrate, and tuned her out as far as possible—and when I'd made it plain I wasn't listening to her, off she went. Down to the rose garden, I think, though I can't honestly say I paid too much attention. I simply thought oh good, she's going, and carried on with my work.''

''About what time would that have been?''

She laughed, extending for his inspection a strong, tanned, bare left wrist. ''I never wear a watch, Superintendent. I'm electric, you see, and they always die on me. So I'm useless to you as an alibi—and anyone in Redingote,'' she added shrewdly, ''will tell you the same.''

Trewley grunted. As the whole village knew of Margaret Brown's idiosyncrasy, had somebody relied upon it? And why had Mrs. Wilford given the impression that she had been helping someone who obviously needed no help from her or anyone else?

Or was Margaret Brown, for some reason of her own, also lying?

''As a woman who's so well-organised, Mrs. Brown, what did you think of Mrs. Radlett's schemes? Not for your own stall, of course, but the general parish improvements we've heard she suggested? Good ideas, would you say?''

''Good enough, but . . . well, the trouble was that she was inclined to want everything done yesterday. She tried to rush people before they were ready, and in a place like Redingote it doesn't do to be too modern too fast. Although I have to say, if the hiring fees are sufficiently attractive to outsiders she could have done us quite a favour with this stall-building scheme—always excepting,'' and she chuckled, ''the feud that seems to have broken out between the people who want the parish rooms renovated, and those who want the lych-gates repaired. Rather a kerfuffle, there's been—and we haven't even got the money yet! Still, I hardly think you're interested in such nonsense.''

''Right now, we hardly know what we're interested in,'' Trewley told her, chuckling in his turn. ''As Mrs. Radlett was involved, however, it might be worth hearing more—not that we haven't heard a little already, from Mrs. Maggs."

"Be warned by me, and take what she told you with a generous pinch of salt! She left home because of it, you know—quarrelled with her sister about whether it should be the parish room or the lych-gates—and they haven't exchanged one word since then." And as Trewley's expression betokened surprise, Margaret added, before he could put the inevitable question, that for her own part she intended to stay strictly neutral in all this. She saw no point in counting chickens before they were hatched. With all the . . . upset this afternoon, there would be little enough money for either, or at least not from the fete—and maybe not from the hiring, now that the moving force behind the scheme was dead. Which could mean there had been a great deal of unpleasantness for no worthwhile reason that she could see.

Trewley, having agreed that it was a waste of effort and emotion, added: "And how about Mrs. Wilford? While you were talking this morning, for instance—did she tell you which side she was on?"

Mrs. Brown shook her head. "I didn't have time to talk to Myra—to anyone, Superintendent, though at least she had the sense to see I was busy. Quite a contrast to Mrs. Radlett: who was a professional woman, and should have known better than to waste people's time. She may have been intelligent"—Margaret's tone implied that she would not care to be pressed for a definite opinion on this—"but she certainly got her priorities completely wrong sometimes. Chatter, chatter, chatter. . . . Myra Wilford knew at once that I didn't want to talk, and was sensible enough to hang about in the background on the off-chance I might need her, rather than hover under my nose trying to gossip. I'm unable to tell you which side she's on, Mr. Trewley—but if she's as sensible as I think she is, she'll keep quiet, like me!"

Trewley stared after her as she took her cheerful leave of them. "There goes one of the ones who didn't care for the deceased, I'd say, though catch her admitting it in so many words—and she didn't admit to hearing the row between Mrs. Pasmore and Mrs. Radlett, either.''

"Maybe the wall muffled it, sir."

"And maybe it didn't. Mind you, even if I'd asked her, she'd have done her best not to tell me—because it wasn't as trivial as all that lych-gate nonsense she was perfectly happy to talk about. Mrs. Brown's a lady, one of the hear-no-evil sort. If they'd screamed blue bloody murder at each other, she'd only have told us she was concentrating on her precious stall and never heard a syllable of anything."

Stone nodded. "She made that point very clearly, didn't she? Not that anyone likes to think their friends are capable of killing, of course. And she did tell us one thing, sir—that Myra Wilford wasn't helping her, for all she tried to pretend to us that she had been."

"Which means she could well have been somewhere else—somewhere, say, like out in the drive?" Trewley motioned for her to push the plan of the fete across for his inspection. "She could," he muttered, "have gone back round the other way—she could even have joined in the quarrel between Pasmore and Radlett."

Stone was quick to voice an objection. "If she did, why didn't Mrs. Pasmore mention it? I don't believe she'd have covered up for her—surely nobody's such close friends they would pretend to forget a thing like that? Especially when it seems Mrs. Wilford's happy enough to try putting the blame on Mrs. Pasmore and her pal Cedric—even if she tried it in rather a roundabout way." She sighed. "How I hate these cases with complicated timetables and motives and alibis and having to work everything out. . . ."

Rarely did she present him with so good an opportunity: perhaps the heat was affecting her, as well. Trewley chuckled. "That, Detective Sergeant Stone, sounds to me like a weak-minded, illogical, *feminine* remark—I'd have expected better from you. Don't scowl, girl! If the wind changes, your face'll stick that way. And everyone knows how particular you females are about your looks. . . ."

"One up to you, sir." Despite herself, she grinned. "Who shall we talk to next?"

"I don't want any more scenes or tears for a while—my nerves can't take it. We'll have a change from the weaker sex, I think, and see that chap who led us through the maze. . . ."

Caleb Duckels had lived in Redingote for more than seventy years—there wasn't much he hadn't seen, one way and another—but murder was clean out of his experience, and he didn't mind telling the detectives he was still pretty shook up by it all.

"But it's poor Doctor Oliver we must feel most for," he reminded them, with a sorrowful sigh. "There's nobody else's feelings should rightly be considered in the case, so do you ask me whatever you're wishful to know, and I'll try my best to help you catch him."

He'd had ample time to think while they interviewed the other witnesses, and now narrated carefully his every action from first having heard those cries of terror from the maze, up to the arrival of the police; and he recalled much of the morning's activities at The Stooks, while everyone was so preoccupied with preparations for the fete. These detailed recollections made the hearts of Trewley and Stone sink. If Caleb told the truth, it seemed that anyone so minded might have lured Ingrid Radlett to the middle of the maze and there killed her: nobody would have noticed. Those who were sober had been far too busy about their own affairs to bother with anyone or anything else; those who were drunk would have been far too fuddled to care.

"Can you give us a rough idea of what time it was when you last saw Mrs. Radlett alive? And whether you got to speak with her, and what you talked about?"

Caleb pondered. "Must have bin half past eleven or so, when she come out of the marquee, poor soul—very stuffy it allus is in there, and this morning not all the judging complete, neither, as I know from what Daisy Hollis said when she had to come along to fetch the parson's good lady from her dinner at my house, to ask for her to finish the judging—on account, you see, of how Mrs. Radlett hadn't come back again after her breath of fresh air. Walked down from the upper lawn, she did, talked to all the stalls on that side of the main ground, then off she went down into the rose garden where the Teas was being set out—and that was the last I saw of her.''

Trewley once again consulted the sketch-plan of the fete layout, courtesy of PC Davers, and showed it to Caleb. The churchwarden drew his finger in a slow clockwise semi-circle round the main lawn. It seemed to tally with other people's memories, though they must check with Mrs. Hollis, whose marquee had been the starting-point for Ingrid's progress in almost royal style about the grounds. . . .

Caleb cleared his throat. ''You'd best be wary of what Mistress Hollis tells you, if there's any word in her talk about me and mine, for she's no friend to the family at the moment, on account of the parish council elections, and her Ernie being passed over in favour of me and Joe Norton, once again. Never really wanted to stand, Ernie didn't, so him and me's good enough friends—but Daisy, now, she and my sister Mildred took it different—the village mostly preferring a man as can stand on his own two feet, which is not what anyone could rightly say of Ernie Hollis. But Daisy, she would have it otherwise. New blood, that's what she kept saying was wanted—but that's not what others thought, and not what happened—and she took it bad. And as for Mildred . . .''

Caleb shook his head, and sighed. ''The sister of a churchwarden, too! Fairly gloated, so Mildred did, when Daisy had to come cap in hand today asking for Mrs. Gregory to come to the judging—and I know she'd bin fussing over the time, because of looking at her watch to leave it to the last minute before coming to my house to fetch the vicar's good lady, you see.''

Trewley and Stone did not dare meet each other's eyes. Village life, it seemed, was every bit as full of excitement as any city's underworld: feuds and quarrels and insults for every possible offence, whether real or imagined. . . .

''And what,'' enquired Trewley, ''did everyone think

when Mrs. Radlett was asked to judge the Flower Show in the first place?'' It seemed an unlikely motive for murder, but in Redingote it might be unwise to take such things for granted.

Caleb looked surprised. ''Ever more ready and willing to play her part, so Mrs. Radlett was, this past year or so—which it was seen and understood to be so, by all concerned. Saving the parish money, with her clever plans—even said how she'd take over the parish books, as were in a sorry state after Old Parson left them, and Mr. Wilford too busy to spare the time they rightly needed—which we all understood—and being Doctor Oliver's wife as well there were a few jealous tongues. But not many, and those mostly belonging to the womenfolk, clacking and complaining. . . .'' He shot a quick look at Stone. ''Women's doings and fandangles, by and large, is what I try to stay out of. Let 'em keep it all among theirselves, and leave me and mine in peace, if so be it's possible to do!''

Which, after his departure, struck Trewley as an entirely admirable sentiment, though Stone muttered of rural back-waters, and male chauvinist piggery. Before he could think of a remark to wind her up even more, however, she jumped to her feet, and waved her notebook wildly.

''Parish books!'' she cried. ''Parish books—and Mr. Wilford—and we wondered what his wife was trying to hide. . . .''

''So we did, girl,'' said Trewley, with a thoughtful nod. ''Yes, you're right—we wondered, didn't we? And now, I'm wondering if we've just found out. . . .''

Eight

STONE WAS STILL standing, as if poised for flight. Trewley flapped a hand at her to sit down again. It made him, he said, weak with exhaustion just looking at her. Before they went charging off after Mrs. Wilford to find out what she'd been playing at, there were other witnesses to see: witnesses who couldn't really be left for the later, less urgent, names-and-addresses types of interview.

He peered yet again at the sketch-map of the fete, with Stone following his pointing finger. "She started off," he said, "in the Flower Show marquee—seems to be the first time anyone noticed her . . . worked her way round the lawn to the rose garden here at the bottom. . . ." He stabbed thoughtfully at the map. "We'll check that out with Mrs. Hollis and the rest, I think. And then, if you like, we'll go farther afield."

"As far as Mrs. Wilford, for a start," said Stone, turning back the pages of her notebook to add cryptic squiggles beside Myra's name. Suspicious behaviour of a bank manager's wife. . . . But the sergeant knew Trewley was right to insist they should talk with everyone on that side of the lawn before they could begin to theorise, and to refine on their theories.

And Daisy Hollis, one of the infamous feuding Redingote ladies, could well have something to say. . . .

Which she did: a great deal of it, woefully repetitious and hard, at first, for Trewley to restrain. Eventually, however, he came to understand that much of the grief she professed stemmed from embarrassment and mingled wrath at having had to apply to her rivals, the Duckels siblings, in the matter of the Flower Show judging. Emergency or not, this fact rankled with Daisy; and her wrathful outpourings made him view parochial life with even more pessimism than before, as he watched from the corner of his eye Stone only noting the barest outlines of what Daisy Hollis said.

"Poor, poor Mrs. Radlett, if only I'd known—so pale and peaky as she was before, and gone for a breath of fresh air when I said she'd do herself no good staying in the marquee—and never come back. . . ." Daisy sniffed, then recovered herself. "Mind you, if I'd known then what I know now, I'd have seen to it as she finished the judging first. Saved me having to disturb Parson's lady from her dinner, which as that Mildred Waskett cooked it you can be sure 'tis no surprise she had indigestion something cruel— and what I was thinking about poor Mrs. Radlett then, I'd not care to repeat—and finding out after what had happened to the dear soul made me feel even worse. . . ."

At last, when she seemed to be running out of breath, the superintendent managed to slow her runaway tongue long enough to ask a few pertinent questions. At what time, roughly, had Mrs. Radlett left the Flower Show? At about half past eleven, near as made no difference, of which Daisy could be sure on account of looking at her watch to check how long the rest might take once Mrs. Radlett had come back again—but of course she hadn't, for no matter how great the honour there were some things nobody could withstand, and if death wasn't one of them—

"A great honour indeed, Mrs. Hollis," broke in Trewley, as she dabbed a handkerchief to her eyes. "But tell me now—weren't people jealous that Mrs. Radlett should be honoured in such a way? You asked the vicar's wife to take her place as a judge, didn't you, so obviously it's not a—a position that's, well, thought light of." Daisy Hollis, though jealous of some people, seemed to have liked Ingrid Radlett; and perhaps would say if anyone plainly did not. . . .

"She was wife to Doctor Oliver, wasn't she," Daisy said, in some surprise that he needed to ask. "With her position in the village to maintain, and showing such interest of late after being chosen president of the Ladies' League—"

"What?" exclaimed Trewley. Stone sat forward. Daisy, startled, blinked at their reaction.

"We hadn't," explained the superintendent, "heard about this, Mrs. Hollis. How long ago was it?"

The turn of the year, it was, when there'd been many a change after the death of the old squire, and his wife selling up and leaving the place open to Lord-knows-who to move in and try to ape his betters. . . .

"We know about Mr. Rowles, thanks," interposed the superintendent, as she drew breath. "It's Mrs. Radlett we'd like to know about now." For instance—he appended silently—why nobody else had seen fit to tell them of Ingrid's recent apotheosis. Most probably it had no bearing on the case—but the general silence on the subject seemed almost conspiratorial. . . .

"Oh no," Daisy said, to Trewley's next question. "It weren't Mrs. Izod as was president before Mrs. Radlett— she's an invalid, poor soul, and no sense in burdening her more than needful. It was Mrs. Pasmore—being such good friends with the Izods, you see—as was president. And high time," she added, "we had some new blood, say I. New blood's a good thing, every once in a while. . . ."

It seemed a likely supposition that the support she hinted at having offered Ingrid at the hustings had been part of her campaign to have Ernie elected as a churchwarden—the campaign which had failed. But would Ernie's wife have wished for Ingrid's death just because her husband lost an election? Redingote people were odd, nobody could deny— but surely never as odd as that. There was the matter of Gwendolyn Pasmore, too. Who had not mentioned her lost Ladies' League presidency as a possible underlying tension to the quarrel that morning with Ingrid—and yet it must, in part at least, have been a reason to intensify any dislike of the dead woman. Perhaps this had been the true cause of her anxiety when she had talked to the police. . . .

"Stands to reason," said Daisy, "there were those as resented Mrs. Radlett—regular stick-in-the-muds as won't make way for modern times when there's little sense in fighting change, which is what most folk know when it's long overdue and try to do something about it. So much younger nor others of her class, so she was, and brought new city notions with her when she come to live among us. Stood up for the modern way of doing things, she did, and told us as we did ought to do likewise, not being duty bound to knuckle under to the menfolk just because that was the way of it in times past. And some of the older folk''—Daisy simpered, letting five-and-fifty years sit light upon her shoulders—''didn't hold with such changes. And them's the ones as would tell any manner of tale to discredit her now, poor soul.''

Cruel rumours, Daisy was sure that's all they were, and she only hoped as no word of them ever reached poor Doctor Oliver, for he worshipped the ground she walked on, and never so proud as the day she consented to become his wife. ''His very words,'' said Daisy, sniffing. ''Hear them now, I can. 'Done me the great honour to consent to become my wife,' that's what he said, and not a man in Allshire happier than the doctor that day. Let her carry on with her job, he did—and talk about proud! Boasted of her clever ways whenever he could, for she was brainful as well as pretty, and him thinking himself the luckiest man in Redingote, as he'd tell any as asked. And she the perfect wife for him, trying so hard to suit the village where he was born—never haughty in her speech, nor scornful to others . . . why, only this morning she had the kindness to talk to that Mr. Rowles, making him feel at home as she didn't have no need to do, but doubtless feeling for him being a stranger, like she'd been herself. . . .''

How should Daisy know whether Mrs. Radlett had previously been acquainted with Mr. Rowles? For her part, she was inclined to think not—how would a lady like her have doings with a shady type like him? Cash down, that man paid for The Stooks—which, if that wasn't enough to make a body think, then Daisy didn't know what was. And of course she had no idea what they'd talked about. She wasn't one to go listening to other folks' private conversations. . . .

''Although,'' remarked Stone, consulting the sketch again after Daisy's departure, ''from the look of this, she could hardly have heard much, even if she'd wanted to. Not if Mrs. Radlett was talking to Rowles right here on the steps—it's too far from the marquee.''

"But the Millages on the Raffle," said Trewley, "could just know something. . . .''

Fiona and Ian, following close on each other's heels, were able to add, they said, so little to the pages of Sergeant Stone's notebook that Trewley was tempted to run them in without delay, on sheer suspicion. They were so quick, so modern, so trendy and liberal and bright—or at least Fiona gave that impression—that his breast boiled with emotion as he listened to what they had to say. They knew nothing, they insisted, of any quarrel between their dear friend Ingrid and anyone else; they kept out of village politics as far as they could; they had overheard none of her conversation with Mr. Rowles that morning on the steps; and, as for her mood when she spoke to them, it had been as normal as anyone could have expected.

"Except," added Ian, with a sigh, "that I thought she looked a bit washed out. The weather. . . .''

"Perky as ever," grumbled Fiona. "Pinched a peach from my prize hamper, right under my nose!" Shortly after which act of larceny, Mrs. Radlett had made, with no sign of haste or distress, for the Produce Stall; and had thereafter been lost to Millage view.

"But if you're looking," said Fiona, her eyes gleaming, "for somebody suspicious—have you heard about Montague Rowles?''

Trewley told her that he had, a little; did she believe she could tell him anything that wasn't just current village gossip? Fiona, to her evident regret, after a moment or two had to confess she could not—apart from the fact that the unfortunate would-be squire had aligned himself with Maisie Tibb on the Tombola. Which proved, said Fiona in triumph, what a very peculiar person he must be. She gave the detectives a potted version of the Millage/Tibb feud, unable to suppress her glee as she spoke of Maisie's sad fate as the object of Montague's charitable efforts.

"Not one word, please," begged the superintendent, once Fiona had taken herself off, preparing to write letters to the *Guardian* about police incompetence. "They're all crazy in this village—you've no need to rub it in. This Tibb woman bumped off the doctor's wife in a fit of jealousy because, in her capacity as Ladies' League big bug, she'd fiddled it so her friends were put in charge of the Raffle. Stark, staring bonkers, the lot of 'em!"

"Only at fete time, sir," Stone said, thinking of his blood pressure. "It's just the Chilmans—should that be Chilmen?—who are crazy the whole year round, by all accounts. Mind you," with a sigh, "this year's fete does seem to have brought out the very worst in human nature, sir. . . ."

He snorted, thinking of his wife, and the Women's Institute. "They always do, girl. There's just one of 'em with the right idea—Mrs. Brown. She does everything by herself, and keeps out of all the arguments. . . ."

"Then she's bound to be the murderer, sir. The least likely character—of course! She could easily have lied when she said they weren't close friends—with friends like the Redingote ladies, who needs enemies?"

"That, my girl, is a sexist remark. You should be ashamed of yourself."

She ventured to pull a face at him before turning back to her notebook. "Could I just sum up what we have so far, sir? Or rather, who. Her husband, of course—the obvious suspect. The local witch, and her sorcerer son—they're bound to come up with some daft reason or other, once we've talked to them. The mad writer chap—ditto. Mr. Rowles—now, I really do like the sound of him. Mrs. Pasmore—a couple of things that make her worth a closer look. Mrs. Wilford, ditto. Ditto! Those parish books—her husband, who's a bank manager—Mrs. Radlett starts to play a larger part in village life, volunteers to check the accounts . . ."

"But how does Mrs. Wilford get her into the maze? It's a place for courting couples and adventurous kids, not for a couple of women going to talk things over—unless you're suggesting that one or other of 'em had tendencies that way, and either Wilford refused her and bashed her out of shock, or Radlett refused Wilford and got bashed out of frustration—both of which seem a bit farfetched.'' He rubbed his chin thoughtfully. ''There are just too many possibilities, girl. And somehow, we have to narrow them down to the probables.''

''Remember, sir, there was some talk of a lover—with the inference that it was male rather than female—so we'd better add him to the list. And Old Cedric Sourpuss, too—the man with strong views about wanton women. If he suspected her of being an adultress . . . and you mentioned wheelbarrows, didn't you? To take the body into the maze,'' as Trewley frowned.

''I wasn't altogether serious,'' he began, but she shook her head.

''You talked about possibilities, and Cedric Ezard wheeling a body in a barrow *is*, sir. It would be, well, almost instinctive for him, wouldn't it? And the same argument would apply to Barney Chilman, too—and we mustn't forget those teenagers who found him, though they're way down on my list. Though I'd put Mrs. Maggs farther up it—''

''For pity's sake, girl, stop! No more theories—you'll drive me as crazy as the rest of 'em. Let's at least finish seeing the other people she must have talked to before she vanished down the steps into the rose garden and was never seen again. . . .''

Elsie Lilleker from Produce was quick to confirm that Mrs. Radlett had visited her stall after talking with the Millages, poor pale thing—and real sorry Elsie was now to have grudged her the peach she snitched from the top of her box, when she was so good-hearted and always willing to be helpful in the matter of government forms, which as a postmistress Elsie had to endure in vast quantities. ''And not a penny would she accept for doing it, you know. Downright neighbourly, so it was—and never mind what others might try to say about her. All slander and lies, that's what it is, and nothing more!''

The voice in which she delivered this remark made

Trewley and Stone wonder what personal cause she had to be so vehement. They were soon enlightened.

"Now, there's that fool sister of mine—you've already talked to her, they tell me—but don't you pay no heed to Ethel and her daft notions! And daft enough she is, too. Wanted to use the money for painting the parish rooms, when they've gone since the Coronation without it and none the worse—and with a new parson coming, it's the least we can do to fix the lych-gate of his church, as a mark of respect and welcome to the man. And then, such trouble there's been about his induction, you'd never credit. . . ."

Trewley and Stone, with their newfound knowledge of Redingote ways, could credit it very well; but before either of them could say so, Elsie was launched upon her shocking tale. The clerical higher-ups, it seemed, wanted to invite all and sundry to St. Swythun's to witness the ceremony—from as far away as Allingham, would the police believe her? The bishop, now—nobody minded about *him*, of course, but when it came to folk having to apply for tickets to sit in the church they'd attended every Sunday since a child, well! Words failed her.

Trewley and Stone wished that they did, as she grumbled on and on. Ethel—her usual spiteful self, of course—had insisted as it was Mrs. Radlett's idea to allocate seats by ticket—as if the poor lady would! Tickets and systems for the fete, that was quite a different matter, saving money and getting things in order as Elsie—working all day with paper as she did—knew only too well was a good idea. "But Ethel's never been *all there*, you see. She was the second born of us two, and the cord came twisted round her neck."

It was Stone, the lapsed doctor, rather than Trewley—despite his wife and three daughters—who grasped the implications of this incredible remark. "You and Mrs. Maggs—you're twins?" Nature's balancing act, she told herself. Large Ethel would make three at least of her birdlike sister Elsie, whose quick tongue hopped from subject to subject and left her listeners dizzy. She had barely acknowledged the truth of the sergeant's guess before offering as her suspect for the murder that Mr. Rowles

who—she knew full well—never sent no letters, leastways
he never bought no stamps—and if Ernie Hollis'd only
sober up long enough he'd say as he never got none, neither,
saving bills for gas and the electric and things of that
sort. . . .

Elsie's fellow Produce worker, Hermione Plenty, was not
so close an echo of her colleague as the detectives feared
she might be. In bulk, she resembled fat Ethel Maggs, and
Stone decided that there must be some subconscious reason
for Elsie's friend looking so much like Elsie's estranged
twin; but, having confirmed all the essential points of her
partner's story, traduced the still-missing Montague Rowles
in the customary manner, and been deterred from a ruthless
recital of the incestuous Chilman genealogy, Hermione
arrived—via a gleeful reference to Abigail Ezard's morals—at
the gratifying goal of Ingrid Radlett's love life.

Her chins thrilled and her eyes rolled as she nodded and
winked her way through licentious speculation, to conclude
that like allus called to like, and Redingote folk preferred to
keep themselves to themselves—the Chilmans being a case
in point—which likewise meant that incomers and strangers
would go one with another. Not, she added, that she'd care
to say for sure, but . . .

The hint sufficed. If Ingrid had indeed played her
husband false, her lover would probably be found among
that group comprising Montague Rowles, Silvester Wilford,
or—a longer shot—Ian Millage. Who, as Stone pointed out
scornfully to the superintendent, once Hermione had departed, was scared of his wife, and would never dare do
anything so rash as to embark on a liaison.

Trewley was still brooding on the general attitude of
Hermione Plenty, comparing it with that of Ethel Maggs.
"Fat women," he mused, "are jealous of thin ones—
specially if they're younger and better-looking, too." Stone
cleared her throat to argue with this premise; he scowled at
her, and she subsided. "Jealousy, though," he went on,
"can come up with some pretty handy bits of information,
can't it? Just think, we might never have known, if Mrs.

Maggs and Mrs. Plenty had decided they'd do better to diet. . . .''

Which was too much for Stone, who spluttered once more, drew a deep breath—and once more subsided. From outside the French windows—by which PC Davers, in shirtsleeved dignity, had been standing guard—came a sudden, shrill commotion. The slow voice of PC Davers rumbled in protest as someone was heard to insist upon entry: a someone who, the detectives heard with sinking hearts, had something to tell them, and would not take no for an answer. Trewley's groan was hollow indeed.

"More bloody women—begging your pardon, girl, but when it takes all day listening to chatter to find out even one useful fact, I despair." He passed a shaking hand over his forehead, and sighed.

Stone cocked an ear towards the distant dispute. "She sounds to me like one of the more determined ones, sir. And maybe she really has something worth telling. . . ."

He groaned again, and briefly closed his eyes. "All right, you win—anything for a quiet life." And he raised his voice above the falsetto demands to 'speak to the superintendent at once,' and called with as much enthusiasm as he could muster: "Never mind, Davers. She can come in."

The rumbled protests died away, and PC Davers coughed in a very marked manner before appearing in the open French windows to usher into the police presence a triumphant and vociferous Edgar Hemingway—at sight of whom Trewley fell back on his chair with a muffled oath. Edgar's piping voice and near hysteria had utterly misled him.

Fortunately, Edgar himself seemed to notice nothing amiss as he plunged straight into his statement with rapturous waves of his butterfly hands. Stone, struggling to hide her amusement, was hard put to it to keep up with his gleeful torrent of words.

"But yes, Superintendent, I assure you, a most *fearful* squabble—and how very distressing it must be for him now, to reflect for the rest of his life that they parted on—ah—on fighting terms!" He tittered. "Not that Mr. Wilford was one of the early birds this morning, I assure you—but that is another story. What I wanted to tell you about was the—the *altercation*, my dear Superintendent, between poor dear Mrs. Radlett and Mr. Wilford, you understand. He was in a positively *furious* mood, I have to tell you—so upsetting for me to observe. Such a *terrifying* change of character, when he'd only a few minutes before been so kind and helpful to me and my dear books—the teensiest bit *pizzicato* last night, I suspect, for he looked utterly *gruesome* when I went to his house this morning—but I never *dreamed* it would come to this! It's dreadful—quite dreadful!''

For once, Trewley found himself unable to reply. Stone leaped into the breach. ''Murder is never pleasant, Mr. Hemingway. For the victim least of all.''

Edgar closed his eyes. ''My dear young lady, please! Such a brutal word—so stark, so harsh—and to apply it to poor, *celestial* Mrs. Radlett! She was sitting in the sun with that guinea-gold hair of hers positively gleaming—too easy to see how poor Barney Chilman might believe her to be a worshipful deity, is it not? And it must have been at High Noon, too—she, poor ignorant dear, in her prime—in her own noontide splendour—so soon to end . . . and I, all unsuspecting, must have been one of the last people to see the poor creature alive! How dreadful!''

Edgar's shudder was one of delight; Trewley's was one of distaste. He threw an anguished glance at Stone, who nodded as she went on with the questioning.

''How can you be so sure of the time, Mr. Hemingway? Noon is a very exact word—you wouldn't wish to mislead us in our enquiries, would you?''

Edgar tossed his head, and replied in sulky accents that it must have been as near to noon as made no difference, for the time of his own arrival at The Stooks was engraved upon his heart. He had been so very concerned about the hour when Silvester Wilford had finally collected himself and his precious secondhand books—he had been counting, positively counting the minutes, if not the very seconds!

At Stone's raised eyebrows, he scowled, and returned to his story. ''Well, anyway—there she sat, poor thing, a veritable picture! If only I were an artist, rather than a wordsmith!'' He simpered. ''What a subject she would have made—so graceful, so very pale and fragile in her beauty— the dying swan—as white, one might say, as the ghost she was so soon to become—ahem!'' He had caught Stone's look. He pursed his lips.

''I can assure you that it was very near to twelve of the clock, you know, because Mr. Wilford and I left his car at the same time, and, in my innocence, I supposed that his intention was to assist me. My boxes of books are heavy, and require transporting as far as the lawn—but he preferred to engage Mrs. Radlett in what I expected would be the customary courtesies. Imagine my *astonishment*, therefore, when I returned from my first solitary visit to my stall— which without any help took *far longer* than I had antici- pated, for I looked at my watch again to check—when I returned, in short, to hear words of *blistering* wrath floating on the summer air, quite destroying its golden purity!''

Reduce the exaggeration by several counts, as Edgar's manner made only too clear would be wise, and Stone still found herself left with a topic worth pursuing. ''Words of blistering wrath by themselves, Mr. Hemingway? No— actions—to accompany them, I suppose?''

Edgar shivered. ''My dear Sergeant, nothing *physical*, I promise you—but nevertheless, so *unpleasant!* The tone—so cutting, so cruel—so devastatingly wrathful! And *he* so much more so than she, by far. . . . I do wonder,'' said Edgar, striving for a spiritual expression and succeed- ing only in looking as nauseated as Trewley felt, ''if she had some premonition that her hours were numbered? She would hesitate to leave this mortal vale in the heat of anger, I am sure. . . .''

Stone shook her head. ''Metaphysical speculations are way beyond the range of normal police enquiry, sir. We'll stick to the facts, if you don't mind. Facts which suggest that Mr. Wilford and Mrs. Radlett quarrelled . . . and I suppose you have no idea of what they quarrelled about?''

With much mincing innuendo and giggling, an apparently embarrassed Edgar succeeded in suggesting that the sus- pected inamorato of Ingrid Radlett was (or until that day had been) Silvester Wilford. And—so far as Mr. Hemingway could make out, between his bouts of book-carrying and eavesdropping—the cause of the quarrel had been Ingrid's wish—her insistence, as Edgar put it—to end the affair.

"Mr. Wilford must have been so *disappointed!* So powerful and manly"—Edgar tittered—"in his frustration, so very *single-minded*, paying no heed to my innocent passage to and fro with my dear tomes! Whereas she, Sergeant Stone, was a veritable *ice-maiden*—so calm, so self-contained—why, she was *eating*, I could see clearly, even as he berated her! So *glacial*—hidden fires beneath, of course, but the facade—so unnerving! Poor Doctor Radlett must have had a most uncomfortable and *confusing* marriage, to say the least. A woman of such very contrasting *moods*." Edgar sighed. "Such a shy man, you know, so slow to make a friend—and for his wife to—to *cuckold* him in so dreadful a fashion! What must the poor man have thought, had he ever found out! Or what dark deed," he added, his eyes alight with sudden speculation, "might he not have committed. . . ."

Stone completed her final outline, and turned a careful page. "Excitable, would you say? Capable of losing his temper and harming her almost by mistake?"

Edgar tittered. "My dear Miss Stone, which of us, in the heat of the moment, might not be so capable? But as for Doctor Radlett—*more* so? Yes, I would say that he is—hidden depths, you know, like his wife. Poor thing," automatically. "A well-matched pair, in more ways than the obvious—she so blond, he so dark—but, though I should have expected him to prefer someone less *exotic*, someone more *comfortable*, no doubt he preferred to live his life dangerously—making up for those many years lost when he lacked even one close friend. . . ."

As Edgar made his mincing exit at last, the superintendent mopped his forehead and sighed. "Thank you," he said. "How you could bring yourself to make notes of that spiteful little twerp's statement—you deserve a medal. If I'd had to listen to much more of our Mr. Hemingway, I think

I'd have started looking round for another statue to bash *him* over the head with.''

Stone grinned. ''We learned about sexual deviation at college, sir. It was interesting to meet a textbook case in real life. I bet he once made a play for Oliver Radlett, and the doctor turned him down! Could have been the same with Wilford, too—notice how he started trying to put the blame for the killing on one, then switched to the other as he thought of it? A subconscious desire to revenge himself for having been rejected by—oh, whichever of them it was. Though he'd never admit it, of course. He doesn't even know that's what he's doing. . . .''

''You're the expert, girl. I don't,'' said the happily married father of three, ''like daisies much, myself—they make me nervous. Still, how much of a daisy would you say he is? Did he make his play for *her*, and do her in when she said no (at least I sincerely hope she did!)—or for *him*, and killed the wife because she got in the way?''

His sergeant stared. ''That's some imagination you have there, sir! I'd never have thought of anything quite so bizarre, but now you've raised the possibility, I suppose it's another theory—to add to all the others. . . .''

She sighed, glanced at her watch, then took a more lingering look through the French windows to the garden beyond. The slightest of breezes had started to ruffle the trailing leaves of creeper, and the air had acquired a slow, gentle, honey-gold hue. ''The sun's going down at last, sir. I feel it wouldn't do either of us any harm to get out in the fresh air. . . .'' She tapped her notebook with a pleading pencil. ''Mr. Wilford, sir. Redingote isn't all that large—he can't live too far way. Might be rather a pleasant walk.''

Trewley started to say something about people who fussed all the time, then stopped, and grinned. ''Maybe you've got a point, girl. We've seen everyone we wanted to talk to—excepting that Rowles bloke, of course. The rest of 'em must be safely on their way home with their statements in a file somewhere. . . .''

A nimble-fingered member of Trewley's team had put the loudspeakers to temporary rights, and The Stooks had been cleared of every witness save the essential few. Most had gone quietly enough, pausing only to give their names and addresses—and some to insist on a refund of their entrance fee. Those who remained were being dealt with efficiently, by uniformed officers whose shorthand was slower than that of Detective Sergeant Stone—and almost as accurate.

All of which the superintendent observed as he left the sitting room to check on the investigation's progress; all of which reassured him that the job was being performed to his own high standard. Whatever he and Stone were planning now would not hinder the investigation at The Stooks. . . .

The police car, obediently waiting, even with its windows open looked stuffy and inhospitable. PC Davers, who had been a distant and fascinated witness of the sitting room interviews, had accompanied the detectives on their quick tour, and now hovered nearby, bursting to be of help. Help which he was able to give when he advised Detective Superintendent Trewley that the home of Silvester Wilford was within walking distance. . . .

"All right, then. We'll walk it," the superintendent decided, amused to find Stone nodding her approval at his side. She looked with far less approval, however, on the scenery through which they passed as they made their way down the long, winding gravel drive.

"Room for any number of suspects to hide here, sir," she grumbled. "Now nearly everyone's gone, the place looks as big as a safari park!"

The superintendent grunted, but did not reply further. His attention had been caught by a rustling of bushes and the sounds of heavy-footed argument on the other side of the drive. A very large, young, eagerly uniformed constable now appeared, escorting an indignant, overly dapper figure wearing a bright floral waistcoat; and on sighting his superior, the bluebottle changed direction and urged his protesting captive towards him.

Trewley regarded the red-faced figure closely. "You're Mr. Rowles, I suppose?" he greeted him, introducing himself and Sergeant Stone, who could not stop staring at the waistcoat. It had lost two buttons, and there was a triangular tear across its left breast pocket. Observing her interest, PC Benson explained that Mr. Rowles had been skulking in the Donkey Field behind a shrub of prickly aspect, discovering far too late that this was inadequate as camouflage. No good is done to a man's attire when he tries to scramble through a hedge with a younger, more vigorous person in hot pursuit.

"We've been looking everywhere for you—sir," Trewley informed Mr. Rowles, who, from being red with anger, turned pale. "We are investigating," continued the superintendent, "an occurrence on these premises—which are yours, if we've been correctly informed?"

Mr. Rowles, who had relaxed only a little, nodded. "You say a—an occurrence? Of a—a serious nature, Superintendent, I infer from your rank." His eyes darted to Stone, then away. "What—that is to say, what has happened?"

"It's a case of murder, sir." And both detectives noted that the expression in the supposed solicitor's eyes was one of apprehension, rather than dismay—of fear, rather than shock. He gulped, and glanced over the shoulder by which PC Benson had held him; and gulped again.

"I'm afraid that in your—continuing—absence," Trewley told him, "we took it upon ourselves to make use of your house. A Mrs. Pasmore, who, er, seems to know her way around the place, showed us the sitting room—"

"You mean you've put the—the body in there?" And Mr. Rowles turned paler than ever. "Good gracious! But—"

"No, sir, we haven't! An interview room, that's all. A sight more official than taking statements in the open air, and a bit more comfortable, too. Which reminds me"—Trewley was almost casual about it—"we've still to interview you, sir. Suppose you come back to the house with us to answer a few questions?"

"Questions?" Mr. Rowles started to go red again. "You wish to question me? Why? No matter what has happened, let me assure you I know nothing—*nothing* about it."

But Trewley took no notice, striding off in the direction of the house without once looking round. Stone and

Constable Benson closed upon Mr. Rowles in such a manner that he was impelled to take several steps backwards, and thence, in logical progression, had perforce to follow in the superintendent's wake. Protesting in muted tones, puzzled and unanswered save with the politest nothings, Montague Rowles was escorted up the gravel drive and in through the French windows of his own home.

In the sitting room, he hesitated, breathing hard. Trewley, too, was puffed, though he carried it off with greater success. He sat down at once upon the chair he had used before, and waited for Montague's reaction.

Mr. Rowles did not appear put out by this rather cavalier treatment. A slight frown creased his brow, but he said nothing, his eyes darting round the room. When he finally chose a chair, both Trewley and Stone observed that he perched on the edge of the seat, rather than leaning comfortably back, as an innocent householder might do. The snap with which Stone opened her notebook made him start.

Though Mr. Rowles sat awkwardly, Trewley did not. He was apparently as calm as anyone suffering from hard work and a long, hot day could be. He stared at Mr. Rowles for some moments before remarking:

"You know, some people would find it odd, sir. Your behaviour, I mean." Montague flinched. Trewley smiled. "I mean, the way that, ever since I told you why we were here, you haven't asked a single question about what's been going on on your property. Some people, believe me, would have been yelling their heads off about civil liberties and all that—but you haven't. Yet it's your home. Your grounds. Your—maze. . . ."

Montague did not succeed in hiding the look of relief which crossed his face. "You're saying that's where—where it happened—in the maze?" Before Trewley could do more than nod, he babbled: "Then I was right: I have nothing to tell you. I certainly don't know my way round the maze. I've been shown, of course—the estate agent, though even he needed Cedric Ezard's advice. And Cedric himself has taken me in a couple of times—but I could never find my way in to the middle and out again without someone local guiding me.''

The superintendent looked at him, his dark eyes even darker in the depths of his bulldog face. ''Well now, Mr. Rowles, what makes you think you'd have needed to know your way to the middle of the maze? How do you know it didn't happen just inside, where anyone could have gone without needing a guide of any kind?''

Mr. Rowles licked his lips. ''But I—I assumed—a maze, you know—always the image of that urn, and the statues in the middle, by the willow tree. . . .''

The superintendent nodded slowly. ''As a matter of fact, sir, that's exactly where it was. Right in the middle by the willow, and the statues. . . .'' He allowed Montague just long enough to start feeling relieved before knocking him off balance again by adding:

''And you mentioned Cedric Ezard, didn't you, sir? Isn't he the old man who drew up a key or plan to the maze—a plan that means *anybody* could find their way around without too much bother?''

''Oh.'' Mr. Rowles blinked. ''Yes . . . some scheme of Mrs. Radlett's—I believe they prepared something of the sort—but I never had a copy! Old Ezard kept careful account of every one of them—he'd know if any were missing, he'll be able to tell you I haven't got one—he and Barnabus like everything to be just right for the fete, I've heard that a hundred times this week—which,'' and his eyes brightened with sudden inspiration, ''is why I've been—been keeping out of everyone's way, you see. All the locals know exactly what they want done and how to go about it, and I'm still a newcomer to the place—no idea at all of how I could best be of help. But the locals—they know the lot. Including the plan of my maze, I'm sure. If anyone is responsible for . . . this crime, it must be one of them!''

Although Trewley and Stone had already worked this much out for themselves, and were inclined to accept it as a working hypothesis, to hear someone like Montague Rowles press such a solution upon them made them both feel like arguing on behalf of the casual passerby as the most likely suspect—Mr. Rowles, with his nervous tic and his flashy clothes, was hardly a sympathetic character.

Yet, for all his unease, the new owner of The Stooks did not appear to be a fool. Worried for some reason which they could not yet fathom, he was still sufficiently in control of himself to have his wits in good working order. And if a suspect had his wits in good working order, the wits of the two detectives would have to work even better. . . .

"Somebody local," murmured Trewley, as if pondering Montague's suggestion. "Mrs. Radlett, now—you mentioned her, didn't you? We know you spent some time talking to her this morning. Would you mind telling us what about?"

"Mrs. Radlett?" Mr. Rowles almost slipped from the edge of his chair. "Is she the—the one who's been . . . killed?"

Stone drew a squiggle to remind herself that this was the first sign of curiosity as to the victim's identity shown by the owner of the property on which the crime had taken place. Had he not asked because he already knew her identity? Or was it because he had other, more pressing concerns?

"That's right," Trewley told him. "Mrs. Ingrid Radlett—and you were talking to her, weren't you? More than one of our witnesses said so. Perhaps you wouldn't mind telling us what you talked about—what kind of mood she was in—the usual kind of thing. As a solicitor, you'll understand, I'm sure, that it's a matter of filling in the background to our investigation. . . ."

Montague's eyes dropped to his pin-striped lap, where his hands had briefly formed fists of annoyance before he forced them to relax. He felt the detectives watching him, and laughed his reaction away: though it was a shaky laugh.

"I'm not surprised she has been—been the victim of an attack. If anyone less even-tempered than myself had had a similar—encounter, and was pushed too far by her—her teasing . . ."

He gave his version of that talk with Ingrid at the top of the upper steps; told how she made him overconscious of being an outsider, rubbed into his spiritual wounds the salt of her own acceptability, contrasting it with his uselessness. She had taken delight in scoring over him several times, under the weather though she had claimed to feel.

"An irresistible urge," he summed up, "like a—like a gadfly. Irritating—almost literally. Even when"—and he flushed—"when I was talking with Mrs. Pasmore in the rose garden, the behaviour of Mrs. Radlett was—seemed deliberately . . . provocative. Obviously, someone else resented her attitude towards him—even if killing her is rather . . . an extreme response. . . ."

"Did you know her before you came to live here?"

"No, I didn't. One could hardly forget such a woman—her looks, quite apart from her—her personality."

"Which was annoying, you said, sir. Well now, annoyance can be the last straw for a certain type of person—can be the motive for a murder. Different people have different breaking points, as you might say. For some, now, it's monetary gain—for others, peace of mind: freedom, if you like—say from a blackmailer. Or jealousy—more than one sort of that, isn't there? Or revenge. . . ."

Mr. Rowles shifted on his seat; he licked his lips again, and coughed. His voice, when it emerged, cracked slightly. "Revenge? A very—drastic—sort of word, Superintendent. Revenge for—for what?"

"Ah, well, we don't know that—yet. We're still trying to find out. Give us time, and we will." Trewley frowned, and gazed at Mr. Rowles from beneath his bulldog brows. "And you say you didn't know Mrs. Radlett before you came to live in Redingote—"

"It's true!"

"And about how long ago was that?" enquired the superintendent, ignoring the interruption. "You're a solicitor, they say. Retired for your health, I suppose, as you don't look old enough to draw a pension just yet." He stabbed a forefinger in Montague's direction, and Mr. Rowles jumped. "How long ago—and where did you come from?"

Mr. Rowles gasped, but rallied. "I tell you, I didn't know

her! And I'm very glad I didn't. Believe me, a little of Ingrid Radlett went a long way indeed. If some of the things she said to me were typical of her attitude, as I said before, it's no surprise to me that she's been killed.''

"How long ago?'' demanded Trewley again, adding: "We can easily check with the estate agent, of course.'' And Montague's eyes fell; his shoulders drooped.

"In the spring,'' he said, with obvious reluctance. "And I come . . . from London. And I repeat that I never met Mrs. Radlett before I came here!''

"Denies any past association,'' murmured Trewley, just loud enough for Mr. Rowles to hear. Then the superintendent blinked, as if rousing himself from a trance. "The past of a murder victim, you know,'' he remarked, "often holds the motive for that murder. We like to be sure about the background of everyone concerned—even if they're only like yourself, on the periphery, as you might say. In a small place like Redingote, you see. . . . But London, now.'' His eyes met those of Mr. Rowles. "That's not a small place, not small at all. Is it, sir?'' Montague gulped. "Is it, Sergeant Stone?''

"Indeed not, sir. Far from small—very large, in fact. Anonymous. You could hide yourself away in London and not a soul would be any the wiser—''

"I protest!'' Montague managed to splutter at last. "Why are you saying—implying—that *I* might have need to hide myself away?''

"The sergeant was just making a general observation, Mr. Rowles—just showing that our minds work along the same lines, so to speak. Pointing out that a man, or a woman, in London can vanish rather easily. So it's hardly surprising, is it, that you and Mrs. Radlett never met? That is, if she came from London, as well. We still have to check on that with her husband, poor fellow—and we're pretty thorough in our checks. Aren't we, Sergeant Stone?''

"Extremely thorough, sir.'' And Mr. Rowles was observed to shrink within the embrace of the chintz armchair.

But apart from Montague's general nerviness, they had so little to go on that they decided to leave it, for now. The chord they appeared to have struck with Mr. Rowles had set up corresponding echoes in Trewley's subconscious; after a few more routine questions, he was ready to let the solicitor go, so that he could try to capture that chord in reality.

The routine questions were soon asked. Mr. Rowles had not noticed Ingrid again after their encounter in the rose garden; he had certainly not been hiding from the police. There was no reason for them to suggest that he had. He was a newcomer still to the village; he had sought the privacy of a distant part of his own (this with emphasis) property, until that property's normal quiet character should return, once the events of the day were over. He had been advised that the house would be open to the public, and, since he had in the first place come to Redingote for privacy, knew this privacy would be destroyed by the presence of hordes of strangers. He looked forward to a resumption of that privacy in due course.

Trewley nodded. "Then you don't mind if we ask you not to leave here without telling us, will you, sir? Just stay on the premises, please. After all, you don't want to get back to find we've pinched the spoons, now. Much better to hang around and keep an eye on us. Protective custody, as you might say."

The little joke fell on unappreciative ears, as Mr. Rowles said nothing, staring at the superintendent with an air of disbelief. Those subconscious echoes were louder now. . . .

The superintendent could hardly wait for his witness to be gone before he was turning eagerly to Stone. "I *know* him from somewhere—right on the tip of my tongue, his name is. We'll run a check on him—description, initials of his name—anagrams, even. Anything to get that computer humming—because our pal Rowles isn't what he makes out to be, I'm sure of it. . . ."

"And so am I, sir. Only—is he a murderer?" And Stone doodled *Montague Rowles* on a fresh sheet in her notebook.

"If we can eliminate a few suspects, girl, we might find out. So—come on, let's get on with it. Starting now!"

Nine

ALTHOUGH IT WAS still hot, it was later in the day than they had thought: interviews, discussions, statements, and cups of tea took longer in lazy July than in brisk December. The coming dusk was drowsy, the full moon sluggish as it struggled into the heat-hazed heavens. Stone stared at the weary amber orb, and remembered Barnabus Chilman. She shivered.

"Something wrong?" enquired Trewley, as they walked on.

"Thunder in the air, sir. At least . . . I know a storm would freshen things up, but . . ."

"Damn!" The superintendent slapped his forearm. "Well, with luck a drop of rain might get rid of these pesky gnats. Blood poisoning, probably. Or malaria. Look at the things hopping about all over that pond!"

For a moment, they stood watching the busy air just above the surface of the pond, a stretch of brown, murky water surrounded by dank greenery. "This must be Doom's Deep," said Stone. "And I can't think of a name that would suit it better. What a horrible, gloomy dump. . . ."

"Doom's Deep." Trewley nodded. "Just to *see* the place is enough to make you want to chuck yourself in—anything to get away from those midges!" He gestured at the crowd of little whining insects that danced and darted about them, blurring the sight. "Malaria," he said again, "if nothing worse—we'd best get on before we're eaten alive."

The two detectives quickened their steps, and the length-ening shadows of the twisted trees around Doom's Deep pursued them in their flight.

"Yuck," breathed Stone, glancing back as they reached comparative safety. "Goodness only knows what foul bacteria breed in that water—typhoid for one, I'd take a bet. You could boil that stuff for a month, and filter it—but you'd never convince me it was safe to drink!''

Trewley frowned at the rising lump on his arm. ''There's something makes me wonder what else besides mosquitoes lives there, and what it might do to you if you hung around too long. The whole place ought to be fumigated— sprayed—anything to kill the little perishers.''

''And if the weather's on the change, it could make them more lively than ever,'' said Stone, more cheerful as the distance between themselves and the Deep increased with every stride. She chuckled. ''When midges dance upon the water, Rain and storm shall follow after!''

''Umph.'' Trewley regarded his sergeant thoughtfully. ''You're kidding—aren't you?''

''Oh yes, sir. I made that up just now! But doesn't it sound good? Authentic folklore from wildest Allshire. I'd rather try making a joke of bad weather than have to think about being out in a thunderstorm.''

A woman's voice spoke suddenly from close at hand, low and harsh and penetrating. ''He who laughs when the weather be dry, He'll have sorrow by and by!''

Trewley and Stone stopped in their tracks, and looked about them. There was a rustle of leaves, and a fantastic figure appeared: a figure who could only be Tabitha Chilman, the Redingote witch. Her clothes were patched, her hair was wild; her eyes beneath the shade of her battered hat glinted with mischief. In her hand, she held a bucket.

''Sorrow,'' said Tabitha again. ''And ill-luck, too!''

Though Trewley had jumped quite as much as Stone at the entrance of the witch, he felt strongly—as the sergeant's superior—that he should be first to regain a modicum of composure. ''That's a bit steep, Mrs. Chilman—er, you *are* Tabitha Chilman, aren't you? Not very friendly talk—if you don't mind me saying so.'' And he stepped back to range himself—for her protection, no doubt—at Stone's side.

Tabitha came a few steps closer. ''You're a witty wight to make so free with my name, but you've a bold spirit and a kindly heart, as I can tell.'' She peered into his face, and the superintendent felt sweat gather in its many wrinkles. Tabitha nodded, and stepped back. "Yes, I can tell—and you show proper respect, what's more. I'll not ill-wish you—for all there's folk in this village will tell you my boy and me bring naught but trouble, and you might think of believing them. . . ."

As the superintendent gulped, Stone said: "Of course, yes, Barnabus. Barney, is that what you call him?" Tabitha clanked the handle of the bucket, and smiled faintly. "How is he?" enquired Stone. "Would you like me to come along and take a look at him? I trained to be a doctor, so—"

"Doctor?" Tabitha shook her head. "Doctor? You'll do my Barney no good, for he's troubled in his mind, and 'twill need more than physicking skills to set such matters right. He babbles in his distress, counting and numbering over and over to soothe his worries—as ever brought him comfort in the past, but not this time—oh, no! Evil, true evil he speaks of, but in his misery he'll talk to none but me. And *I* will talk to the ones who would destroy the evil, to those who do not fear to remain in my company, though the name of witch is bandied about. . . . But, witch or wisewoman, what are they but words? Words meaning one who has wisdom—and they that have wisdom know of much that normal mortals may more likely miss."

She set down her bucket to gesture upwards. "The moon, now—my pale lady with the changing face. She knows much, for she oversees all, she knows even the deepest secrets in the hearts of men—and women. . . . She sees all, I say—and sometimes, so do others." Once more she pointed to the great, low-lying lunar orb. "She smiles down upon my boy and me, she sees him and he sees her—once in the fullness of every month, every four weeks she comes to gladden his heart. But—when she hides her face—when she comes no more . . . at her staying away, he'll grieve. And others there are, others who will grieve and worry in their hearts, when the moon comes no more. . . ."

She fixed her wild gaze full on Stone, and nodded, very slowly. Then, as the sergeant seemed on the point of speaking, Tabitha broke the spell by bending to pick up her pail. "Moon-water's best for brewing, as the wise know. And it's for that purpose I come here, to bring good fortune to your true intent. But I must be mindful too of my Barney's wants—he lies sick, troubled in his heart, and he rambles in his wits and talks overmuch of the doctor—it's a burden to his soul, poor lad. Doctor Oliver understands well enough the ways of my poor Barney's mind . . . and, when you speak with the doctor, do you tell him that my boy is wishful to see him, for the easing of his torment. Will you say these things to him, when you speak with him?"

Stone looked at Trewley, who cleared his throat. Every crease of his bulldog face was damp with perspiration, and his voice, try to control it as he might, quivered a little as he replied: "Well, the poor man's just lost his wife—so I don't think he'll want to, er, work as a doctor for, well, a few days, anyway. But we'll pass your message on, when we see him," he added, as Tabitha scowled. "We'll pass it on—though it won't be just yet, I'm afraid. Because we're going to Mr. Wilford's house first." His final words sounded unnaturally loud in the still evening air.

Tabitha hesitated, then smiled a sideways smile, beginning to back away in the direction of the pond. "Remember, moon-water," she said, "has a good magic to it. And a very powerful magic it will work—as you," to Stone, "must know. Three times three, in the fullness of the moon!"

And then, with no more than a rustle of leaves, she was gone.

Trewley drew in his breath with an effort, and rubbed a shaking hand across his forehead. "Well, now . . . if that's the mother, girl, d'you reckon it's worth going to talk to the son? Poor devil! She gave me the regular creeps, not to mention the way she kept staring at you. How did you manage to face up to her like that?" And once more his damp handkerchief was brought into play.

Stone said, after a pause: "I think, sir, there was some method in her madness. I think she was trying to hint at what she didn't like to make too obvious—it wasn't just a load of nons—Oh!"

Tabitha had once more materialized from a gap in the

hedge before them. Instead of her bucket, she now held a bunch of flowers, with which she beckoned to the detectives to draw near. And, as they warily did so—Trewley even closer to Stone's side than good manners might require—the witch stepped forward.

"Flowers," said Tabitha. "Flowers picked in the fullness of the moon. Three times three, and all comes right once more, as you should know. . . ." She proffered the posy to Stone, who, startled, stretched out her hand. Tabitha smiled, and withdrew a few yards, still smiling. "Here's flowers for you: carnations and streaked gillyvors. Which some call—nature's . . . bastards. . . ."

She thrust the posy into the sergeant's hands, and once more vanished. Stone studied the flowers for a moment, puzzled; then in her turn she smiled, and called softly into the shadows: "Thank you very much, Tabitha." But her only answer was a shrill, fleeting giggle, followed by the slam of a nearby door.

"She's gone," breathed Trewley, mopping his forehead yet again. "And"—he glanced about him—"good riddance, too!"

"Oh no, sir. We really should be grateful to Tabitha. She's helped us quite a lot. Call it an educated guess, or intuition, if you like"—and she grinned—"but I'll bet the autopsy will show Mrs. Radlett was pregnant. Three times three moon months, you see. And from this"—she brandished the flowers under his nose—"I'll risk another bet. The child wasn't her husband's—or that's what Tabitha thinks, anyway. A gillyvor—a bastard. . . ."

For a moment, he stared at her. Then he, too, grinned. "Well, well, you don't say. Those couple of years weren't wasted, were they, girl?"

She shrugged. "I'm female too, sir, don't forget, which has rather more to do with understanding her, if you think about the hints she was dropping—not, of course, that I'd say for one minute she's bothered about slander. . . ."

"And we're on our way to see Wilford," mused Trewley, as they set off again in the direction of the bank manager's house. "I wonder, now. Might she have guessed where we'd be going, and decided to wait for us and spin that rigmarole to get us thinking about him? Like calling to like, everyone's kept saying. Silvester Wilford. . . .''

The two detectives walked on, in a silence broken only by the sound of their falling footsteps through the lonely summer dusk.

The Wilfords lived in what Redingote natives scathingly spoke of as Foreigners' Fork: a neat, genteel, neo-Georgian estate built between the village's main street and the lane which led to wilder, wooded areas. All the houses had bow windows, acres of white paint, panelled front doors, and—because their back gardens converged upon Doom's Deep—damp-courses, cunningly concealed behind creepers, reconstituted stone troughs of assorted plants, and decorative urns. Nothing so vulgar as a gnome was permitted to grace any garden in Foreigners' Fork.

The paved path to Silvester's front door was set in a long, artistic curve, and edged with flowers of impeccably matched size and contrasting colours. Was this, wondered Stone, as she gazed about her for one sign of neglect or indifference, all the work of Myra? Or did the Wilfords employ a gardener of so rare a nature that he justified the exorbitant sums generally demanded by the species?

Myra did not open the brass-knockered door until Trewley's second or third rapping, and frowned as she saw who had disturbed her: what, again? She said nothing out loud, however, and stood waiting in silent challenge for the superintendent to make the first move.

"Good evening, Mrs. Wilford. Is your husband at home?"

"Can't it wait until tomorrow? He's—we've had a shock—we're both very upset. Do you really have to come bothering us at this time of night?"

"Yes." Trewley glanced at his watch. Night? Trying to make them feel uncomfortable, was she? A quick thinker, Mrs. Wilford: her switch from singular to plural had been skillful. Was she a quick enough thinker to have worked out, on an earlier occasion that day, the risks involved—

whether for her husband, or for herself—and to have acted accordingly? "Yes, we do, though I'm surprised you see it as a bother. In cases of murder, you know, unless there's a very good reason why not, we like to talk to everyone who might be . . . involved, as soon as possible—and it all helps to bring the criminal to justice, which I'd have thought would be what everyone—the victim's friends—wanted."

Her hesitation was slight: the look in his eyes and the tone of his voice told her it would be useless to demur, and she lowered her eyes in a brief acknowledgement of defeat. "Very well, if you insist—but I must warn you he's . . . not himself at all. The shock—he isn't overstrong. His—his nerves. . . ." And she led the way through the narrow hall to a fug-filled room at the back of the house, where Silvester Wilford was discovered.

He sat in a deep armchair of studded leather, clutching a glass filled with pale golden liquid, a nervous cigarette held between gray lips. His black hair, and the shadows beneath his eyes, made his face seem very white as he gave the newcomers no more than a quick glance, a brief nod; and then resumed his interrupted blank gazing at the carpet.

Trewley performed the introductions and, still without a word from Silvester, turned to the bank manager's wife. "We'd prefer to speak to your husband alone, Mrs. Wilford, if you don't mind."

At this, for the first time Silvester's attention became focused on the superintendent. "Alone? You want to talk to me—but why? What about? Myra"—his eyes fastened on hers, desperate—"have *you* any idea why the police should want to see me? I wasn't even at the fete this afternoon, was I? Tell them!"

"Ah," interrupted Trewley, "then you know it's about Mrs. Radlett's murder we've come to see you, sir. Good, it all helps to save time. Mrs. Wilford—perhaps you could wait in another room? After all, we managed to speak to you without your husband there, didn't we?"

This argument appeared to quench any protest she might have made before it was uttered, for she looked at Silvester—from him to Trewley—and then, without another

word, left the room. With her hand on the doorknob, she
glanced once more at her husband, uttered a quiet sigh, and
pulled the door shut behind her.

Silvester's eyes had followed her as she went, but as soon
as she was gone he drew deeply on his cigarette, coughed,
and gulped a large mouthful of whisky. He set the tumbler
down on the curved arm of his chair and some of the
contents came splashing over the rim to stain the leather.

"Oh, yes," said Trewley, as if replying to some earlier
remark, "it's a very distressing business, isn't it? The
murder, that is. I suppose you knew the dead woman well?"

"Well? She and her husband were our friends, if that's
what you mean. Naturally we're both upset—do you take us
for unfeeling brutes?"

"Oh no. But you do seem, Mr. Wilford, to be rather
more . . . upset than your wife. Different temperaments,
no doubt. People seeing things in different ways—like
that . . . talk you had with Mrs. Radlett this morning."
Silvester went very still. "Now, you, sir, might just have
thought of it as a friendly chat—but several people have told
us it was an out-and-out quarrel, you know. Only goes to
prove my point about people being different, doesn't it?"

The smoky spiral from Silvester's cigarette quivered at its
base as he took a deep breath, coughing again. "Edgar
Hemingway, I suppose." Mr. Wilford tried to sound scornful. "Great gossiping old woman the man is—always
exaggerating. Says it's his artistic temperament! You'd be
crazy to pay any attention to a prosy old fool like him—and
Barmy Barney, too. Crazy isn't the word for that one.
Whatever he may have told you he—he heard while he was
prowling round this morning, believe me, it's of no use at all
when it comes to investigating a . . . a—serious crime."

"A murder, sir." Strange how people always found it
hard to apply that six-letter word to anyone they
knew. . . . "Well, then, if you say we can't rely on what
other people may have told us, how about giving us your
version of what happened, Mr. Wilford?"

Silvester stubbed out his cigarette with such force that the
ashtray went sliding to the far end of the low table in front

of his chair. He looked with longing at the whisky in his other hand, then forced himself to look away as he said: "We—we talked, that's all. People do, when they meet—friends—it's not unreasonable, is it? Or suspicious? Is it really so surprising that when Hemingway and I arrived, and she was sitting by the Tea table, we should stop to—to pass the time of day?"

"Both of you? You and Mr. Hemingway together?"

"Oh, well . . . he may have said hello, or something more than that—he was so preoccupied with his infernal books, I shouldn't suppose he remembers clearly."

"Whereas you, being such a close friend to Mrs. Radlett—and to her husband as well, of course—you'd remember talking to her rather better than Mr. Hemingway would? He'd be more of an acquaintance, perhaps, than a friend."

"All four of us were close friends—my wife and I, the doctor, and Mrs. Radlett. It's only natural we should be." Silvester's grip on the whisky glass tightened, and he took another gulp almost without noticing. "In a place the size of Redingote—not many other professional people. . . ."

"Like calling to like," said Trewley, nodding; while Stone leaned forward, and took the tumbler from Silvester's hand.

"Excuse me, sir, but that really won't do you any good at all. Too much, too quickly—bad for you." And she set it down on the table just out of his reach. "You might say something you'd regret afterwards, if you aren't careful."

"I have nothing to hide! I know nothing about—about—Ingrid's . . . death—and you've no right to accuse me!"

"Why, sir, Sergeant Stone wasn't making any accusations—were you, Sergeant?" And Trewley nodded in her direction. "But she does know about these things. If she says you're liable to do yourself no good—in whatever way—then I'd be inclined to listen to her."

As Silvester turned even paler, the superintendent's eyes met those of the sergeant. They recognised clear signs of a guilty conscience: wouldn't a truly innocent man have snatched back his whisky and demanded an apology?

But was what Mr. Wilford had to hide the same secret at which Tabitha had so obliquely hinted?

"Look, sir, there's no sense in messing around. Your—friendship with Mrs. Radlett was intimate, wasn't it? Much more intimate than your wife, or her husband. She was your mistress, wasn't she?" And, even as he made the accusation, Trewley found time to reflect that if only Abigail Ezard had remained in Redingote, Silvester might not now be suffering this uncomfortable disclosure of his not-so-private life.

The bank manager opened his mouth. No sound emerged except a gasp; his breathing was noisy and uneven. He looked towards the whisky where it stood just out of reach, and licked dry, bloodless lips.

"She was your mistress, wasn't she? Come on, sir, there are other ways we could find out, you know. Far more embarrassing than a quiet chat like this?"

Trewley settled himself on his chair, for all the world as if he were happy to wait in Silvester's study for days, if necessary. His bloodhound expression betokened infinite patience; his bulldog features showed resolution. Silvester realised that denial was pointless.

"It's no use my saying she wasn't, is it?" He flopped back against the arm of the chair, and struck his head with the heel of his hand. "You wouldn't believe me, would you? Oh, what a fool I've been! I suppose everyone in the whole damn village knew about it, except—except Myra." He lifted his head to stare at the closed door. "They'll have kept it from her, won't they—the mutual protection society . . . and the effort was all wasted, because now she'll find out from you—and it's too late . . . there's no point to anything now. . . ."

He closed his eyes, buried his head in his hands, and groaned. There was a sudden crash as the door burst open, and Myra ran in, a fury of protective love as she glared at the detectives. It was obvious she must have heard every word of the interview. She flung herself on her knees at her husband's side, and cradled him in her arms. Silvester shuddered as she drew him close, and groaned again.

"I told you to leave him alone!" Her voice was shrill. "You see how right I was? You should have waited until tomorrow!"

"She should have died hereafter," muttered Stone, before she could stop herself. Myra rounded on the sergeant, her eyes blazing.

"How dare you make cheap jokes about this—this terrible business! Our friend is dead—murdered—and you should be helping your superior to look for the culprit, not tormenting innocent people like this!"

"We are," Trewley told her, "looking for the culprit— and we have to look in many different places, Mrs. Wilford. And at many different people, innocent or not. But we can't prove their innocence—or their guilt—if they refuse to answer our questions as your husband has done, you know." The superintendent was revolted by the spectacle of this middle-aged, pelican-spirited, over-devoted wife hurrying to defend her spineless husband. She could, he thought, have killed quite as easily as anyone, in order to rid herself of her rival for Silvester's love; but why she loved him in the first place, he was unable to guess. The man couldn't even stand up for himself without her: he was snivelling now, and clinging to her, even though by keeping her at his side he would expose her to the sordid truth he had hoped to keep hidden. The man was more a child than a man. . . .

Trewley's involuntary snort of irritation penetrated even Silvester's shock and misery, for he raised his head and addressed Myra in a voice that shook. "Innocence, guilt— what's he saying? You didn't—you couldn't have killed her! Or—or did you do it to save me from myself, to save me from her—when you know I'm not worth it. . . . You've always been far too good for me, Myra—you've never known, never believed what I'm really like, deep down inside. . . ."

"I know all that I need to know about you, Silvester. And even that is not enough to make me kill. Stop talking this nonsense—giving the police such ridiculous ideas!"

He stared at her. "Then—you knew—about Ingrid and

me? And you said nothing! You didn't mind—you didn't need to harm her, even though I—we . . . ''

Myra's voice was sad. "What else could I expect you to do, after I'd refused to . . . cooperate with you any longer? You know how I tried to . . . accommodate your . . . to put up with . . . to please you for the first few years of our marriage, but I wasn't . . . a great success, was I? Of course I knew you'd have to go . . . elsewhere for your—your pleasure . . . my one regret is that you were apparently less than discreet about it. Your affair with Ingrid is no secret from anyone, is it?''

Above Silvester's bowed head, his wife's sorrowful eyes met those of the superintendent, while her arms continued to hold close her errant spouse, who shuddered, and groaned. There was a long pause.

Trewley broke it by remarking: "So you've known about your husband's involvement with Mrs. Radlett for some time, Mrs. Wilford. And you claim it didn't bother you?''

"It is no claim, Superintendent, it is the truth. As it was a direct result of—of my . . . failure, how could I let it bother me? So I did not let it. I . . . understood.''

"Oh,'' moaned Mr. Wilford, "you understood—you always understand! So generous, so forgiving—when I know I don't deserve your kindness—when I should be punished. I should be made to suffer for the wrong I've done. . . .'' And in her embrace he trembled, his face lit with a gleam of pleasurable anticipation.

Myra was unable to suppress the look of distaste which flickered in her eyes, but banished it almost at once, and stayed at Silvester's side, glaring at the detectives. They were puzzled now. If indeed she had known of his affair with Ingrid, and claimed not to have been worried by it—what had been worrying her when they first questioned her? Could it have been the fear that they, knowing as much as they must do of sexual preference, might yet be scandalised and disgusted by Silvester?

Then Trewley recalled her exact words during questioning—her response to his request to tell him what she could of Ingrid and her movements, her actions, her conversations that day. "What do you mean," she had said, "did I overhear anything this morning? It is not my habit to eavesdrop. . . ." But he had said nothing about eavesdropping.

It was her use of that word, her unconscious hint as to what was really worrying her, which now prompted him to turn his thoughts rapidly in a different direction. The one occasion about which Myra was known to have prevaricated had been when she was not, as she had implied, helping independent Mrs. Margaret Brown with her Prize Every Time: which was the stall next to the Bottles run by Mildred Waskett, sister to churchwarden Caleb Duckels.

And the churchwardens had been discussing with Mrs. Radlett the possibility that she might take over caring for the parish books, those erratic accounts which, until now, from the time of his arrival in the village had been in the care of Silvester Wilford: one of those difficult jobs dumped by wily locals upon newcomers eager to fit in and flattered to be asked . . . and never checked up on since.

Trewley took only a few moments to work out his theory, and now tried to give the impression of an inquisitor much embarrassed by the torrent of emotion unleashed at his instigation, eager to change to a less contentious topic.

"Mr. Wilford, how long have you lived in Redingote?"

It was Myra who replied. "Five years—nearly six."

The superintendent rubbed his nose. "Well, now, I'd be interested to know how you managed to fit into a close-knit community like this. Was it hard?"

It seemed a harmless enough question; Myra shook Silvester by the shoulders, gently encouraging, then released him. It was his turn to answer: which he did in a voice which was almost steady.

"I suppose we managed as well as anyone new would have done. A job like mine didn't hurt, of course—being socially acceptable." And a faint sneer twisted his mouth.

Trewley nodded. "Of course, yes. Banking. And that was why they made you responsible for keeping the parish finances in order, wasn't it?"

Myra drew in her breath. Silvester froze, and turned even

paler than before. He swallowed once or twice, fixing his eyes on Trewley's face, unable to look away.

"The churchwarden—Mr. Duckels, isn't it?" said the superintendent. "Lives near here, does he?"

Myra pulled herself together first, though with an effort lost neither on Trewley nor his sergeant. "It's not far from here—but he won't thank you for visiting him so late at night." She glanced at the clock which stood on the overmantel. "We keep early hours in the country, you know—which is why I—we—would prefer it if you continued this conversation tomorrow. . . ."

And give them time to concoct some story? Would it be easier to break them if they confused themselves with even more convolutions they would find hard to remember under the pressure of questioning—or should he strike now, while the iron was reasonably hot?

Now, the superintendent decided. "Police business, Mrs. Wilford—a case of murder—background information, nothing more, as far as we know. Always useful, of course. Perhaps—if you don't mind—we could talk to your husband alone? As we asked you," he reminded her, "once before."

She rose from her protective crouch at Silvester's side to face him squarely. "I don't think my husband should answer any more questions without—without our solicitor here. In fact, neither of us will answer any more questions without our solicitor!"

Trewley shrugged. "As you wish. That is your prerogative. Is your solicitor Mr. Rowles, by any chance?"

The surprise on both faces seemed genuine. "Certainly not!" snapped Myra, while Silvester blinked, and shook his head, his grey lips tightly shut.

"A pity," said Trewley, rising to his feet. "He'd have been nice and handy for a visit this evening. Well, we'll just have to wait until tomorrow, won't we?" And he nodded to Stone, who made a pointed note in her book before putting it reluctantly away. If they'd only been able to talk with Silvester by himself, she felt sure they would have learned the truth.

"Oh, before we leave you, Mr. Wilford"—the superintendent was having one last try—"could I just put it to you that your quarrel with Mrs. Rad—"

"It wasn't a quarrel!" But his tone was not convincing.

"Your . . . discussion," amended Trewley, with what Stone thought of as his old-fashioned look. Silvester squirmed on his chair as his inquisitor demanded: "Was it about the parish books she was going to do a proper audit on, in time for the new vicar's induction?"

"You don't have to answer that!" cried Myra, shrill and suddenly pale. Silvester gave her a startled glance, then turned to Trewley.

"No—no, it wasn't. In fact—if you really want . . ." He looked at Myra again more slowly, calculating, weighing up which would be the lesser of the two evils. Both detectives now suspected that the parish books, in Silvester's professional care for so long, would be worth close inspection—and so, if her current behavior was any indication, did Myra. Indeed, she seemed more anxious about the state of the books than about the fidelity of her husband: who, having thought for a few frantic moments, said:

"She'd let me down—the night before, without warning—and I'd been so . . . I'd had to go to a—to pay for . . . and now she said she wanted to stop seeing me. She insisted on ending . . . everything—suddenly! Finished, done, over! But I need—I can't do without—I've always wanted . . . and of course I spoke angrily to her! Leading me on like that—giving me everything I asked for and then . . ." He shivered. "A man like me can't—can't bear to be teased that way. . . . But I didn't kill her. And you can't prove that I did. When I left her, she was still alive!"

Ten

"FRESH AIR," GROWLED Trewley, as they left the Wilford residence for the interview with Dr. Oliver Radlett. "That's what I need right now!" And he strode along at such a rate that Stone, fit as she was, found it hard to keep up with him—and certainly did not dare speak to him.

"Damn the woman," she heard the superintendent exclaim. "If she hadn't shoved her blasted oar in, we might have got somewhere with that jellyfish husband of hers. . . ."

"Slow down, sir!" gasped Stone, fearful they would have rounded Foreigners' Fork and arrived at the bereaved doctor's house before Trewley's mood had mellowed. Oliver Radlett had suffered quite enough already for one day. "Sir—I'm getting a stitch!" And, as he looked back, she twisted her body sideways and her face into contortions indicative of pain. "Sir. . . ."

Once she'd seen him halted in his headlong rush, she straightened, breathed deeply, and ventured to grin. She approached him warily. After an awful silence, he chuckled.

"Top marks for acting, Sergeant Stone. For a moment, I almost believed in that stitch of yours! Worried about my blood pressure again, are you?"

"Yes, sir. It's been a long, hot day, remember."

"And we're about to pay a call on a doctor. But we'll take it at a more gentle pace now, if you prefer. . . ."

The front door of the doctor's house was ajar as the two detectives turned up the short paved path. Trewley closed the gate behind him, and followed his sergeant the few yards to the bottom step, where she hesitated. "Anyone about?" he called, just loud enough.

The bulky form of Caleb Duckels loomed along the

hallway to greet them. He had heard their arrival, and welcomed them in a hushed voice.

"Me and the new parson was just leaving the poor soul to his grief in private, but I know you'll have things to ask him—and maybe it'd be better for him to talk with strangers such as yourselves, rather than them as knows him well. Bottled it all up, so he has—not a word can we get from him beyond yes and no, for all our sympathy. Poor Doctor Oliver, proper stunned, he is. If you could sort of . . . encourage him to let it all out, he'd maybe overcome the worst of what's happened. But he needs treating gentle, mind."

Trewley nodded. "We'll try not to upset him, but there are things we must ask—and we'll try not to take too long. We'd like a word with you and your sister, later on, if that wouldn't be too much bother."

"Gladly, gladly. Anything we can do to set this terrible matter to rights . . . and it's not so hard to find my cottage. Me and Parson, we'll be on our way now, and see you there—not," he added, with a faint grin, "as I'm in any great hurry to get back. If things has gone aright, I could have myself a new brother-in-law by the time we're home." He shook his head, and chuckled. "Or maybe not, for the truth is that Joe Norton's no quick worker. Right glad I'd be of an excuse to tarry a while longer, Mr. Trewley—so suppose we both wait for you here in the hall, and you do your business with poor Doctor Oliver? Then we could show you the way to my place, and no fear of losing yourselves." And Caleb favoured the superintendent with a slow, knowing wink.

Trewley at once returned it. "We wouldn't want to get lost in a place as large as Redingote," he agreed solemnly. "The police are always glad of good news, Mr. Duckels, and try to help it along where we can. After a day like today," he added, "I reckon everyone could do with something to cheer them up."

"They could indeed," said Caleb, with a sigh, leading the way through to the study.

Oliver Radlett's house was the mirror image of Silvester

Wilford's: all the properties on Foreigners' Fork, or so it seemed, had been built to the same plan. Trewley recalled the bow windows and white paint that had caught his eye earlier in the evening; his mental map suggested that the doctor's home and the bank manager's might well back on to each other. A boundary, as well as a woman, in common?

Oliver's study was identical in size and shape to Silvester's, and even in their looks the two men were not unalike. Stone thought it odd that it should be Silvester, with his desk-bound job, who was the more muscular, while Oliver inclined to plumpness; but both were tall, though Oliver was taller; and dark, though Silvester had been darker. His face had already shown a prickly shadow of tomorrow's beard, while Oliver's, strained and white as it was, looked almost fresh in comparison to that haggard, tormented countenance she had watched writhing with emotion. Oliver Radlett might well be stunned, but was in greater control of himself—perhaps too much so. When the dam broke, the release of his pent-up feelings might be devastating.

Oliver, too, held a tumbler in his hand, though it contained some clear, anonymous liquid and not the rich gold of Silvester's scotch. Vodka, probably, Stone decided, since there was no recognisable tang in the air. If everyone in Redingote took to the bottle at the first signs of stress, the doctor must do a brisk business with liver complaints. She wondered who would minister to his own: physician, heal thyself. . . .

"G-good evening," the doctor greeted his guests, in a voice that was thick, and slightly hesitant, though not slurred. Silvester, with less reason to be distressed, had been in far worse shape. Caleb Duckels made the introductions, and Oliver nodded, with no sign of recognition that he had seen the two detectives earlier, at the centre of the maze.

The Reverend David Gregory, who was hovering quietly in a corner, nodded a brief greeting, and murmured a low farewell to Oliver. He then accompanied Caleb out to the hall, leaving Trewley with Stone to ask the stricken widower whatever questions they thought fitting.

"Do . . . sit down," said Oliver, looking round him at

the several chairs which stood in various parts of the little study. His hallway was clearly the waiting room, for there had been a row of low benches along one wall; this must be his consulting room, for the chairs were more comfortable, designed to set his patients at their ease before they began to discuss their problems. Trewley caught Stone's eye, and indicated the chair nearest to Oliver's desk, where she might rest her notepad. For himself, he collected a chair from over by the wall, and placed it carefully at his sergeant's side. Together, the two detectives regarded Oliver Radlett with as much interest as he was obviously not displaying in them.

Trewley cleared his throat. "We're very sorry to have to bother you at a time like this, sir," he began; and Oliver's blank eyes drifted from one strange face to the other, as if wondering who they were. "But we've got our job to do—and I'd like to start by saying that you have all our sympathies, sir, over the loss of your wife."

"My Ingrid?" A faint spark of animation seemed to rouse Oliver from his trance, though it was clearly with a major effort that he continued: "Yes, of c-course—I understand. She's dead—dead—and that means you have to find out . . . who did it. . . ." He shook his head. "Ingrid—my wonderful wife—the perfect marriage . . . too perfect to last, I suppose. Unrealistic of me to expect . . ." He sighed. "But I was the happiest man in Allshire while it did, I promise you—I'd g-got everything I'd ever dreamed about at last, you see. My work—my wife—my home. . . ."

"And your garden, sir?" Trewley gazed round at the many bookshelves lining the study walls. They did not all, or so it seemed to his inexpert eye, hold medical tomes: there were other, brightly jacketed volumes of coffee-table format, bearing pictures of plants and flowers. "Your hobby, is it, Doctor?"

Oliver nodded. "*Mens sana in c-corpore sano*, you see. Fresh air as well as exercise, and books to read afterwards—the perfect c-combination. I've always preferred my books to people—I don't make friends easily—until I met Ingrid, of c-course. But after then, well . . ."

Trewley said quickly: "That was your prescription for

Barney Chilman, wasn't it, Doctor? To stop him making a nuisance of himself over your wife.''

''Poor Barney! Yes, he had to be stopped—he upset her, following her about and singing under her window at night. He adored her, in his own strange way, every bit as much as I d-did. But I knew he had to be k-kept under c-control, and Cedric Ezard was a reliably strict overseer. Barney was a different boy from the day he started work at The Stooks.''

Beside the superintendent, Stone stirred. He looked at her enquiringly, and she smiled at Dr. Radlett. ''Would he be likely to relapse, despite your prescription? We've heard about the full moon—and that's tonight. . . .''

''He'd never have harmed Ingrid! I'm sure he wouldn't. He was devoted to her—and, as I said, since Cedric took him in hand he's been . . . much improved.'' And Oliver sipped from his glass, frowning.

Trewley said: ''Barney's, er, mother tells us he's in a very odd sort of mood right now, Doctor. Asking to see you, and talking a lot of nonsense. I explained it wasn't really very likely at the moment—I mean, you've enough on your plate without, well, ordinary people upsetting you. And if his, er, mother's anything to go by . . .''

Oliver's face twisted into a faint smile. ''You've heard about the Chilmans, I g-gather. Redingote folk like to k-keep themselves to themselves, you know.''

Trewley muttered that if he hadn't before, he did now: and added, leaning forward: ''If they're so—so parochial, if that's the word I want, might it be they'd resent an outsider to the extent of—excuse me, Doctor—ridding themselves of one in a—well, a rather drastic way?''

Oliver looked shocked. ''I'm sure they wouldn't. Why, when I announced that she had done me the signal honour of c-consenting to accept my hand in marriage, everyone was as delighted and proud as myself! As an outsider, you see, Ingrid was so obviously foreign—not from a c-couple of miles down the road, not from the next c-county. I doubt if anyone they'd known all their lives c-could have won anything like the same general approval.'' He smiled again. ''I'm *Doctor Oliver* to Redingote, remember, son of the Old

Doctor. They all watched me g-grow up, and I don't believe anyone, in their eyes, would ever really be c-considered g-good enough for their Doctor Oliver. So . . ." He shrugged expressively. "Besides, they elected her president of the Ladies' League. They c-can't have disliked her that much, c-can they?"

"And asked her to judge the Flower Show this year, so we understand," Trewley prompted him.

Oliver's eyes were misty with reminiscence as he seemed barely aware of what the superintendent had said. "We were so very happy this morning—I went with her into the g-garden to pick the perfect rose for one of the c-classes in the Show. She wanted the best—nothing else would do— not for boastful reasons, not flaunting her presidency in everyone's face, but because that was a—an integral part of Ingrid's nature. She and I were so very alike, in that respect . . . nothing second-rate, nothing flawed. When I first met her, she was so polished, so g-groomed, so g-good at her job. . . ."

He frowned, and coughed. "I chose the best I c-could find, a rose I had been nursing along just for today; but in c-case something even better had blossomed overnight we had to search the whole g-garden before she was satisfied—or myself, either. Then we c-came back to the house, and she hunted high and low for the right vase to display her rose to the best advantage. It must have presented a fine sight in the marquee. . . .

"How I wish I'd had time to g-go with her! But I was so busy in my dispensary. Redingote still prefers bottles to pills—Ingrid used to love teasing me about it, saying I was too c-conscientious, at everyone's beck and c-call, working odd hours and neglecting her—but of c-course she didn't really mean it. She believes, as I do, that at your job—at everything—you must do your utmost. There must be no half measures. . . ."

Suddenly, he returned to the present, and the realities of his situation. "Dear C-caleb Duckels! He insisted on taking my phone off the hook—he's like you, he thinks I need to be left alone for tonight. But I'm not sure that's wise.

There's nobody else to c-care for the village except Tabitha Chilman, and—''

"Then let's hope," broke in Trewley, "that if there's an emergency they'll have the sense to call in a doctor from outside. I wouldn't ask that Tabitha of yours to take my temperature." He raised despairing eyes to the ceiling, and looked more like a bloodhound than a bulldog. "I wouldn't trust her to treat even a cold in the head!"

Oliver nodded. "Yes, they're a—a strange family, until you're used to them. But, well, I know them both—have done all my life—and I won't believe Barney had anything to do with . . . with what's happened. I won't believe it!"

"Umph." Trewley rubbed his chin, scowled, and looked sideways at Stone as he ventured: "Maybe, when he's got something definite to occupy his mind—clipping hedges or gatekeeping or mowing the lawn—he's all right, but there's still the matter of his behaviour this evening to explain. Tabitha says he's babbling, whatever she means by that. Mightn't it be from a guilty conscience? He wants to talk to you to—well, to confess, and to ask you to forgive him. Maybe." Stone nodded quietly at his side as he added, when Oliver's look of polite interest turned to a slow stare: "Don't forget, it's the full moon tonight. . . ."

"No," said Oliver, having thought over this suggestion. "Not Barney. Not Barney, of all people. . . ." But, for the first time, a note of doubt might be heard in his voice. "He adored her. Adored her. . . ."

Stone said: "How about if he'd bumped his head on a low branch, or something? Couldn't that account for his acting out of character in such a—such a dreadful way?"

Oliver sat up. "Has he had a bump on the head?"

Stone glanced at Trewley, and said: "We haven't seen him yet, Doctor Radlett—but Tabitha never mentioned that he had. Still, could that be a possible explanation—assuming he committed the crime?"

Oliver, however, was turning over this new idea in his mind, and did not reply. Trewley looked anxiously at Stone. Her eyes were fixed on Oliver Radlett's drawn features; her frown hinted that she thought the interview had almost come to its limit. Before that limit was reached, though, he had one or two more questions that could not be left for later.

"About what time this morning did your wife leave here to go to The Stooks with her perfect rose, Doctor Radlett?"

"What?" Oliver passed a hand over his eyes, blinking. "Oh, yes. I'm not sure—I was busy. Around ten, perhaps."

"Weren't you worried when she didn't come home for whatever meal you planned to have at midday?"

Oliver shook his head. "I was working, remember. I had no time to notice—and it wouldn't have been a c-cooked meal on a day like this, to spoil if she c-came back late—or not at all," he added, in a lower tone.

Before Stone could stop the interview altogether, the superintendent said: "So you weren't worried at all by her absence. But what about when you yourself came to attend the fete—weren't you even a little concerned that she'd never come home?"

Oliver closed his eyes, and sighed. "I thought . . . she had decided the walk back was too much for her, on such a hot day. She'd been looking very pale earlier, I remember I told her she'd been overdoing things—somebody had asked her back for lunch with them, I thought. At least, I suppose I did. Anyway, I was sure she'd be there when I arrived at the fete myself. . . ."

"And when was that exactly, Doctor Radlett?"

"I suppose—about two-fifteen. . . . I walked to the house—such a beautiful day, after being c-cooped up indoors dispensing all morning. . . . I planned to g-go straight to the Flower Show, to see her in all her g-glory as a judge. A beautiful setting for a beautiful woman—the perfect woman . . . and for old times' sake I felt I should like to visit the maze, as well. It was there that I had asked her to become my wife, and she had g-graciously c-consented—on such a day as this, too." His eyes misted over as he gazed into the past. "Happy memories, indeed. But today, I was a little early as I arrived at The Stooks— nobody around, so I thought I'd g-go first to the maze, I didn't want to interrupt the judging . . . only, just as

I arrived, I heard—I heard someone—screaming—
hysterics . . . so much noise and c-confusion . . .''

The silence seemed almost unbearable as he shuddered to
a halt. He raised his bowed head, and met Trewley's eyes
without flinching, though his own were full of tears. ''Of
c-course, I went in at once to see if I c-could help.
And—and then . . .''

At last, Oliver's grief, so long suppressed, was showing
itself in his disjointed speech, his ravaged expression, his
working features. Trewley shot an anxious look at Stone,
who was regarding the doctor with compassion. She sensed
the superintendent's silent enquiry, and, as Oliver buried his
face in his hands, spoke in a quiet voice.

''He's had about all he can take for now, sir—couldn't
we leave the rest until tomorrow?''

Trewley rose at once to his feet. ''Doctor Radlett, we'll
be on our way. We've other people to see, more questions
to ask—but will you be all right on your own? Is there
anyone you'd like us to call?''

Oliver raised vacant eyes to the superintendent's face,
and forced the courteous, stiff, desperate smile of bereavement, concealing his wish for privacy. Stone said gently:

''Would you like me to fix something to help you sleep?
I'm sure I could find my way around your dispensary—''

''No, thank you.'' At her words, Oliver's smile had
become even more desperate. ''I—I'll be all right. And I
always make up my own medication, Sergeant. But it
was—it was a very k-kind thought. Thank you.''

They shut the door on his grief, and went out to where Caleb
Duckels and David Gregory waited for them in the hall. The
vicar seemed inclined to return for a few more words of
consolation, but Stone dissuaded him. The four made their
thankful way out of the house, and down the narrow road
leading from Foreigners' Fork. Even in the stress of the
moment, they remembered to walk only two abreast along
the unpaved road, in case of traffic; but they did not speak
to each other. It was a silent, brooding little procession.

Inside Caleb's cottage, three people greeted them with
pleasure: Cherry Gregory, whose eyes sparkled as she saw

her husband; Mildred Waskett, whose frown betokened thoughts of the larder; and Joseph Norton. The latter pair hailed their friends with relief, but hesitated to enquire after Dr. Radlett; Cherry, however, was more forthcoming.

"How is he, darling? Will he be all right?"

David's tone was solemn. "I did what I could, but he'll weather this storm much better with his many good friends among the villagers. When someone has grown from childhood in a small place, his roots are deep. A stranger such as myself can be of only limited help."

Mildred suddenly became vocal. "What a terrible sad time of it you must have had with poor Doctor Oliver, I'm sure. You'll all be glad of a nice cup of tea—I'll make one directly." And she bustled away. After a few seconds of furious cogitation, Joe Norton sidled after her, blushing at Caleb's wink.

As he disappeared behind the closed kitchen door, Cherry smothered a giggle. "Thank goodness you've come. I've been feeling so horribly in the way here—I began to think my parents should have baptised me Gooseberry, not Cherry."

"What? Do you mean . . ." But Caleb could say no more, dissolving into laughter. "Do you tell me," he managed to splutter at last, "as that daft beggar's not put the question to her even yet? Every encouragement Joe Norton's had to make an honest woman of my sister—and she as willing as anyone could be, I'm sure—though I can see, ma'am, meaning no disrespect, but you might have cramped his style a bit, so to speak."

Cherry chuckled. "Please apologise to him from me, once it's all safely arranged, won't you? And I promise we'll do something really splendid by way of a wedding present, to make up for it."

David murmured his agreement, but added sadly that proposals of marriage seemed to be having a hard time of it that day. "Those two youngsters who found the poor woman . . . a day they'll never forget—and such a terrible introduction to our new parish, my dear."

Which reminded the detectives that for form's sake they

must make routine enquiries of the vicar and his wife, even if as confirmed strangers to Redingote they seemed unlikely suspects. Indeed, their alibis—vouched for by the cream of the parish (whose curiosity had been immense)—were so perfect that for one wild moment Trewley longed to arrest them on the spot. They had motored from home some forty miles distant in the neighbouring county, to reach Caleb's cottage at around twelve-fifteen; from which time they had been constantly in the company of witnesses. Mildred had prepared and served their lunch; Daisy Hollis had come, much upset, to beg Cherry to deputise at the last minute for the missing Mrs. Radlett at the Flower Show. If by any outside chance either of the Gregorys had sneaked off to The Stooks before the hour of their nominal arrival in the village, they would have been marked down as strangers, their every move noted.

"And until," concluded David, "I came upon that unhappy sight in the middle of the maze—through which, incidentally, I had to be guided by Caleb here—I'd never seen either of the Radletts before in my life, as far as I know. Yet I hope I was of some comfort to the poor husband. . . ."

"I'm sure you were, sir." And Trewley required confirmation of only one more point which had been at the back of his mind all afternoon. "How was it you took so long to get out of the maze after we arrived? I understood that Doctor Radlett, like all the locals, knew his way straight through, but judging by the rumpus from Barney Chilman when Mrs. Maggs said her piece, it was quite a time before the pair of you finally emerged."

David sighed. "He was . . . lost, Superintendent—dazed, like a man in a trance—sleepwalking. At first, I thought it was natural reluctance to face the inevitable crowd outside that made him move so slowly—but he walked right into a dead end and tumbled down in front of me—a seizure of some sort. He blacked out completely, and I wouldn't waste time calling for help until I had tried first aid—and by God's grace I was able to bring him round. When he surfaced, he told me there was nothing to worry

about. And he seemed normal enough, afterwards—there
were no further lapses at the house. . . . I understood this
sort of thing to have happened in the past, when the stress
of outside events has been too much for him. . . .''

He looked enquiringly at Caleb, who nodded. ''And
that's true enough. The poor lad. Born with the roof of his
mouth missing, he was—or his face twisted, something of
the sort, they said—not that we saw the child till the hospital
had put all to rights, but these operations may do unbalanc-
ing things to the workings of a man's body. Always been
one for these terrible heads when matters crowd upon him,
has Doctor Oliver—but he's always soon over them, for
which we're all thankful. I suppose I should have warned
you it might happen, but I never thought of it.''

''Not too surprising, considering,'' Trewley began—but
was interrupted, by a bump and a clatter at the kitchen door,
which swung slowly open. In came Mildred, bearing a tray
laden with glasses; behind her, a sheepish proud grin on his
reddened face, came Joseph Norton.

''We've kept you waiting for your tea, and shame on the
one as distracted me from my guests,'' remarked the lady
with a blush and a bridling. ''Fair parched with thirst I've no
doubt you must be. . . .''

She set down the tray with a cheerful bang. A quick study
showed no cups and no teapot, but in their place an
assortment of glasses and a large bottle. ''What d'you
reckon this time-wasting juggins here did''—indicating Joe,
who smirked shyly behind her—''but ask me to marry him?
And me in such a whirl with having visitors, I'd say
anything as come into my head to quiet him and let me get
on about my business! The shame of it, when Mildred
Waskett neglects her guests. . . .''

''Mildred Waskett for not much longer, mind,'' said Joe,
a tentative arm creeping about his lady's waist for a squeeze
and a cuddle. ''Mildred Norton has a fine sound to it—and
if you didn't think so, why else did you fetch out your best
elderflower? Seems to me you must have had it in mind to
celebrate something!''

She blushed again, and told him to get on with him, do;

but she did not push his arm away, and he chuckled. Caleb laughed loudly and clapped his friend mightily on the shoulder. David Gregory looked delighted, his wife relieved. Trewley glanced from Stone to the glasses, and smiled.

"If my sergeant and I are being asked to drink the good health of the happy couple," he said, "then we're delighted to accept the invitation. Today's not been too cheerful so far, has it? Thank you!"

They were as near off-duty as made no difference, and it was entirely up to him how he ran his investigations. What did it matter, so long as he got results? He had a few more questions to ask—but not quite yet. . . .

The elderflower wine was poured. Caleb raised his glass with a happy bellow. "Mr. and Mrs. Joe Norton as is to be, and the many years together we're wishful they should have!" And the sentiment was echoed all around the room.

It was hard, amid the excitement and goodwill, to think of constabulary duty, and Trewley told himself he would do just as well to wait until, at least, the Gregorys had gone. They could know nothing—and yet, perhaps it had been the imminent arrival of the Reverend David as vicar of Redingote which had led to the murder of Ingrid Radlett. . . .

The Gregorys were gone, the glasses primed for a nightcap nobody was refusing; and the questions must be asked before much longer. "Mr. Duckels, Mr. Norton—one thing, if you'd be so good. Mrs. Radlett was all set to take over your parish books, wasn't she? From Mr. Wilford?" Caleb and Joe looked surprised, but agreed. "Mind telling me why?"

It was Caleb who replied: Joe had drifted back into a happy dream at Mildred's side on the sofa. "Well now," said Mildred's brother, "with the new parson on his way, it would never have done for 'em to stay in the ramshackle way they'd become, and we'd not the ability to put things to rights ourselves—nor expecting it of Mr. Wilford, on account of how he's—he's been not himself of late." Even now, the churchwarden would not stoop to repeating gossip—which had still not been proved, and with Mrs.

Radlett dead would probably remain unproved. Besides, if it had been true, she at least had made some reparation for her sin by her recent interest in parish affairs. "Poor Mrs. Radlett," he said, sighing. "She was willing to oversee things for us, and it's good to know she had such an act of Christian charity in her heart as she died."

"Did she offer," enquired Trewley, "or was she asked?"

There was a pause. Caleb blinked, and rubbed his chin. "Well, I believe as it was her that offered. . . . Joe, am I right?" The elderflower was affecting Caleb's memory. "She was the one as offered, I think, but . . ."

Mrs. Waskett nudged her suitor with a loving elbow, and Joe coughed. "True enough, she did. When she come to talk to us working on—Mildred's Bottle Stall," delighted at the chance to employ his lady's given name. "Yes—she said how she'd been wondering about it, and what did we think. And we said we thought 'twas a good idea."

The Bottle Stall. Trewley conjured up his mental map of the fete layout. "She'd walked down from the Produce Stall, hadn't she? And from talking to you, she went on to Mrs. Brown's Prize Every Time?" Assenting nods from all three Redingotians. "Then she went into the rose garden, and nobody saw her again?"

"That's exactly the way of it, sir," said Joe brightly. Mildred nodded, and Caleb, frowning, nodded also.

"Which," said Trewley to Stone, as the two detectives left their new friends to their revelry and headed for The Stooks, "proves that Mrs. Wilford could easily have over-heard them. The Prize Every Time stood near enough for that, and Mrs. Brown's no talker when she's working, remember. Mrs. Wilford could have heard everything—Mrs. Radlett suggesting there's something wrong with the books, Duckels and Norton slow to get what she's hinting at—but Mrs. Wilford's not slow at all, is she?" He yawned. "A quick thinker, our Mrs. Wilford."

"The elderflower has inspired you, sir," said Stone, a laugh in her voice before she, too, yawned. Under the full moon, the superintendent observed her expression.

"Dammit, girl, I'm not drunk—I'm as sober as you! And

even if I'm not," he added, yawning again, "it's worth it, because it's given us another suspect."

"I'd have thought we had enough already, sir, never mind motives. What do you suppose Wilford's been doing with the money—if he's really been fiddling it, I mean?" Stone let her elderflowered imagination run riot. "A compulsive gambler, perhaps. Or paying blackmail on account of his sexual habits. . . ." She smothered a second yawn. "Maybe he's one of those weak characters who can't resist the chance to show the world they're secretly not as wet as people think. . . ."

Trewley was unable to stifle yet another yawn and followed it with a rubbing of his eyes. "Too late at night to worry about all that now, girl. Better to sleep on it—but remind me to get Davers to add the Wilford place to his beat tonight, will you? We'll have unsettled him and his wife a bit this evening, or she wouldn't have started yelling for their solicitor like that. . . ."

"Davers," muttered Stone, and made a mental note.

The pair walked on in a companionable silence until they reached The Stooks. The French windows were still open, and Trewley stalked into the sitting room.

"Clear off now, would you, there's a good girl? I want to think, and with you hovering round I can't concentrate."

"You mean you want to sleep it off, sir. I'll let your wife know, shall I—that you've been partying with the suspects and won't be home for breakfast?"

"Oh, tell her what you like." He sighed, stretched, and headed across the room to sit down on the sofa with a thump. "The heat. . . ." he excused himself wearily. "Lie down for a spell, and I'll feel better. . . ."

He swung his legs heavily up and round, swore, kicked off his shoes, and closed his eyes. Stone shook her head, smiled, and went into the kitchen.

She returned with a glass of water, which she set beside him on one of the low tables. "Fluid replenishment, sir!" He remained with closed eyes, motionless. "Sir. . . ."

"You're a good girl," he mumbled. "Leave the doors open for some fresh air. See you in the morning. . . ."

But morning came earlier than he expected. At half past five, PC Davers, wide-eyed and breathless with his boots damp from dew, rushed in and cried him violently awake.

"Sir! Mr. Trewley, sir—wake up, please! Sir!"

The superintendent sat up, gazed about him, blinked, and cursed with fluency. His beard rasped horribly on his collar as he shook his head several times to clear away the elderflower cobwebs. Glancing at the watch he had forgotten to remove from his wrist, he groaned aloud.

"Have you got any idea what bloody time it is, Davers?" Then he managed to focus on the constable's face. His heart gave the odd leap that generally heralded bad news. "What's wrong, lad? Come on—what's happened?"

"Oh, sir—it's Ernie—Ernie Hollis, you see. . . ."

"No, I don't. Not yet. What about Ernie Hollis?"

"He was up early, sir, on his rounds—and he found him, sir, found him dead—dead and drowned in the ditch!"

━━━━ Eleven ━━━━

TREWLEY SHOOK HIS head once more, slowly. "That's no way to make a statement, Davers, no matter what time of day it is. Let's start again. Who's been found drowned, and what ditch were they found in?"

Davers took a deep breath, and swallowed. "Sorry, sir—a bit of a shock, you see. It's Barmy Barney—I mean Barnabus Chilman. Ernie found him, with a—with a rope and a stone round his neck—like he'd done himself in, sir."

For a long moment, Trewley said nothing. Deep rage was welling up inside him: rage at the waste of yet another life—rage at the loss of whatever it was Barney, yesterday, had wished to say. If he himself had been bolder with Tabitha—if he hadn't let the Wilfords choke him off with their talk of solicitors. . . .

But it was far too late to do anything now. "Give Detective Sergeant Stone a ring, will you? Tell her to get the whole gang out of bed and over to the spot as soon as they can—she's to come here, though. And I'll see Ernie Hollis now, I suppose, though with me in my whiskers it won't feel altogether right. . . ."

Ernie was ushered in, pale of face, his coat buttoned tight to his chin, and even the feathers on his lugubrious hat drooping with shock. The first thing Trewley did was to arrange for tea (sugared) with biscuits, an ample supply of both. He knew he would need to be fully alert to cope with this latest tragedy.

He apologised first for not having had time to speak with Mr. Hollis yesterday, pleading pressure of work, though his true reason had been the general consensus that Ernie's inebriated state would make the effort of interviewing him worthless until he'd sobered up. Which now, it seemed, he had: to bring news of another sudden death. But—was this death, too, a murder? And was Ernie's evident nervousness merely because he knew that the person who discovers a body is always subjected to rigorous questioning? Mr. Hollis sat on the very edge of his chair, and replied in a barely audible monotone to Trewley's opening remarks.

After a few minutes: "Ah, tea," said the superintendent, with relief. "Sugared and strong—you need it for the shock, so drink up, Mr. Hollis!"

"Shock?" Ernie shrank deeper into his coat, high-pulled collar hiding his ears. "I'll say it was a shock, to find him there with that rope about his neck, and a look on his face like all the devils of hell had chased him there. . . ."

"Chased him where, exactly?"

"Down in the ditch I found him, dead and drowned, by the copse, and that's the truth of it."

"By the cops? That's a serious allegation, Mr. Hollis."

"Doom's Copse," groaned Ernie, not listening. "Drowned there as ever is—a place fitting for such deeds, but a sorry end to the lad, whatever he may have done. The full moon, you see. . . ."

"Doom's Copse!" Trewley sighed thankfully. "I understand now. Your village pond—the, er, haunted place?"

"That's the way of it, sir. Ever a site for self-destructors, Doom's own places—and now another to add to their number. 'Tis in Doom's Deep they mostly drown theirselves, but the Ditch runs into the Deep, and the Copse through which it do flow stands black as night with the shadows of sorrow and sin. . . . Human sacrifices, there used to be in the Deep in times past."

Trewley's face creased in a deep-furrowed frown. "Then it's a—a sort of ritual place for someone born in Redingote to kill themselves? You're not surprised? Apart from the shock of finding him, of course."

"No, sir, I'm not." Ernie set down his cup with a clunk on its saucer, and hunched his shoulders again. "A true son of the village was poor Barney, faithful to our ways right to the end. . . ." And, having imparted all he seemed prepared to tell of Redingote's death customs, he began to look nervous again. Trewley eyed him with interest. What was bothering the man? More than simple distress at having found Barney's body, the superintendent guessed.

"Well now, Mr. Hollis, how about a statement? Nothing formal for now, the details can wait—just the basic facts will do." If he could persuade Ernie to talk, he might worm out of him whatever it was that troubled him. . . .

Ahem. Ernest Benjamin Hollis was aged sixty-three, having been postman to Redingote district these forty years or more, and had been proceeding about his lawful business—

"At five in the morning, Mr. Hollis?"

Ernie shuffled his feet and sank back into his still-fastened coat. "These fine summer days, I likes to be up betimes, rather nor wasting the God-given air in idle slumber." He coughed at Trewley's look of disbelief, and hurried to resume his statement.

"Proceeding about my lawful business and anxious to be finished early—so as to spend the rest of the day otherwise in doing good, such as the reading of letters to folk as lack the gift, or helping 'em put pen to paper for their reply."

He paused expectantly, and the superintendent nodded. "Very public-spirited of you, Mr. Hollis. Go on, please."

"Well, yes. Yes . . . now, poor Mrs. Radlett, she had her faults like all God's creatures, and especially the—the weaker vessels—but she, like me, was glad to help out them as couldn't understand they plaguey government forms and such. Mostly those as neither Elsie Lilleker at the Post Office nor I couldn't make no sense of—and that reminds me, talking of letters—what about this Mr. Rowles"—with a wary glance around the room, in case Montague might appear from behind a bookcase—"as come into the village not six months since?"

Ernie had nothing to add to the web of suspicion already spun about the noncommunicative Mr. Rowles, and Trewley listened with only half an ear, wondering how long Records would be in getting back to him. . . .

"And poor Mrs. Radlett," Ernie was saying, "ready and

willing to play her part in Redingote life in these and other matters, so she was.''

''And Barney Chilman adored her.'' Time to make the garrulous—nervily so?—old man come to the point. ''Might he have committed suicide because he was so upset by what had happened to her? Or might he just have killed her himself—under the influence of the moon, say, and was taking the best way out?''

''It's traditional to the village,'' Ernie insisted.

''So you said. Doom's Copse and Ditch and Deep . . . where exactly was it you found the body?''

''Closest to the Copse, he were, well away from the Deep. I reckon he didn't want nobody to come upon him till the deed was properly done, for it's an out-of-the-way place and no mistake. Set in a tangle of thickety hedge, so he was, half in and half out of the water. A terrible sight. . . .''

''Well-hidden, was he? In a tangle of hedge? Then,'' demanded Trewley, as Ernie nodded, ''how did *you* manage to come upon this terrible sight? Does the Post Office normally expect its employees to carry on its business right in the middle of a wood?'' Ernie flinched. ''And, in any case, is the GPO in Redingote such a slave driver that it forces its workers to go to work *on a Sunday*?''

Ernie yelped, and rolled his eyes, and huddled himself frantically inside his coat. Trewley awarded himself a silent kick for being so slow to remember what day of the week it was—to remember that the murder which had first brought him to Redingote had occurred at yesterday's church fete, and that the customary day for a church fete is Saturday. He sat upright on his chair, and favoured the hapless Mr. Hollis with a stern look.

Such silent authority soon had its reward. Ernie drew several deep breaths, scowled, and released the topmost button of his coat. With a sigh, he reached for a confidence-boosting biscuit, and grinned. ''Got me fair and square, sir, you have, I don't mind admitting. But I'd take it as a kindness on your part to remember as I did my duty by poor Barney as a Christian should—and he being the very last person to wish trouble upon me on his account. It's a—a matter of respecting a confidence, sir.''

Trewley could hardly commit himself to respecting any such thing without full knowledge of the facts, which so far in his talk with Ernie could only be described as confusing. Barney's death had caught the superintendent unawares, and he had no wish to make a further error of judgement: he was angry enough with himself already. ''Suppose,'' he said, ''you tell me the truth—the whole truth, mind—and I can think it over. But I'm promising nothing, understand.''

Those large brown eyes in the bloodhound face evidently persuaded Ernie that the superintendent could be trusted, for he dropped his voice to a hoarse whisper, and leaned forward. ''Some calls it prigging, sir, and some will say it's poaching—but hereabouts we go trading, and few can say they've never tried their hand at the trade. But there ain't nobody to beat Ernie Hollis!''

He rose to his feet, unbuttoned his coat the rest of the way down, and revealed to Trewley's startled eyes a fine set of poacher's pockets, suspiciously bulging.

The superintendent had experienced several surprises in Redingote, and was becoming immune. He gazed at the pockets, then at Ernie; then at the ceiling, which he studied for some time.

''Must have been a real shock for you, Mr. Hollis,'' he said at last. ''Finding the body like that—a real shock. Strong sweet tea's one way of treating shock, but I'm sure my sergeant—she knows about these things, you see— she'd tell you it helps even more to keep yourself from cold. Now suppose you fasten that coat of yours again? Then you won't run any risk of catching a chill.''

With a grateful wink, Ernie subsided onto his chair, no longer perching but able for the first time to relax, and to pay full attention to the matter of his statement.

Which was straightforward enough. At half past one that morning—a fine clear night, to be sure, but with everyone occupied with the murder it was unlikely as they'd be snooping—he'd gone to Doom's Deep to give their normal signal to Barney. The lad had been a willing and able pupil, for all his manifold strange ways, and Ernie had thought he might care to forget his sorrows in some healthy . . . outdoor exercise (he winked), such as Doctor Oliver had said would always help to settle him, and with not working on Sunday likely enough to be at a mischievous loose end, or so Ernie supposed.

Mr. Hollis grinned, and gloated over his happy turn of phrase. "Outdoor exercise," he said again, with another wink. Trewley found himself winking back at the old reprobate, and was thankful Stone could not see him.

Then the grin faded from Ernie's face as he remembered. "A promising youngster, poor Barney. A sad loss. . . . Well, so I give him the call—two owl-hoots and a scritch— more than once I summoned him, but he never did come. I had the sudden notion as he'd tooken one of Tabitha's witch-bottles to help him sleep, and small surprise in that—so I come down alone past the Chilman house, no sign from Barney, and along the Ditch where it do flow past the bottom of they new houses—but out of sight of the road, you understand." He favoured the superintendent with a reproachful look. "On account of Ben Davers keeping watch in the area all night."

Trewley rubbed his chin. "This ditch goes past the houses where Davers was keeping watch—the houses on the new estate, with the gardens that back on to each other?"

"That's the way of it, sir. Foreigners' Fork, so it is, them places set either side of Doom's Ditch, right by Doom's Copse. Redingote folk, see, we're not so wishful as ignorant newcomers to live close to the spirits of the restless dead . . . nor to Tabby the Touched, neither."

This reluctant honesty brought a faint grin of fellow feeling to Trewley's face. "Umph. Very lonely roads, both of them. And is it a very long ditch? Where exactly was it you found Barney's body?"

"Depends what you call long, sir. It comes flowing down through the thickety woods from far away in the hills, then mostly through the manor lands till it reaches Redingote. You might say as Doom's Deep sets on the edge of the old houses, with the Copse stretching away from the Deep between they two roads as make up Foreigners' Fork—''

"Yes, yes, Mr. Hollis, but until I've got a map, or gone there myself, this means nothing to me. Let's try again. Whose house is nearest to where you found the body of Barney Chilman?"

Ernie frowned. Why could this policeman not see what was so obvious to him? "Why, Mr. Wilford's, of course. Went past there cunning as any fox, I did, screened by they bushes and seeing no light from the houses—not, mind you, as I'd rightly expect it, them being mostly full of town folk with small wish to be early from their beds. And even them as were out of their beds, young Ben Davers for one, he saw neither hide nor hair of me as I passed him by—though," he pointed out with some pride, "'twould have been shame to my calling if he had, indeed."

"Indeed," muttered Trewley, who was thinking. "You say it was near Mr. Wilford's house . . . and you went past there at about what time?"

Ernie shrugged. "Twoish, I reckon. And I'd take my Bible oath there was no sign of young Barney anywhere in the Ditch then, poor lad."

He might well have to take an oath, reflected the superintendent: as a key witness at the inquest—and also at the trial, if Barney's death turned out to be murder, and not the suicide Mr. Hollis had evidently supposed it to be. But Trewley was unhappy with that supposition: something was wrong, he had a feeling. Yet he tried not to let his feelings show as he enquired:

"Well, then, when you came back from your . . . exercise, were there any signs of life in any of the houses? In Mr. Wilford's, maybe?"

Another denial, very firm. "Signs of death, more like," said Ernie. "Happening across poor Barney in such a fashion—must have been around half past four, when I found him. And I hopped out of that Ditch quick enough, you're sure, and went to seek out Ben Davers, only it seemed he was round the other side of the Fork, and it took more time than I'd bargained for, to find him."

"And, when you had," concluded the superintendent, striving to suppress his excitement, "he brought you here at once. Because he knew I'd want to know that you'd found Barnabus Chilman dead in a ditch . . . drowned at the bottom of Silvester Wilford's garden. . . ."

When Stone arrived at The Stooks, she was muttering with irritation over PC Davers, who was at that moment showing his Allingham colleagues the precise location of Barney's body. As soon as the team had concluded their preliminary investigations, Trewley and Stone should be there: but the superintendent waxed loud and angry against the Wilfords, and was keen to visit them at once to hear what they had to say. Stone, too, was brooding.

"Whatever Davers was doing to let poachers and corpses wander about the countryside right under his silly nose, I shudder to think! He was told to keep an eye on Wilford—he must have kept it shut!"

Through the haze of his own emotion, Trewley recalled how PC Davers had merited his sergeant's wrath yesterday afternoon, and smothered what might, in happier times, have been a chuckle. "Come on, be fair to the lad. Ernie boasted to me there was nobody around here who could equal him for poaching—and he said Barney was his prize pupil. And take a closer look at those snaps. A place like that, in the middle of the night, full moon or no full moon—you can't be too hard on poor Davers. . . ."

Stone studied once more the Polaroid scene-of-crime photos, acknowledged (grudgingly) how very damp and dark the site appeared to be, and admitted (eventually) that—maybe—she could see the superintendent's point. "I suppose," she said, "that if Hollis made a habit of creeping about through all that lot, I should take my hat off to him. It looks perfectly horrible!" Which was as near to forgiving PC Davers as Trewley could expect her to go.

"Horrible, but traditional—for a suicide," he said. "If that's what it was. Mrs. Wilford messed things up a bit too much for my liking last night—"

"But would the Wilfords have known about it, sir? About the suicide tradition, I mean."

"They've lived here five or six years, remember. I'm sure they would. Rowles, now—he'd be a different matter. The locals don't talk overmuch to him. He probably doesn't even know where the place is. . . ."

Stone was shaking her head. "Barney was Cedric Ezard's assistant, sir, and these naturals can be very biddable in many ways. He'd have no inhibitions about talking to people like Rowles—who's his boss, and would have tried to learn all sorts of things about his new home. Barney could have chattered away for ages without much bother. My mother's the village witch and we live in the haunted wood by the local suicide spot—you can imagine, can't you? He'd probably say it more than once, too—for reassurance, like the counting and so on. Oh, I bet Rowles could have known all about Doom's Deep from Barney, sir."

"I wish," muttered Trewley, "that I could remember where I've seen our Montague before. On our way down there, we'll put in a chase-up call, I think. Come on!"

As she pocketed the photos, Stone turned her thoughts to the previous day's death, since that of the morning was too recent, too confused. "Montague Rowles," she murmured. "Suppose I Pelmanise, sir? To give your subconscious a helping hand. Montague—Capulet, I suppose. Rowles—Royce, of course. Let's ask Records if there's anything on a Capulet Royce, shall we?"

"It's too early in the day for your nonsense," he grumbled, conscious not only of the matter in hand but also of his unshaven, sleepy state. "No mother in the world would give her son a crazy name like—"

"Tabitha!" Stone broke in. "Sir—does she know what's happened? And—if she doesn't—shouldn't she be told?"

"Umph." The superintendent halted, his hand reaching for the car door. "Yes, well . . . we could drop in on our way, I suppose. . . ." He sighed. "She seemed to take a fancy to you, girl, didn't she? Might make it a little easier to break the news. . . ."

In the event, they had no opportunity to break it. No

answer came to their knock at Tabitha's door, which was not locked; the witch trusted in her reputation to deter visitors. After trying the handle, Stone suggested they should enter—just in case, as she put it. Trewley, who knew he was getting out of his depth, reluctantly agreed; he insisted that he was not superstitious, yet nonetheless stood aside with unaccustomed courtesy to usher his sergeant into the house well in front of him.

"You take a quick look upstairs, will you, girl? I'll—I'll wait here and keep an eye on the outside. You never know, after all. . . ."

And he hovered by the open door as Stone called out, swiftly searched each room in turn, called again. "She's not here, sir—unless she heard us coming and hid in the garden somewhere."

"Unless she's in Doom's Ditch, drowned, and nobody's found her yet. Maybe the full moon affects her as well—she was odd enough last night, wasn't she?"

Stone was shocked. "Surely not, sir! Her son? She'd never want to harm him—remember how she tried so hard to keep him out of the loony bin by getting Doctor Radlett to say he wasn't dangerous—if she'd wanted to, she could easily have been rid of him then. But the doctor found him that job at The Stooks, and Tabitha was grateful. She'd never harm him, after all that!"

The superintendent looked quickly over his shoulder. "Yes, he was her son, but that wasn't all he was, was it? How about shame—and guilt—and harbouring a secret grudge against him, ever since he was born? Suppose she suspected him of having killed Mrs. Radlett—whether or not he did doesn't matter—but Tabitha sees the chance to be rid of him once and for all, and for a reason nobody would blame her for, whereas if she'd had him certified people might have—well, been funny about it. Enough to turn any woman's head, a son who's a brother as well—and that head of hers is full of odd notions, you can't deny. . . ."

He glowered about him at the empty garden. "Come on, girl, we're doing no good here. We'll call back later." And he strode down the path in a great hurry, anger mingled with unease in his every step.

The radio was calling them as they returned to the car, and Stone was quick to reply. "Listen to this, sir—good news! One thing you can stop worrying about now—there's a message from Central Records. Let's have it again, please." And the radio duly obliged.

"Your description," it crackled, once the preliminaries were over, "fits Mortimer Reeves, supergrass squared, who skipped from, quote, inadequate police protection, open bracket, is that slander or libel, query, close bracket, last winter and not heard of since, stop. A very popular person whose many friends are looking for him to invite to a special party, stop. We do not expect to be officially asked to attend, stop. Shame eh, query. Regards, end."

"On a Sunday morning, too," groaned Trewley, though he had brightened. "Didn't I tell you I knew him? Mortimer Reeves, without a doubt—that's who our mysterious retired solicitor is!"

Stone tried to recall the details. "Reeves really was a solicitor, wasn't he? Before they struck him off. Which is how he managed to fall foul of—"

"That's right. And a lovely bunch they were, too—no wonder this murder kerfuffle's scared him rigid! Coppers everywhere, his lovely cover blown to bits—can't you imagine the headlines? Murder at the Manor, they'll say—"

"And a very nice manor it is, too. I always thought," said Stone, "that he must have got away with more than he let on. A numbered Swiss bank account, do you suppose, sir? But then, what's the use of all that money when you can't be sure of living long enough to enjoy it. If you try pulling a stunt like that. . . ."

"Some stunt, girl. And yet—Reeves was soft, wasn't he—that's why he did a bunk. He's not a killer. Would he be likely to have clobbered Radlett, a man like that?"

"In a panic, perhaps he would. She recognised him, sir—teased him—tried a spot of blackmail or something, and was bashed over the head for her pains. . . ."

Trewley rubbed his chin. "Maybe, maybe. But how

would she have recognised him? The publicity on that case wasn't any too sensational, as I remember it."

Stone pondered for a while. "I know, sir! Money mixes with money, after all—and she wasn't just a tease, she was an accountant. She didn't know him before—and she didn't know now when she'd pushed him too far—she enjoyed watching him squirm—and then he overreacted. A panic reaction, like when he skipped from our tender loving care when things got a little dicey."

The superintendent still had doubts, but it was, he had to admit, a theory—yet another of them. . . .

"Perhaps he only wanted to threaten her," he suggested, "wanted to keep her quiet, didn't realise that garden ornament was as hefty as it turned out to be. It could have been an accident—it slipped, or something. But—no, wait—that's impossible. The middle of the maze—how did he get out again after he'd killed her? Granted, she might just have gone in with him—but I shouldn't think he'd be able to find his way around without a guide, and I don't suppose he'd have had anyone waiting to show him out."

"Those printed sheets of instructions, sir, remember? He could easily have taken one, and used it—and then put it back, so that when anyone counted them there wouldn't be any missing."

"Barney and the rest would have seen him put it back," objected Trewley; then stopped. "Barney. Now, I wonder if he *did* see something—and that's why he died. . . ."

Stone allowed him a few moments' brooding before saying: "And what about the yew twig, sir? Definite local knowledge needed for that, I thought we'd agreed from the start. Maybe Rowles could have known of that particular superstition from talking to Barney, but . . ."

"I'm not sure. Remember, *I* knew about it—you did too, more or less—I'm not sure the argument holds water, Stone. Young Gary King was from Allingham—but he'd learned the plan of the maze from a library book." He rubbed his chin, and frowned. "I wonder if we haven't been too . . . dogmatic about all this."

"Well, sir, we need *some* starting suppositions, or we'll

just get bogged down completely and never advance at all. There are other things besides motive and opportunity: character, for instance. Rowles is hardly the premeditated sort, is he? And to learn the maze from a book, or to pinch one of the plans on the way in, before killing her . . ." She shook her head firmly. "He's too soft for that, sir, as you yourself said. He'd—oh, he'd buy her off, or do another bunk—maybe even tell her to publish and be damned, rather than add murder to the list. Wouldn't he?"

"Umph. Well, I'm not sure about that. . . ." Trewley, who had so roundly demolished Stone's theory, realised that he now found a perverse pleasure in trying to uphold it. They were spared further discussion, however, by the radio, which announced that it had news of vital interest to impart. Stone urged the radio to impart it without delay.

"So," said Trewley, as she signed off, "Mrs. Radlett was six weeks gone, was she? Your friend Tabitha guessed right, girl—and things are starting to look a bit sticky for the Wilfords, one or other or both of 'em. Very sticky indeed."

"Him, sir, for preference. I don't like him—too kinky by far, and not in a—a normal sort of way," said Stone, in decided tones. Medical textbooks were one thing, real-life perversions quite another. "He's not like Barney and Tabitha, who are, well, just natural about being strange. Let's go and get him!"

Her enthusiasm was as great as his own. He nodded. "If we turn up before they've heard the news, we can spring it on them and see if it loosens their tongues—and I'm not having any nonsense about solicitors today. This visit's an entirely different matter: I'm sure Barney's death wasn't suicide." He frowned. "I wonder if Tabitha knows? She was clued-up enough to know about the baby. . . ."

"Yes, sir, but if you think about it, we should have guessed, you know. People said Mrs. Radlett looked sickly—she had a craving for sweet things—those butterfly wings weren't just spite . . . and a woman would be far more likely to work it out than a man, sir. Really, I should have spotted it myself—and I bet that's how Tabitha knew."

"So Mrs. Radlett breaks the news of her pregnancy to Wilford out in the drive, uses it as the reason to end their affair—or else tries to blackmail him over it somehow . . . anyway, they quarrel. He says he'll have to think it over—asks her to meet him later, somewhere more private. . . ."

Stone was almost dancing with impatience. "That's it, sir—that must be how it happened! Oh, do come on!"

───── Twelve ─────

DETECTIVE SERGEANT STONE darted along the winding path to Silvester's front door, leaving Trewley far behind her. By the time he had reached the step, she had rapped and rung several times with no reply. She turned to him in a temper.

"If Davers has let them slip away, I'll—I'll have his guts for garters! He can't use the excuse about poaching skill with a pair of town-bred types like the Wilfords!" She knocked again, and jabbed her finger on the bell push. "Nobody home," she concluded grimly. "Had I better try the door?"

"Hold it." A curtain had twitched upstairs. Trewley stepped back into full sight of the unseen watcher. "Someone'll be here before much longer, I reckon. Think," he said with a twinkle, "of your blood pressure, girl!"

Stone muttered something, and jigged from one foot to the other as the long wait continued. "Sir, please!" she begged at last, but he raised a warning hand. Footsteps were approaching Silvester Wilford's door.

It was Myra who opened it to the detectives, wearing a dressing gown over her nightdress, her hair unbrushed. She had evidently been nerving herself for her greeting, which was stilted and stiff.

"This is a very early visit for a Sunday morning, Superintendent. And we told you last night that—"

"Last night was different, Mrs. Wilford. Things have changed since then. A lot. We'd like a word with your husband immediately, please."

Some note in his voice she had not heard before made Myra suppress her planned protest before she had opened her mouth. Trewley was a large man, heavily built; he loomed on her doorstep, his shadow darkening her hall. His brown eyes bored into hers, and she found herself unable to refuse him entrance, though even as she moved aside to let him in she made one final objection.

"My husband is still in bed. He needs his rest, and we had a—a late night, after you had gone. . . ." Trewley and Stone wondered whether the Wilfords had been talking together until all hours—or whether they had had a midnight caller. "We do not," said Myra, "expect visitors at such an ungodly hour. . . ."

"Not so ungodly for us, Mrs. Wilford. We've already paid one visit this morning—to Tabitha Chilman." Trewley regarded Myra closely, but she gave no sign that this intelligence meant anything to her. She led the detectives down the hall towards the back of the house, but instead of directing them to the study opened the door of a sitting room they had not entered the previous night.

"You may—wait in here," said Myra, waving them to the chairs near the rear window of the room, which ran the full depth of the house. Doubtless she had no wish for neighbours passing on the road outside to observe two police officers interrogating the Wilford family so early on the Sabbath morn. . . .

"I will fetch my husband—if you insist," Myra said, as Trewley's raised eyebrows showed surprise at the bleakness of her tone. "But I would prefer it if you could first discuss your business with me—and quietly, please. His room is directly above this one."

"Separate rooms, Mrs. Wilford?"

"Our private sleeping arrangements can have nothing to do with whatever has brought you here today, Mr. Trewley!" Did her frown and angry flush betoken a guilty conscience? Did she, or did she not, know that Barnabus Chilman had met his death late last night, close to this house? Someone who slept in a single room had every opportunity to slip unnoticed outside for a rendezvous with fate . . . as, earlier, he or she could have had a rendezvous with Ingrid Radlett. . . .

Trewley's voice was stern. "Will you please ask your

husband to come down at once, Mrs. Wilford.'' It was not a request.

Myra dropped her eyes, and left the room. There came the sounds of hurried dressing: feet pattering, sinks gurgling, the to-and-fro sliding of drawers: all somehow muted, yet with an air of desperation. Did Silvester feel this could be his last chance to spruce himself up before being hauled off to Allingham police station? Or . . .

''Sir!'' hissed Stone, suddenly alert. ''Suppose he's told her to pretend he's still here, while he slides down a drainpipe and makes a dash for it?''

''Relax, Sergeant.'' Trewley pointed through the window towards the nearby view of more houses, built to the same pattern, on the far side of the wooded hollow. ''No drainpipes on the outside of the house—not near the windows, anyway. Look at the backs of those. He's stuck upstairs, all right—and so is she.''

''Until they come down, and we grill them, sir. I want to find out what they have to say. . . .''

From outside the room came sounds of descending feet: two pairs, Stone was relieved to hear. Silvester Wilford entered the room, with his uxorial shadow close behind. They were both fully dressed, though a small dab of foam under one ear bore witness to the speed of Mr. Wilford's toilet, and Stone's quick eyes noted that Myra's stockings did not match. She reflected on how many women, in this era of comfortable and convenient panty hose, still wore stockings. Had the suspenders appealed to Silvester's fantasies—a final attempt on the part of his wife to keep him from straying?

Silvester seemed more in control of himself today. Perhaps he was resigned to whatever might happen: he would bluster his way through until the police case seemed overwhelming, then collapse as suddenly as he had done the night before. Trewley took a quick look round for any decanters, but none was to be seen. He probably kept the drinks in his study. Would Myra think to fetch one for him?

She had lost some part of her original bravado, and her eyes were under too strict a control as she took her seat at her husband's side. Did she, now that she had had time to think things over, realise how black the case looked for him—and for herself? Had she wished to rehearse with Silvester just once more the story they should tell—and had the police insistence upon entering deprived her of her final opportunity?

Silvester leaned back on his chair with a studied air of calm cooperation. For the first time, his manner reminded Trewley and Stone that he was Mr. Wilford, bank manager, as well as Silvester, the sexual oddity, weakling, adulterer. "And how," he enquired, "may I be of help to you this morning?"

He even managed a smile. It was an impressive performance: Trewley wondered whether it might be harder to break this witness than he had anticipated.

"Well, sir, for a start, it would help us to know what time you went to bed last night."

Silvester's jaw dropped. He rallied quickly. "I fail to see, Superintendent— Oh, very well, if you insist. About an hour after you left—maybe a little more."

"So you didn't go straight up to bed?"

"I would have thought that even the police"—Silvester was starting to lose that air of almost unnatural calm he had somehow adopted—"would realise we had a great deal to talk about. This has hardly been the most restful weekend my wife and I have ever known."

"Would you say, though, that you had a—a relatively undisturbed night?" But Trewley's only reply was Myra's flush, and Silvester's scowl. He pressed on: "No visitors?"

Surprise which seemed genuine appeared on both faces. Silvester leaned forward. "Why are you asking these questions, Superintendent? You gave my wife to understand that this was some kind of emergency. Pestering us about our sleeping habits does not strike me as particularly urgent."

Trewley's eyes narrowed slightly. "Did you have any visitors last night, sir." It was not really a question.

"No, we did not. In the circumstances, it isn't likely anyone would want to call, so late at night. If you remember, Superintendent, we were . . . disturbed enough by those who did."

"You're saying that apart from Detective Sergeant Stone and myself, you had no visitors last night?"

"I will keep on saying so, Superintendent."

Myra chimed in bitterly: "Why should we want to talk to anyone else? We were only too glad to go to sleep at last—to forget . . . everything. And can you blame us?" It was the first time she had spoken since Silvester had appeared. Had she, until that moment, decided to let him play the man's part in this way, if he could do so in no other? Myra became aware of Stone's speculative gaze, and blushed.

"You went to sleep," repeated Trewley. "But as you and your husband don't—excuse me, Mrs. Wilford—share a room, how can you be so certain you both went to sleep? One or other of you could have had a visitor when the other was out for the count."

Myra replied through clenched teeth. "We may not share a room, Mr. Trewley, but that doesn't mean we are indifferent to each other's welfare. Since my . . . failure as the sort of wife Silvester . . . seems to prefer, I try my best to ensure he lacks none of the . . . comforts I am prepared to give him. We both sleep with our doors open, and I would hear at once if he called out—or if he moved around."

She sounded more like a mother discussing a favourite infant than a wife discussing her husband. The problems of her unusual marriage must certainly have been exacerbated by her maternal instincts, which clearly were strong: the sexual practices which Silvester favoured accorded not so much with the behaviour of a mother as with that of a mistress. Some wives might be able to act the part, but Myra, she had made plain, could not—and, in his frustration, Silvester had turned to Ingrid Radlett. . . .

"Which presumably explains," said the Superintendent, "how you came to know of your husband's affair with Mrs.

Radlett. As you're such a light sleeper, you'd have heard him sneaking out of—''

"I resent the use of that word, Mr. Trewley!" Silvester sat bolt upright on his chair, closer to losing his self-control than ever. "My private life is of no possible concern to the police!"

Now that he was so nearly off balance, it was time to tip him over. "Even," enquired Trewley, "if your dead mistress happens to have been pregnant?"

Silvester's face drained of colour. Myra's eyes opened, her lips went white. "She—she was having—a—a baby?" And the look which she turned upon her husband as he sat, stunned into silence, was bleak indeed.

"She was going to have a baby," Trewley said; and saw tears in Myra's eyes. Had her maternal instincts been touched by this child, dead before it had even lived?

Or had she already known of its existence, and killed its mother in a fit of jealousy that Ingrid had something she herself could never have?

"A baby," she repeated softly, shaking her head, blinking the tears away. "A baby. . . ." She clenched her hands into fists, and beat herself upon the thighs. "A baby!" And she turned in a fury to Silvester.

"Oh, this explains everything—why she refused to carry on with your—your sordid relationship: she knew it wouldn't be safe! The sort of . . . disgusting things you enjoy would be much too dangerous for a woman expecting a child—the child," her voice broke, "you said you could never give me . . . but you were lying. . . ." And, with a sob, she buried her face in her hands. "I hate you—hate the sight of you, for what you've done to me. . . ."

This dramatic change from the devoted, protective mother-wife to the broken, deprived mother was frightening. The bitter words Myra hurled at her husband had been uttered in a voice throbbing with passion, revealing to the world the secret sorrow of the strange Wilford marriage: the younger husband, the childless wife needing someone to care for; the resulting obsession, the destructive, despairing renunciation.

Though Silvester was clearly shaken by his wife's altered attitude, he tried to recover himself. "I didn't know she—she was—pregnant, but—yes, it could have been why she—she decided to . . . stop—it might have been—unwise to continue, I don't know . . . but she wouldn't say why, she refused to give any reason. That was what made me so angry. . . ." He realised too late what he had said. "But I didn't kill her! Why should I want to do that? It wasn't"—he tried to catch Myra's eye—"my baby! She was a married woman, for heaven's sake! Oliver adored her. . . ."

"Enough," enquired Trewley, "for him to accept another man's child as his own?"

Myra's sobs grew louder, and she turned her back on Silvester. She, at least, believed the baby had been his; and the news had overtaken her so completely that it was entirely credible she could have killed Ingrid—if she had known of the pregnancy yesterday.

As Tabitha Chilman, for one, had known. . . .

"I didn't kill her!" Silvester's denial, with his wife ignoring him, was as much as he could manage: without her support, he was utterly lost. Myra, too, was speechless, struggling to stifle her sobs.

The shock treatment had so far worked well, and Trewley decided to apply it once more. "Before we came here today, we visited Tabitha Chilman, Mr. Wilford. We wanted to tell her"—he and Stone studied Silvester's unchanging expression for any hint of foreknowledge—"to tell her that her son Barnabus was dead. . . ."

Silvester remained motionless; Myra uttered a little cry—of horror? Shock? "Dead," repeated the superintendent. "Found drowned earlier this morning—in the stream that runs past the bottom of your garden!"

He stood up to point an ominous finger towards the sinister tangle of bushes and darkling trees which sheltered the hollow where Doom's Ditch ran.

Silvester swallowed, and licked his grey lips. "Poor Barney," he said, after a pause. "He was—he was devoted to Ingrid, everyone knew that. The shock must have—must have unhinged him. . . .''

"You fool!" Myra's voice throbbed with emotion. "Can't you see they don't believe it was suicide? They wouldn't be asking so many questions if that's all it was—they're softening you up to make you confess to both murders! They think you've killed two people, Silvester— two people in the last twenty-four hours! And to think"—a note of scorn—"that I used to worry you were too quiet, too shy, unsociable! How close do you have to get to people before you can kill them?"

By now, he had recovered from the initial shock. "What do you mean, I've killed two people? You must be mad! As mad as Barney, to suggest that I—I could . . . and as for Barney, what nonsense! It was the full moon—everyone knew he'd be even more out of his wits than usual, never mind the . . . what happened to Ingrid! Are you *trying* to make them arrest me? Getting your own back because of this—this baby—which I repeat was not my child?"

"I mean it all right. I can't cover up for you and your—your nasty little habits any longer! Horrible. . . . Making me pretend I didn't know and didn't care when you went prowling like an alley cat for someone—anyone—to join in your fun and games . . . leaving me with nothing—nothing! Oh, I don't care so much about Ingrid. She deserved all she got, for treating her husband like that—she was a tramp. But the—the baby . . . and poor Barney, who never harmed a soul in his life—how could you kill him? Yes, he was a Peeping Tom—he might have told the police about your—your carrying-on with Ingrid— but everyone else could have told them about it anyway! And whatever he saw—whatever he knew—nobody would have thought of him as a serious witness. And Tabitha, too—how could you deprive her of her only child, just to save your—your disgusting, perverted skin!"

Trewley was appalled at what had been unleashed; yet he could see that Myra's accusations had merit. And surely, nobody could act as well as (if indeed she was acting) Myra was doing now? The shock—the horror—the growing hysteria. . . . He looked anxiously at Stone, whose pad seemed no more than a blur of hieroglyphics as she noted down what she could of poor Myra's tortured outburst. The superintendent lacked the courage to slap Mrs. Wilford round the face, but his sergeant, with her medical background, could do so with impunity. Hell had no fury, he told himself, like a mother scorned: Myra had accused her child-husband for the sake of those other children, Ingrid's unborn baby and Tabitha's incestuous offspring. How the inability to procreate could warp an otherwise normal mind! It might have been better for Silvester Wilford if he, with his unorthodox desires, had never married the wife who seemed now to have turned from absolute devotion to unbridled hate.

Poor Myra Wilford. Once this tragic business was resolved, would she—if she was innocent—be able to live with the memory of her treacherous collapse? Or would suicide solve all her problems—as at first glance it seemed to have done for Barney Chilman?

Trewley needed to collect his scattered wits, to think over what had been said—and to give both Myra and Silvester some breathing space for their emotions. And a change of subject might help to clear the air; or might make one or other of the unhappy pair embroil themselves yet more deeply in the lies and distorted truths which could eventually build the case against them.

Stone had nodded in silent reply to his questioning look, and now he said: "Mrs. Wilford, I'd like to ask you something now. Yesterday, you said you went to help Mrs. Brown on her Prize Every Time, didn't you?"

This was so unexpected that Myra was startled into sensible speech. "Why, I—that is, yes. For a time, that is, I was there. . . ."

Trewley observed Stone making a note of this modification. Myra must guess that the police had heard from Margaret Brown that her offers of help had been refused; she must wonder whether he supposed that she had hastened to the sitting room of The Stooks to be alone, needing time to think over what she had found out. Which had been . . .

"Did you at any time overhear a conversation between Mrs. Radlett and the churchwardens, Mrs. Wilford?"

Her hesitation, and the look she gave him, confirmed the superintendent's guess. "Yes," she said, in a low tone. "I did. . . ." And her glance flicked towards Silvester, over him—and away.

Today, she was prepared to protect him no longer: but yesterday, when she had overheard that conversation, she had still been the wife who would do almost anything for her husband—including murder? Or had she, drawing the line at another's death, merely warned Silvester, so that he could take action on his own behalf?

"They were talking about the parish books," Trewley said; and she nodded. Silvester saw that nod, and turned pale again; he tried to read the expression in her eyes, and whatever he saw there made his own darken with apprehension.

Trewley turned to him. "Mr. Wilford, we haven't had a chance to look at the books yet, but we can't help suspecting that your financial methods have been, well, less than accurate. And that any of the inaccuracies always work out to your advantage—"

"I inherited the books," broke in Silvester, "in a very muddled state. It may be that I—never sorted out all the errors, and continued them by accident, as it were—"

"Oh, come on, Mr. Wilford! With your banking background? Not very plausible, is it—the simple affairs of a small parish too muddled for you to deal with, when you handle huge sums every day . . . and suppose," said Trewley, as inspiration struck, "we were to check at your bank, Mr. Wilford. Would we find the same . . . muddle there?"

"I—I don't know what you mean." But the protest sounded unconvincing. Trewley continued as if it had not been uttered.

"Great oaks, Mr. Wilford, so they say. From the one little acorn of the old vicar's carelessness. Did you try your hand with the parish books, and go on to the big time once you'd worked out a complete system? Your life-style—this house, identical to the Radletts'—professional people, all of you, yet *your* wife doesn't need to go out to work, does she? But Mrs. Radlett did—and she," he reminded his enthralled hearers, "was an accountant. . . ."

Though Silvester was speechless, Myra managed to say: "I wondered—when he paid off the mortgage . . . new clothes for me, presents . . . I thought—I hoped it was his way of apologising for—for our marriage, but . . ."

The look on her face told Trewley that now, at last, she was willing to speak the truth; that she would shelter Silvester no longer. "How long has all this been going on, Mr. Wilford?" he enquired; and Silvester, knowing as well as the superintendent that his wife's support had been lost to him, sounded a beaten man as he replied.

"Four years or so—soon after we came here. Whenever it was they asked me to take over the books, because the old vicar was getting past it. . . ."

"And the bank?"

"Just over three years, I suppose. But I—I . . ."

"You admit it, then?"

Silvester's broken look met Myra's eyes, all tension gone—all pretence over. "Yes, I do," he said wearily.

"And you'll pay for it," Myra reminded him, goading him. "You'll be punished for it—you'll enjoy that, won't you?" She was almost triumphant as she said this, seeming unaware that suspicion still fell upon her as well as upon her husband: her change of attitude towards him had come long after the grim events of yesterday. There were more questions yet to be answered. . . .

Trewley cleared his throat, and Stone flexed her wrist for what she supposed would be the final outlines in her notebook. "Mrs. Radlett offered to take over the books, and the churchwardens agreed. She was bound to notice any discrepancies—she was a threat to you, Mr. Wilford, and she had to be stopped. Your quarrel wasn't about ending your affair at all, was it? As you yourself said, no married woman can have an illegitimate baby. Who was to say, short of blood tests, that it wasn't her husband's? But once she found out about the swindle''—Silvester winced—''you'd have been skating on very thin ice indeed!''

Instead of yet another denial, a bitter laugh burst from Silvester's grey lips. ''Ingrid and her systems! Why did she have to start interfering? She said it would be good cover—she wanted to keep up appearances, to stop these bumpkins guessing about us—I was always afraid they'd find out in the end, but not Ingrid! And it wasn't enough for her to act out the lie discreetly—she had to go overboard, flaunting her damned newfound helpfulness—the do-it-yourself stalls, the rolls of tickets, offering to audit the books . . . if only she'd kept quiet! The village had managed fine for years without anything of the kind—I tried to tell her!

''But I didn't kill her. Oh, I can see I have the best motive, so far, but . . . and Barney. What good would killing him do me, if I'd killed Ingrid? He was a—a simpleton. Nobody took any notice of what he said. Unless it was one of the routines he was used to, he always got confused by anything he wasn't used to—he was fit for nothing except gardening and helping Cedric get the place tidy for the fete. I had no need to kill him—and I most certainly did not kill her!''

Myra jumped to her feet, her voice trembling. ''You're lying—lying! You killed them—you know you did—''

''Mrs. Wilford—sit down!'' Trewley feared she might be about to inflict serious damage on her husband, and his tone was sharp enough to make Stone look up from her notes. ''Mrs. Wilford!'' Myra had ignored that first instruction and taken several steps nearer the overcome Silvester. The superintendent held up one large hand, halting her in her tracks. ''Mrs. Wilford, there's no need . . . we have to finish questioning your husband. This kind of behaviour doesn't help.''

She choked back another outburst, and retreated a few steps before insisting once more: ''He killed them both—I know he did!'' But she sat down again, shuddering.

Trewley remained standing, his eyes moving from Myra

to her husband, who huddled pale and apprehensive on his chair.

"Mr. Wilford . . ." began the superintendent at last.

And Stone, with a flourish, wrote in her notebook: "*The usual caution.*"

━━━━━━ Thirteen ━━━━━━

"MR. WILFORD," THE superintendent began. Silvester sat bolt upright on his chair, a look of utter disbelief on his face. Myra uttered a little cry. Of fear? Dismay? Relief? Or—of pleasure?

A sudden pulse beat at Trewley's temple, and he paused, his forehead creased in a tremendous frown. A few seconds of silence lasted a thousand years.

"Mr. Wilford. All these new systems Mrs. Radlett brought in—she dreamed them up as cover for your affair?"

Silvester could only nod in dumb amazement.

"Last year some time, that would have been?"

He nodded again.

Trewley's smile was thin. "Let me guess, now. This was in the summer—but *after* last year's fete, not before."

Silvester found his voice. "Why—yes, it was. But—"

"You're sure nothing was suggested, nothing said or done at all for last year's fete?"

This line of questioning was so unexpected that Silvester found himself relaxing from sheer bewilderment. "Well, of course I'm sure. It was only afterwards that she thought about the repeated cost of hiring the market stalls and, er, so on. Cover or not, Ingrid had a professional pride in her abilit—" And he broke off, flinching, remembering how the indirect results of this same pride had made him Trewley's prime suspect.

"Well, now," said the superintendent. "If these systems were so very new this year, there was always the chance that mistakes might be made?" He turned to Myra, who had started to mutter. "Yes, Mrs. Wilford?"

"Not much of a chance, I would have said. It was only that everyone was having so much trouble setting up these famous new stalls they hadn't the time to spare to help us put the tea tables out. Although . . . although in fairness to the woman, she wasn't the one who designed the stalls. And the men were all drunk, what's more.''

Trewley nodded. ''So we've been told. Room for any number of mistakes, that sort of thing, if you ask me—''

''Oh, no,'' protested Silvester. ''I tell you, she was good at her job. Her ideas were so simple, a child could use them—like the Donkey Rides and the maze, for instance. You paid your money, you took your ticket, you queued for your turn. What could be easier?''

''True, sir. But Barnabus Chilman wasn't a child. Maybe he wasn't even as bright as the average child about lots of things—certainly slower than a normal adult. But he could cope with routine work and systems—and, if he thought long and hard enough, he could make sense of what he knew, in the end. And last night, after he'd been thinking, he got his answer—but the answer didn't seem to make sense. And so—he went visiting. . . .''

He rounded on Stone, who had stopped writing to wonder what it was that he had spotted and she had missed. ''Come on, Sergeant—it's obvious, isn't it?''

She tried to look knowing, and decided to keep silent. Myra was not so strong-minded. ''Do you mean that Barnabus . . . died because of Ingrid Radlett's new systems? That he was . . . murdered—that it was a cover-up—that he knew of my husband's . . . little escapades? But you said yourself—''

Trewley was shaking his head. ''Oh, I'll allow that Mr. Wilford disguised his fraud''—once more, Silvester winced—''cleverly enough for nobody in Redingote to find it out, let alone the likes of Barney Chilman. But''—as Mr. Wilford sighed with relief—''I say Barney was murdered, and that it was because of Mrs. Radlett's new systems—and if I'm right, I also say that without his murder we might never had got at the truth of the matter. I hope he gets some satisfaction from that, wherever he might be.

''Sergeant Stone, come on!'' And, as she thrust away pencil and notebook before scrambling to her feet, he turned to the Wilfords. "And you two—don't you leave the village, do you hear?"

"But where are we going, sir?" demanded Stone, as they hurried from the house. They'd been within a whisker of an arrest—and now they had left without so much as a caution! "I don't understand. You mean we've got to look at Barney's body before you can say anything more? Is that where we're going now—Doom's Ditch?"

"No, it isn't," he said, waiting for her to unlock the car. "Make it snappy, girl!"

In her confusion, she dropped the keys. As she fumbled for them, she asked: "You *do* think it was murder, sir—that Barney was killed because of something he saw?"

"Yes . . . and no. The opposite, in fact. Hurry up!"

She opened the door and climbed into the driver's seat, leaning over to let the superintendent in. "So was it suicide, after all? Did Barney kill Mrs. Radlett?"

"Oh, no. He was murdered, all right, if what I think is true—and the same person who murdered Barney murdered Ingrid Radlett as well. Only poor old Barney wasn't bumped off because of something he saw, Detective Sergeant Stone. No, it was because of something he *didn't* see."

She started the car, her mind furiously working. "Something he didn't see—oh. Well . . ."

"That's what I think, but I need to prove it. So get a move on, girl, and we'll go and find out!"

"But where are we going, sir?" she repeated.

He turned to grin at her. "Three guesses, Detective Sergeant Stone. Give up? Back to The Stooks, of course!"

He stood for a long time at the entrance to the maze, studying the card table, now bare of its ticket roll, float tin, and sheets of instructions. He stared just as long and hard at the opening in the thick, high hedge; and then he requested the presence of Old Cedric Ezard.

The ancient gardener was winkled from whatever hidey-hole he had found for himself, and persuaded—not without difficulty—that it would be in the best interests of all concerned if he could lead the superintendent to the centre of the maze, and back.

"You stay here, will you, Sergeant?" said Trewley, as Stone prepared to accompany them. "If I'm making a mug of myself, I'd rather not have too many witnesses. And, if I'm right . . ." But his grin told her he was sure of his rightness, and she tried to look suitably impressed.

Cedric stumped away, followed by the superintendent, and Stone stood reading her notes, brooding; without success. When the maze-threaders eventually emerged from the green yew fastness, Trewley's look of triumph and gleaming eyes told Stone she had no real need to ask. "Oh, yes," he said, before she could. "Yes, I think so—come on!"

And he began to lead the way towards the house, Stone hurrying after him. "Sir—sir, what are we doing now?"

"Going to check some statements, of course."

"Which statements?" she panted, having given up even trying to pretend she knew what was going on.

"From the people who found Mrs. Radlett's body—oh, and I must check the contents of the table at the entrance to the maze as well, of course."

"Of course," muttered Stone, wondering again what she'd missed; and hovered at his shoulder as he leafed through the pile of statements, chanting the names as he did so.

"Gary King, Debra Jarvis—Gibbins One, Two, Three, Four—great heavens! Ethel Maggs . . . Pasmore, Wilford, Brown, Duckels, Hollis. . . . Nothing," he said, "from Barney Chilman, girl, and there never will be, now. So we'll just have to make an educated guess, won't we?"

"Yes, sir," came the dutiful reply. He chuckled.

"You're a fraud, Detective Sergeant Stone—you haven't got it at all, have you? As for me—well, the only thing I'm not sure of now is the motive. . . ."

"Oh, that's all, is it, sir?" she retorted, as he pored over the neat list she herself had prepared of the contents of Cedric Ezard's official table. He ignored her, and rose to his feet with a satisfied grunt.

"Come on, girl. . . ."

"Where to this time, sir?"

"To make an arrest, of course. What else?"

"But where—who—" she began; and there came an interruption at the French windows. PC Benson stood there clearing his throat, a paper in his hand.

"Beg pardon, sir, but the doctor's done his preliminary report on Barnabus Chilman—said to bring it along to you, as you, er, hadn't been along yet, sir." The hint of insubordination in his tone was, Trewley guessed, a muted echo of Dr. Watson's original comments.

"Oh, yes? Anything interesting to say, has he?" Trewley enquired, with a grin: which startled PC Benson, though not Detective Sergeant Stone, who recognised the euphoria of her superintendent's end-of-case mood.

"Doc's of the opinion, sir, it was some sort of dope. Not exactly poisoning, though—but not exactly drowned, either. More like a bit of both. . . ."

Trewley grinned again. "I thought as much—doesn't surprise me one bit. Or you, eh, Sergeant?"

"Not in the least, sir," she replied, bluffing nobly.

He chuckled. "Tell 'em all I'll be along in a few minutes, will you? After I've arrested the murderer!" And, beckoning to Stone, on this triumphant exit line he made his exit.

Montague Rowles was nervously wandering about the garden; Trewley ignored him. Cedric Ezard muttered and growled as the two detectives went by; he, too, was ignored. And when Stone, for the umpteenth time, asked their destination, Trewley paid no heed. He was too busy pondering the final part of the puzzle. What had been the motive for Ingrid Radlett's death?

"I'll drive," he said, thrusting his sergeant absently out of the way. She buckled herself into her seat belt without a word; and they drove in silence until—

"Oh, no, sir!" she cried, as they reached the house of Dr. Oliver Radlett. "It can't be him—he adored her—he's heartbroken by it all—"

"So was Barney Chilman, girl—and Wilford too, in his own way—but that didn't stop us suspecting them, did it? And you know as well as I do that the husband's always the obvious suspect—right?"

"Yes, sir, but—in this case? What motive could he have? He worshipped the ground she walked on!"

"Now, there you've got me," he admitted, as he rang the doorbell a second time. "I hope that once we've got him to confess, he'll tell us why—it's what a jury would prefer. But the evidence points directly to him, so I think. . . ." For the third time, he rang the bell. "Hope he hasn't done anything daft," he muttered.

"I think he's coming, sir." And, as the door opened slowly, she took a good look at Oliver Radlett, still hardly able to credit the superintendent's accusation. Oliver's face, as he recognised his visitors, did not change. He was neither surprised, nor worried—almost, she thought, as if he had been expecting them. His eyes were weary and resigned. Suddenly, Stone understood that Trewley's theory had been correct.

"Good morning, Doctor. Do you think we could come in?" Trewley's normal robust tones were muted, in recognition of the man's exhausted appearance: he wore the same clothes as on the previous night, clothes which now hung crumpled on his tall frame as if he had slept in them—or failed to sleep, if his haggard face bore faithful witness. He leaned against the frame of the door and looked down on the two detectives through half-closed eyes. Stone marvelled that he seemed to have found time to shave. Did he fear that, once he was arrested, such luxuries as soap and razor blades would be denied him?

Unlike Myra Wilford, who had ushered them into the sitting room, Oliver once again led the way down the hall to his study. In the morning light it looked just as it had done the night before; even the same glass tumbler was balanced on the arm of his chair. The cushions of the seat were still springing back from his rise to answer the doorbell: evidently he had spent a sleepless night here, brooding, silent and alone, on what had happened—or what he had done—to his wife.

Without a word, he motioned the newcomers to sit down, and himself sank back on the cushions, picking up his tumbler of clear anonymous spirit with a sigh. It was as if they were frozen in time: it was all just as it had been yesterday. Stone half-expected to hear again the murmurs of Caleb Duckels and David Gregory as they waited in the hall for the end of the official interview with the bereaved husband.

But now it seemed that the bereaved husband was the murderer of the wife he had adored. . . .

"Just a few more questions we'd like to ask you, sir," said Trewley. Oliver nodded, and managed a faint smile. The superintendent smiled back. "I'm not daft enough to ask if you slept well, Doctor Radlett, because it doesn't need a detective to see you didn't," and his glance encompassed the whole tormented room. Oliver grimaced.

"I've been down here the whole time—I c-couldn't bring myself to g-go up to bed. I never c-closed my eyes at all."

"A disturbed night, then."

"You said yourself, Mr. Trewley, it doesn't need a detective to work that out. Very disturbed indeed—and are you surprised?"

"A visitor, perhaps?"

Oliver shrugged. "Apart from you, and your c-colleague, and C-caleb and the new vicar, I saw nobody last night. After all, who in Redingote g-goes out when there's a full moon? Especially after a day like yesterday."

"Umph. How about the local poacher, for one? And Barnabus Chilman, for another."

Oliver stiffened, and frowned. "Barney? Yes, the full moon does tend to bring him out on the prowl—and, between him and the g-ghosts, no wonder the village prefers to stay indoors."

Trewley shook his head, very slowly. "Oh, Barney didn't stay indoors, Doctor. Far from it, in fact. Otherwise, how could they have found him dead in Doom's Ditch—at the bottom of your garden, Doctor Radlett!"

Stone gasped. Of course. . . .

"All the houses," said Trewley, "in this new part of the village are designed the same: this room, for example, is the double, except in reverse, of the study in Mr. Wilford's house. And the gardens back on to each other, don't they—with that stream, Doom's Ditch, separating them. The trees on either bank give plenty of privacy. . . . Now, the houses on what I'll call the Wilford fork are set *back* from the road, nearer the stream—but those on your side, Doctor, are much closer to the road, which is almost a lane, it's that bit quieter—not even a proper pavement. And it isn't the lane you need privacy from, it's your neighbours out the back. . . .

"So the bobby we had watching these houses last night could see yours more clearly than Mr. Wilford's. He walked backwards and forwards between the two houses, to and fro around Foreigners' Fork—and, when I asked Ernie the postman whose *house* was nearest to where he found Barney's body, he said Mr. Wilford's—as, of course, it was. But it was just as close to your *garden*, Doctor Radlett! The garden of a house which is close enough to be visible through the trees from Silvester Wilford's house—close to the stream where Barney was found murdered!"

Oliver blinked. "It's news to me, Mr. Trewley, that Barney is dead. Surely not by someone else's doing, though? If he was found in Doom's Ditch—well, that's the traditional place for suicides in Redingote. It's easy to drown yourself when the water's so deep, and the banks are steep and narrow. The trees overhang everything, and make it hard to c-clamber out if you change your mind. . . ."

"And hard for anyone to be noticed, too. Noticed putting a body there for other people to find—people who'll believe it's just another suicide. . . . Putting it there as you did this morning, Doctor, not last night. What you said about having no visitors *last night* was true—Barney came to talk to you after midnight, didn't he? You heard what he had to say, and you knew he was dangerous—so you doped him—he'd have taken anything Doctor Oliver gave him, you could rely on that—and you left him in the ditch to drown!"

"If," said Oliver slowly, "all you say is true, what reason c-could I have had for g-going so much against my whole life's work as a doctor? What g-good would it do me to—to remove Barney in such a way?"

"I notice you don't say *kill*, Doctor. Very literal-minded, you are. Our police doctor says Barney wasn't dead when you put him in the water—you left him to drown, but you didn't drown him yourself. And''—he raised his voice above Oliver's attempted protest—''if I'm wrong, why hasn't Tabitha come to ask for your help today? She couldn't talk to the vicar, because Redingote's without a parish priest at the moment. But you took care of her son, you stopped them putting him away, you found him his job at the manor—she owes you a lot. She trusts you. And the—the common bond of bereavement ought to make her feel even closer to you. . . .

''But she hasn't come. You said you didn't know, you said it was news to you, that Barney was dead. Another of your—your playing with words, I think; but Tabitha hasn't told you, she hasn't been here—and I say that's because she knows you were the one that caused her son's death!''

''This is utter nonsense, Superintendent.'' But, though Oliver's voice was steady, his hand was not; and the drink in his glass splashed on the leather arm of the chair. ''You have no possible proof of such a—a ridiculous theory. You are g-guessing, Mr. Trewley!''

''But you're not denying it, are you? Tabitha Chilman knows you killed her son—just as she knew, last night, that you'd killed your wife, only we didn't understand her when she told us. She wrapped it up in a load of garbled, sorcerous talk—but that's the way she was hinting, all right. You killed them both. Didn't you, Doctor?''

He leaned forward, and jabbed a finger in Oliver's direction, so unexpectedly that both the doctor and Stone jumped. Oliver flung up his free hand across his face to block out the intrusion of Trewley's piercing gaze: the palm was clearly visible, the deep red marks of his nails mute witnesses to his tension. Stone stared at him in sudden sympathy, and knew that her superior had pressed this man as far as he could, in all humanity, go. She put down her pencil, and motioned to Trewley to let her speak.

''Doctor Radlett, you look utterly done in.'' She reached out and took his wrist firmly, feeling the pulse thunder beneath her touch. ''I think you've had about enough, haven't you? For now, I mean. You need a drink—shall I mix something for you, or freshen that one? I used to be a medical student,'' she explained, as he looked at her enquiringly.

"Oh," he said, and hesitated. "This will do fine, thank you, Sergeant. I'll—I'll be all right, I think. . . ." His eyes met hers, then fell beneath her look of quiet understanding. He sighed, and turned to Trewley. "Sorry to have been—hysterical, Superintendent. I c-can promise you it won't happen again. Now, you were saying?''

Trewley looked at Stone, who nodded her permission for him to press on with his reasoning. "I was saying, Doctor, that you killed both your wife and Barney Chilman—and I was waiting for your answer, plain yes or no, without any more of your . . . prevarication.''

"Shall I prevaricate a little longer, Superintendent, to ask you my reasons for so doing? My wife—my own dear, wonderful, perfect Ingrid—and poor, simple Barney. Why?''

Trewley could supply only part of the answer, though of this part he was sure. "Barney knew you'd killed her, you see. I expect it was a while before he worked out what was bothering him, but he'd told Tabitha something of it by yesterday evening, enough to make her stop us and talk in her daft riddles—she couldn't, or wouldn't, explain straight out. You were Doctor Oliver, son of the Old Doctor—you were born in Redingote, you'd looked after her son—but, Doctor Radlett, you had killed. If you'd killed one of the locals, I reckon she'd have come right out with it, but your wife, now—that was a different story. . . .

"Still, Tabitha was worried; and she'd only had it secondhand, from Barney, who'd be confused enough anyway without a murder on top of everything else. So she told us to tell you he was worried—muddled—wanted you to go and see him, to set his mind at rest one way or another, to know if his guess was correct. But you didn't go. We passed on her message, but we didn't understand it properly until it was too late. . . .''

"I don't c-claim to understand it even now, Superintendent." Oliver's eyes had drifted almost closed. "Do tell me more, won't you?"

"Oh, it's easy enough, once you know. Barney couldn't sleep for being so upset and confused about what he'd seen—or rather, what he *hadn't* seen, that made him think you'd killed his own adored Mrs. Radlett. Of course, he didn't want to believe it—couldn't believe it, probably. You were her husband. So, some time after midnight, he sneaked out of the house—he was Ernie Hollis's poaching partner, nobody would notice him—and he turned up here, to put the matter to you as he saw it—to ask for an explanation."

He paused. Stone had stopped taking notes, her gaze upon Oliver as he sat, saying nothing, with a faraway look in his eyes as if he had heard not one word of the superintendent's charges. Trewley coughed.

"Now, I don't know for sure why Barney came to see you. Blackmail, maybe—or just to accuse you—maybe even to warn you. Or to ask your advice—or to avenge his idol's death. Would you like to tell me?"

"No, Superintendent, I would not. Why don't you c-carry on with this . . . ridiculous speculation, and see what you c-can deduce on your own account?"

Trewley sighed. "I'll do my best, sir. You had to kill Barney because he knew too much. You talked him into taking some drug or other, something strong enough for you to get him down to Doom's Ditch without a struggle; then you threw him in to drown, to look like suicide. He was dangerous—which is what you remembered yesterday evening, when you tried to blame him—oh, it was cleverly done—for your wife's murder—insisting you couldn't believe he'd done it!

"But it was meant to make us think the exact opposite—and we nearly did. But, just in case we didn't, you had to make sure. Lucky for you he came to see you when he did! And something still made him trust you, right to the end. You faked his murder to look like suicide—you do your own dispensing, don't you? Easy for you to mix something. . . ."

Oliver opened his eyes to stare at the glass in his hand. "Oh, yes, Superintendent. Very easy indeed."

Stone studied the blank page of her notebook; Trewley was concentrating on his theory.

"I suppose you knew that whatever Tabitha could say in evidence was likely to be twisted by a clever defence counsel—and would be hearsay, in any case—but Barney's evidence would have been a real threat. Barney, who was on duty at the maze when your wife's body was discovered by that young couple who'd gone to the middle to get engaged, poor kids. The girl had hysterics, and Cedric Ezard barged in to sort things out. And he left Barney on guard, with orders to let nobody past. . . .

"But Barney *did* let somebody past—two bodies, in fact: Mr. and Mrs. Gibbins, whose twins were in the thick of it all. The parents charged in to the rescue—and Barney remembered that they did—*but he didn't remember you, Doctor Radlett!* He knew how many tickets he'd sold, he knew how many people had gone into the maze . . . officially, we'll say—and he knew that only three people went in afterwards, and you weren't one of them. But—he saw you coming out. . . .

"He didn't have time to think it over then, because someone let slip what had happened, and he went into his own hysterics and was taken home by Tabitha. But afterwards, at home, he thought about it—counted things over in his mind to steady his nerves, I expect. The sort of routine that had always worked before—but this time the routine wouldn't add up. . . . So he came to see you. And you drugged him, and drowned him in Doom's Ditch. You're pretty traditional-minded yourself, Doctor!"

Oliver opened the weary eyes he had closed unnoticed during the last part of Trewley's exposition. "Yes," came his low-voiced agreement. "Yes, I am." And before either of the detectives could stop him, he raised his glass to his lips, and drained its contents.

"Hey!" cried the superintendent, jumping to his feet. "What have you—Stone, do something!" For his suspect— surely now proved beyond doubt?—was smiling, even as his hand fell, releasing the empty tumbler with a clatter to the ground. Trewley picked it up, and sniffed. ''Radlett, what was in this glass?''

But Oliver shook his head, still smiling, as Stone sat motionless, watching him. ''Something,'' said Oliver softly, ''that I've been wondering all night whether or not to drink—and now, well, I've d-drunk it. And it's all over. . . .''

''He mixes his own potions, of course!'' Trewley seized the smiling Oliver and began to shake him by the shoulders. ''For heaven's sake, girl—come here—do what you can, and I'll go and phone for an ambulance!''

''Oh, I can't do anything, sir.'' And the manner of her saying it made him spin around to stare at her. ''I'm sure it's far better to leave well alone. . . .''

''You,'' he snarled, ''may think so, but I don't. I'll get the ambulance anyway—'' But Oliver's mocking voice stopped him in his tracks, as Stone remained where she was.

''The ambulance will c-come far too late, as your g-good sergeant knows. Your c-clever sergeant—who's been a medical student—and knows . . . knows . . .''

Trewley glared from one to the other in baffled fury. Stone watched Oliver's face, saw his eyes close, and rose at last from her seat. She laid a gentle hand briefly on the doctor's wrist as if checking his pulse, then bent to pick the fallen glass from the floor, and said to Trewley:

''I'd appreciate a private word with you, sir.'' And she led the way, with a last backwards look of sympathy, out of Oliver's study into the hall.

He turned on her before she had shut the door. ''You'll be back in uniform by the end of the day, girl, for playing such a bloody fool game with me—what the hell possessed you? We had a cast-iron case, apart from motive—and you—you deliberately . . .''

As words failed him, she broke in: ''Yes, sir, but if you would only let me explain—''

''Explain? Cast iron, it was! He goes in the maze with his wife, kills her, has some sort of collapse like the one he had later, so he can't get out in time before Cedric Ezard and

Barney take up action stations on the gate—he couldn't climb a seven-foot hedge, so he had to stay inside till he had some excuse for being there—and what could be a better excuse than hysterics? Nobody's ever surprised if a doctor turns up with a load of screaming going on—and nobody was! I checked every statement, didn't I! But Barney worked it out later—the same as I did. And I almost got a confession out of him. And then—you . . ."

"I'm very sorry, sir." She had edged him, without his being aware of it, along the hall and away from the telephone: she had to keep him talking for a while longer yet. Oliver Radlett, she felt sure, had trusted her.

"He adored his wife, sir, no doubt of that—he laid her body out in a dignified manner, sent her on her way with the emblem of hope on her breast—no matter what had happened, he still had some feeling for her. In his eyes she was perfect. Didn't he tell us that nothing second-rate would ever have done for him? Only he was *too* fond of her, unbalanced about her—look at the highfalutin phrases he used when he told us how she agreed to marry him. No man I've ever met talks like that, unless he's kidding—but Doctor Radlett was absolutely serious. Besides, no man's going to crack jokes when his wife's dead—when he's just killed her. . . ."

"What! You agree he killed her? And you still let him—do that? What kind of a detective are you, Stone—as crazy as those Chilmans? The man killed Barney, he killed his own wife. A double killer, with a glass of save-yourself in his hand, and he drinks it right under our noses—while you sit there watching him! In heaven's name, girl, why?"

"Why did he kill her, sir, or why did I let him—let him do what he did just now? Though the answer's the same in both cases," she added, as he turned almost purple. "If you'll only let me explain, sir! I—I felt sorry for him."

"Sorry for him? *Sorry for him?* Stone, I ought to—"

"Please, sir! Yes, sorry for him—as I think you'll be when I tell you. He killed his wife when she betrayed him, sir—betrayed his trust in her with another man, and then tried to pretend she hadn't. She led him to the centre of the maze—a place with the strongest sentimental attachment for him, at least—and she told him she was going to have another man's baby. Only she wanted to persuade him it was his child, sir—so he killed her.''

Trewley was floundering now. "A married woman—a baby—how could he know for certain it wasn't his?" Then he stepped back, and stared at her with sorrowful eyes, seeing, in place of her neat features, the fat, angry face of Ethel Maggs as she grumbled about Ingrid Radlett. "Mumps," said the superintendent. "You're telling me the man had mumps at the wrong age. . . ."

And once again, he reflected on how the inability to procreate could distort an otherwise normal mind.

But Stone was shaking her head. "No, sir. It's worse—horribly worse—than that. Much rarer than mumps, which in any case needn't have that effect on an adult male. But one in five hundred males, if I've remembered the statistics right, has . . . Klinefelter's syndrome, sir.''

"Has what?" He stared at her as if she'd suddenly begun to speak in a foreign language: as, in a way, she had.

"Klinefelter's syndrome, sir. Mumps, you can catch—it's an accident, and could happen to anyone, and at least you're born . . . normal to start with. But with Klinefelter's, you've never . . . been a proper male at all, if you see what I mean. It's a genetic thing, a chromosome defect which is untreatable—and which means you can't ever father a child. With mumps, before you caught it, at least you had the chance—and only ten percent of the population catches mumps in the first place. And even then, there's no reason why it should . . . damage you. But Oliver Radlett must have known all along he wasn't a—a perfect male, sir, and that's why he insisted so much on the perfect wife, to compensate. And when she turned out not to be perfect, well . . .''

"Klinefelter's syndrome. One in five hundred. And you say Radlett is suffering—used to suffer, I suppose, thanks to you—from this? How can you be so sure?"

"Physical indications, sir. They needn't appear at all, and until tests are done you might never know about it—but poor Doctor Radlett exhibited several of the classics. He was unusually tall—plumply built, with a rather feminine fat distribution—had a slow beard growth. Didn't you notice how clean-shaven he looked, even though he'd spent all night downstairs? While you, sir, with due respect—and Mr. Wilford . . ."

Trewley passed a rueful hand over his face, nodding as the stubble rasped against his fingers. "But I know plenty of men who don't show heavy overnight beards. I've always envied them. You can't mean that they all—"

"Oh no, sir. I bet most of them are blond or redheaded—whereas Radlett and Wilford were equally dark, weren't they? But it wasn't just that. Oliver Radlett had a slight speech impediment, remember—and Caleb Duckels told us he'd been born with a cleft palate, or something of the sort—it isn't positive proof, but it's another indication. But what made me realise for sure was when he threw up his hand like that, and I saw the palm. . . . It only had one line across it, sir. Look at your own—at mine—at anyone's. Three, aren't there? But one of the signs of Klinefelter's is having a single line. If the little finger turns in, that's another sign, though I didn't notice that. Just the single line on his palm—and then I remembered about Klinefelter's, sir, and when all you needed was motive—well, there it was."

"So you let him know you knew. Telling him you'd been a medical student—letting him get away with it!"

"Yes, sir." She turned imploring eyes towards him. "But what else could I have done? Imagine it all coming out in open court—"

"He could have pleaded guilty, then none of the medical details would have needed to come out. Especially if he'd agreed to be tried on the Chilman charge alone."

"But to do a deal like that, sir, he'd have had to know that other people knew about the Klinefelter's. Not just us, but the lawyers—he'd have felt they were thinking of him as a freak—whispering behind his back—only half a man at the most, sir, and knowing it would follow him after his release. . . ."

The superintendent scowled at his feet, and cleared his throat with great violence. Stone held her breath, waiting for his decision.

He coughed. "He was sitting up all night, wondering if he could bring himself to drink that stuff, wasn't he? And then he heard us at the door—guessed who it was and why we'd come—and swallowed it before we could get to him. We never thought he'd do such a thing, did we, girl? After he seemed so levelheaded when we left him last night?"

"No, sir, we certainly didn't." Her eyes were bright, and she could not meet his gaze.

"He'd lied to us about his movements yesterday," continued Trewley, having thought a little more. "He guessed we were suspicious of him—that we knew he left his dispensary before lunch, and walked up to meet his wife, and killed her in the maze when she confessed to her affair with Silvester Wilford. Couldn't bear the deceit any longer, could she, and wanted to get it off her conscience and wipe the slate clean at the start of her new career in village life . . . didn't realise he'd put her on some daft pedestal and she'd tumbled herself off it. For a moment, he went crazy—he picked up that statue and hit her with it, panicked when he saw what he'd done—fainted, I expect, then went on to automatic pilot when he finally recovered, acted just as a doctor should when he heard that girl scream. . . ."

"That's absolutely right, sir."

There was a pause. "I need some fresh air," he said, opening the door. He seized her by the wrist. "We could go for a walk to the gate and back, then try ringing at the door again—I mean, we could ring at the door. How else are we to let the man know we want a word with him?"

"That's right, sir," she breathed, and smiled shakily. They went out into the front garden, pulling the door almost closed behind them.

A stealthy movement in the bushes halted their thoughtful progress down the garden path. "Tabitha?" called Stone, without turning her head. A high-pitched moan answered her. "He's gone, Tabitha—he won't hurt anyone else the way he did poor Barney."

"I set a curse on him," Tabitha said, stepping from the bushes nearby. Trewley's hand clutched his sergeant's arm, and he tried not to yelp. "A curse on him," said Tabitha, "for though he may once have been a good friend to my poor boy, he killed him—I know he did!"

Trewley was speechless. "We know it too," said Stone.

"And his wife, as well—my Barney's pale lady with the lovely bright hair, gone! Golden lads and girls all must as chimney sweepers, come to dust . . . so now *he's* dust with the other two, and with my curse on him!"

"You can leave your cursing, Tabitha," Stone told her. "He suffered in his last hours every bit as much as you could want—and at least you have your—your craft to console you. He'd lost everything he ever needed—everything in the whole world."

"Children of shame," she said. "My boy—and *she* with a babe beneath her wanton breast. . . . I told you, but you paid me no heed!"

"We're sorry, Tabitha. We didn't understand, at first."

"My boy might still be alive . . . child of shame that *he* was, too. Poor Barney. Shame. . . . So, maybe 'tis all for the best, then?" And she disappeared into the undergrowth as quickly as she had come.

"Strewth," muttered the superintendent, and mopped his streaming brow. The sun was climbing high in the sky—but Stone did not believe that this was what troubled him. She smiled.

"Tabitha's quite a philosopher, isn't she, sir? Rather more than a witch, I think. Rustic wisdom. . . ."

"Umph. It—it takes all sorts, girl, and you can't say more than that. Which reminds me—didn't we come to have a word with the doctor? How about going and—and getting it all over?"

They turned, and went back up the path. There were many loose ends to tidy, but between them they had finally unravelled the puzzle of the murder in the maze. Their main task was complete. . . .

Trewley looked up again at the high summer sun, and gave a loud sigh. It was going to be another hot day.

———— About the Author ————

Sarah J. Mason was born in England (Bishop's Stortford) and went to university in Scotland (St. Andrews). She then lived for a year in New Zealand (Rotorua) before returning to settle only twelve miles from where she started. She now lives about twenty miles outside London with a tame welding engineer husband and two (reasonably) tame Schipperke dogs. Under the pseudonym Hamilton Crane, she continues the Miss Seeton series created by the late Heron Carvic.